G-11

Nanne Tepper

was born in 1962, and is the .... published novels. *The Happy Hunting Grounds* is his first, for which he received the Anton Wachter Prize, given for the best debut of the preceding two years. He writes about British and American literature for a leading Dutch newspaper, *NRC Handelsblad*, and currently lives in Groningen in the northern Netherlands.

From the Dutch reviews for *The Happy Hunting Grounds*:

'The work of a real writer.'   *NRC Handelsblad*

'An engaging novel . . . full of lively, often funny dialogues and shamelessly moving scenes.'   *De Volkskrant*

'A debut novel which is both magnificent and intriguing.'
                    De Groene Amsterdammer

'Fast-paced and teasing dialogues alternate with ironic and lyrical descriptions. Over that lies a boyish glow that reveals Tepper to be a truly inspired writer.'   *HP/De Tijd*

THE HAPPY
HUNTING GROUNDS

NANNE TEPPER

translated from the Dutch by
SAM GARRETT

Flamingo
An Imprint of HarperCollins*Publishers*

Flamingo
An Imprint of HarperCollins*Publishers*
77–85 Fulham Palace Road,
Hammersmith, London w6 8jb

Flamingo is a registered trade mark of
HarperCollins*Publishers*Limited

www.**fire**and**water**.com

Published by Flamingo 2000
9 8 7 6 5 4 3 2 1

First published in Great Britain by Flamingo 1999

First published in Dutch under the title *De eeuwige jachtvelden* by Uitgeverij Contact, 1995

Copyright © Nanne Tepper 1995
Copyright in English translation © Sam Garrett 1999

Nanne Tepper asserts the moral right to be identified as the author of this work
Sam Garrett asserts the moral right to be identified as the translator of this work

This novel is entirely a work of fiction. The names, characters and incidents
portrayed in it are the work of the author's imagination. Any resemblance to actual
persons, living or dead, events or localities is entirely coincidental.

Translation of this book into English has been made possible with the financial support
of the Foundation for the Production and Translation of Dutch Literature,
Singel 464, NL-1017 AW Amsterdam, for which Flamingo is extremely grateful.

Photograph of Nanne Tepper © Harry Cock 1999

ISBN 0 00 655146 7

Set in Postscript Linotype Aldus with Bembo and Frutiger display
by Rowland Phototypesetting Ltd,
Bury St Edmunds, Suffolk

Printed and bound in Great Britain by
Clays Ltd, St Ives plc

All rights reserved. No part of this publication may be
reproduced, stored in a retrieval system, or transmitted,
in any form or by any means, electronic, mechanical,
photocopying, recording or otherwise, without the prior permission of the publishers.

This book is sold subject to the condition that it shall not, by way of trade or
otherwise, be lent, re-sold, hired out or otherwise circulated without the publisher's
prior consent in any form of binding or cover other than that in which it is
published and without a similar condition including this condition being
imposed on the subsequent purchaser.

For Annette

Ainsi je voudrais, une nuit,
Quand l'heure des voluptés sonne,
Vers les trésors de ta personne,
Comme un lâche, ramper sans bruit.

Pour châtier ta chair joyeuse,
Pour meurtrir ton sein pardonné,
Et faire à ton flanc étonné
Une blessure large et creuse,

Et, vertigineuse douceur!
À travers ces lèvres nouvelles,
Plus éclatantes et plus belles,
T'infuser mon venin, ma sœur!

BAUDELAIRE, 'À celle qui est trop gaie'

BOOK ONE

Langsam, schleppend, wie ein Naturlaut

On a cloudless but by no means clear day, at around four in the afternoon on 1 August 1989, a long greenish-yellow train pulled in to the Gare du Nord in Paris. Victor Prins, inclined more to stagger than to stumble, held his leather valise (more shirts than manuscripts) clenched tightly under one arm and stepped down carefully onto French soil. He regarded the way light fell in the station hall, then strolled over to the first kiosk he saw. An unfamiliar song played in his head as he paid for two postcards. He sat down on a bench, laid the valise across his knees and twisted the cap off his Rotring. On the card with the photo of a half-naked Hamilton nymph – big grain, little girl – he wrote: 'Dear Veen. The boar has landed. It's a well-known fact that travellers end up as beasts. So far, the Parisian custom of welcoming Prussians with open arms is relinquished to the realm of myth. This is the last you'll ever hear from – Your Victor.'

It took him half an hour to write the other card. A picture of W. R. Sickert's 'Mornington Crescent Nude Reclining', a prone, naked figure who seemed to rest with fists clenched: 'Boo! I've seen you like this. Others have seen you this way too, it seems. What are you doing there in your slumber, that's what I want to know!'

*

———

3

Victor tried out a grin but felt it drip off. He mailed the cards, lit a cigarette and wandered out of the station. A smoky glow hung over the city. The odor of exhaust fumes and grilled meat. The noise was a mixture of traffic, voices and summery, yet untraceable, sounds. Something in Victor crowed, sounding like a child moving up the scales: higher, higher, and then . . . what a view! The final note a thin cry flying at the horizon.

Real travellers, he thought while studying his directions, don't feel the tourist's urge to mingle with the local inhabitants. A real traveller wants an aura that makes the native start and rear back. The lonely one who makes them ask: 'Where does that man come from?', 'What's happened to him?', 'What on earth does he want?'

He crossed a square. Cars tore by him, honking, scraping and sucking their dry tires over melting asphalt. Drivers with elbows out of open windows, all of them, it seemed, wearing a frown. A sidewalk café veiled in blue gases beckoned him pause. He ordered a double Calvados. While his muscles relaxed, tears welled up in his eyes.

Paris, the city he'd longed for for years. Here roamed angels who would teach him: the souls of the great minds of the Left Bank whose wanderings along the Seine and wild forays from bar to bar he had followed in his mind. He listened and tried to catch the whispering.

What he heard was his memory.

His father shaking his hand at Groningen station (the mind's eye never clouds with tears): 'But what are you really planning to do there, boy?'

4

The sky above East Groningen, the ceiling of his youth, perhaps of his ability.

Voices across a kitchen table: 'So, cap'n, big plans in the offin'?'

A final hiccup before summoning the *garçon* for another double:

'Victor, just what the hell are you up to?'

Victor emptied his first glass, took a sip from the second, opened a map across his knees and tried to concentrate.

A cool hand on the back of the neck startled him from his dream. Louise. She'd looked for him and found him, in the heart of Paris. While interiors and landscapes in the mist dissolved before his squinting eyes, he saw how a young girl he'd once known had changed into an old girl, as only French girls can. The beauty of the face that had come back to him clearly until he was seventeen (after that he'd daubed with fading impressions to paint a phantom portrait) was hard to locate amid the sharp cheekbones and thin cheeks, the teeth tinted by wine and smoke (quite charming, really), the tired bosom in a printed T-shirt (what a horrible get-up). She'd thought she'd find him here. If one thing had stayed with her from that vacation long ago, it was that 'Victòòòr', her summer love, and his incredible 'papááá' had 'occupied' every sidewalk café they came across. She looked at him, nodded approvingly and blushed. The blush cut him to the quick. She dropped down into a chair, and within a second had a cigarette in her hand and her lungs full of smoke.

A bit later she sat slurping at her coffee. She kept looking at him: Victor, overpowered by fatigue, could find nothing to say. How was his family? Oh, you know. How was he doing? God, he looked great, he hadn't changed – almost hadn't changed, that's right, not her, she knew that too. Victor smiled.

The apartment was in a flaking street. Rue de la Fauvette. The walls an old yellow with here and there a soot stain, the trelliswork on the cramped balconies black and shiny as anthracite. One long row of lindens. No gardens.

They climbed a blinding white staircase. Louise unlocked a door on the third floor and led him through the rooms. She smelled strongly of sweat, and it was as though she filled each room – enormous spaces, one containing a grand piano – with her odor. Her friend Simone ('She has stayed much prettier than me.') would come home late, and the boys would be back from Brittany the next day.

Well then.

This was his room. A bed, a window that looked out on the street, chandelier, cupboard, floral wallpaper. A window that opened. She left him to unpack, and when she stuck her head around the door a little later, blushing again – come on now! – she looked at him tenderly, a new experience for him. He opened his valise, laid Jack Kerouac's *Desolation Angels* ('bad, but good,' as Lisa would say) on the floor next to the bed, on top of the black notepad.

The next day, the boys (he'd never met them, and he didn't recognize Simone: Louise was the one he'd written to all those years) would dismiss Old Jack with a perfunctory French shrug as 'the discoverer of the dead-end road'.

The rest of his books, videos and LPs arrived five days later; another five days and he knew no letter was on its way.

*

He roamed through the streets and imagined himself an exile. Late in the afternoon he met Louise in the Bois de Boulogne. They drank lukewarm beer from the can, and she sounded him out. How were his parents and sisters, really? Why, in his long letters through all those years, had he tried first and foremost to be funny? Did he realize that, all that time, she'd thought she was writing to someone who no longer existed? Who had turned out to be a – excuse the word – cliché? That she had a photo of him and his sisters in which he was fifteen, Lisa holding one hand, Anna the other, and that she had never been able to make that face of his rhyme with what he wrote? Victor shrugged his shoulders and smiled.

'Well,' he said, 'I try to keep 'em laughing.'

The meals at the table in the living room, the windows open, the roar of the city as muzak, gave him a chance to be silent. He could barely follow his companions' rapid French. If he withdrew to his room after dinner it was seen as a burst of inspiration. He was a 'European bard'. He had things to read. The boys – men, really, impeccably dressed philosophy students – brought him books and looked at him with a mixture of pity and repressed amusement. To be a writer in a dying language on a dying continent: *c'est absurde*. Victor felt the urge to write to Veen ('Here, in this country, high-school students take to the streets for better education; try explaining that to someone from East Groningen!'), but held himself in check.

One evening he asked to see the photo. He'd had a lot, a whole lot, to drink. Blind-eyed he looked at the picture held before him by a cackling Louise. A magic lantern went on in Victor's head. And while Louise and Simone told the attentive-looking philosophers about that vacation long ago (Greece, 1975), Victor saw himself driving down a road, turning a corner: Oude Huizen, East Groningen.

The Boss was there in the field. Leaning against a combine, he spoke to the boys, who had ceased haying, like Old Man Jesus Hisself: 'If Man was made ta give Nature a helpin' han', than tell me who's the goddammed boss?'

In the yard of Café Stik, where a little carnival (Crack-the-Whip, carousel, donut stand and cotton candy) parked during the village fair each summer, Victor and Lisa combed the ground for exotic refuse: an intact beer glass on a stylish foot, wine bottles of obscure origin, a roll of Oranjeboom coasters disposed of accidentally. In their own garden, which bordered on the fields, their mother was making sandwiches. Further along, out by the fen, was the manor house of Farmer Valk. There in the boathouse was where he'd found Lisa, filthy and undone.

Oude Huizen had always consisted of a single street, a long straight road lined closely with houses and, a ways out into the fields, the farms. There was a greengrocer, a butcher, a bar and a bank. Progress had obtained only one foothold: a shop where a biology graduate sold free-range meat. Not long ago, when Victor and The Boss – old as the hills by then – had gone to that butcher's shop, Victor's neighbor had dealt with the modern meat *boutiquier* in his old familiar fashion.

''N' cut o' dead hawg, nothin' better'n that.'

The dazed Hollander had proceeded to sing the praises of an entire spectrum of pork products, until the old man, in a steely voice and his most up-market Hooghaarlemerdijk enunciation, had put an end to it by ordering a chop 'with plenty of fat to it'. Pork was the only thing The Boss bought at the butcher's. He claimed to have half a bull in the freezer at all times, in case of 'sudden visitahs'.

A nudge to the shoulder snapped him out of it. He looked vacantly at Louise, who was trying to wangle a story out of him. But Victor stood up, excused himself and locked the bedroom door behind him, window wide open. The whispering of the trees, and further away the raging of the city. He took a new notebook from the valise and lay down on his bed.

When he was submitted to a vocational test at fourteen, the following conclusion was drawn: film director, conductor or writer. The fairy tale began that day. His parents had other thoughts, and dragged him to a professional guidance counsellor. After asking a few absurd questions ('Have you ever been to France? Did you like it?'), the man turned to Victor's parents with the announcement that he was perfectly suited to be a travel guide. This revelation didn't comfort them in the least, but would, they thought, at least put a damper on the enthusiasm with which their son had embraced his fate. Nothing could have been further from the truth. That he had been waylaid in his calling after only one week by a man whose beard grew out of his ears made Victor all the more determined.

Three days after receiving the joyful tidings ('I'm a born artist!') he decided to inform his neighbor, the director of the local bank, of his calling. He was anxious to hear what The Boss had to say to this giant rabbit pulled from the hat of destiny. In the waiting room of glistening wainscot which reeked of lacquer and cigar (as like the passenger lounge at Hoogezand station as two places could be), he waited until the last customer had stepped away from the cashier's window. Then, not entirely at ease, he sauntered to the door of the biggest room in the house, the room that served as office. Before he could even knock, the door was opened by the same smiling girl who'd been watching him from the window. The Boss was sitting in his grayish undershirt with sleeves rolled up. His snowy white forearms stood out like they'd just been painted. He was smoking a cigarette, staring out the open window over the top of his glasses, and seemed not to notice Victor approaching his desk.

'How you?' Victor said.

'Ah . . .' The Boss said, roused from another world, 'the champion of the noisebox. No school t'day?'

'Vacation.'

The quiet of late afternoon hung at the open window like a cloud of flies. Victor could have sat there for hours, but The Boss looked around and asked no one in particular: 'Wha' time is't?'

'Quarter past four,' one of the girls said.

'That's enough for one day,' The Boss said, 'I'll be 'cross the street.'

They left the office. Victor waited in the long hallway. A few minutes later The Boss came back, dressed in his Sunday best, cigarette in one corner of his mouth, thumb hooked in vest pocket in the classical mode. They crossed the Hoofdweg and climbed the steps to Café Stik.

Stik was sitting on a stool behind the bar, close to the tap. He wasn't the kind of barman you'd ever catch polishing a table or emptying an ashtray.

''N' drop of the pink, Boss?'

Victor got a half of Oranjeboom. As usual, they were the only customers at this time of day. Victor pulled the report from his back pocket.

'Wha's that?'

'Vocational test.'

'Vocation? Yer still at school, aren't ya?'

'For later. I can be a writer, a conductor or a film director.'

The Boss looked away, pinched his nose closed, but didn't burst out laughing.

''N' what's yer pa say 'bout it?'

'He wants to go to school with a gun and blow some sense into 'em.'

Once again, The Boss didn't laugh. Victor, who'd always blushed whenever he noticed that his words were actually being mulled over, wondered if his childless neighbor was granting him this honor because he enjoyed the presence of a vassal, or if he really put stock in Victor's concerns.

'You were plannin' to go to The Coast, weren't ya?'

'But I'm no good at math.'

'What?' Stik asked. 'Conductor? With that wailin' o' yours? Oh, yu'll be beatin' the bank, yu'll.'

'That's 'n electric guitar,' Victor said, 'a conductor does classical.'

'Wavin' a stick,' his neighbor confirmed, pointing to his glass for a prompt refill.

'Oh, one o' those,' Stik nodded. Victor got another glass. (Beer in the afternoon puts evening in the legs, his father always said.)

No-one spoke. The propeller on the ceiling did its best to blow the roof off the café. The warmth became heat. Stik drummed his fingers on the bar. They lit cigarettes. They took a slug. Men together. Then an odor reached him. In the doorway stood Lisa. She was wearing her black jogging pants and a gaping old-man's undershirt: she was fourteen, and she looked like a sleaze.

'I'm gonna tell,' she said, pointing at his glass of beer before strolling over to them.

'Aw, shove it,' Victor said.

'Come now, Liesje child, don't be like that,' the Boss said. 'Stik, give the kid a popsicle.'

The barkeep disappeared into the back and returned with a Moo-Moo bar, raspberry flavor. Lisa took it and, with a disapproving look, slid up onto a stool. In a flash her mouth was as red as if she'd been drinking blood.

'So, Missy,' The Boss said, 'what brings you here?'

He addressed her like she was a lady and he was some farmhand. Her undershirt sagged open, you could see budding breasts. Victor itched with annoyance.

'Victor has to come home. Anna's sick. Victor has to tell her a story to quiet her down.'

'Well,' The Boss said, 'ya' heard her, fellah. Home is the huntah from the hill. Come by this evenin' with that paper o' yours.'

'Can't you,' Victor snapped at Lisa once they were outside, 'put on something decent for a change?'

'If I were you,' Lisa said, 'I'd shut my mouth about it.'

She stopped at the back door.

'Smell your breath?'

Victor breathed against her forehead.

He got her popsicle.

Mornings in Paris. Victor visited the Louvre, walked the quays along the Seine, drank wine with a *clochard* and felt out of place. He couldn't shake the feeling that he'd run away. The conviction that he was after something seemed to fade. He was twenty-nine, considered himself an artist, and wondered what it was all about.

Pathos.

All he had was his past, the Dutch writer's treasure-trove. He had no desire to cast aside that paltry tradition – provincial life, the wrath of many fathers – with a careless, haughty gesture. But he was after something very different: the grandeur of bereavement, an exquisite derangement of the senses, the battlefield of the obscure.

When Louise found him that afternoon in the meagre but stylish wood close to the tennis courts, she thought she saw something in his eyes that tempted her to a kiss. Victor took it, but his teeth were clenched.

Their house was next to the bank, circled by chestnuts at the corner of the Hoofdweg and the sandy path that wound its way into the land, kitty-corner to Café Stik. The garden behind the house, that possessed a roof of leaves in summer, flowed over into the land. The vegetable patch was the line. Visitors always came around the back, because the front door symbolized death and decay: Victor's father was a doctor.

The house was cool, dark and moist. Half the ground floor was taken up by an enormous kitchen that looked out on the gardens and the land behind. Then there was a little parlor, a waiting room and an office on the street side. The center comprised a toilet. Up the stairs were four bedrooms and a bath, and when one pulled down the ladder above the landing one could enter the junkroom attic, where one risked decapitation by Lisa or Victor, who had founded their dwindling fairy tale village here when they were four and five. Most toys had now been moved to Anna's room, and the doctor, with his wife's caustic grimace at his back, had built a little bar so his children could throw parties.

Anna was sick. She had a fever and diarrhoea. Anna was nine and almost always sick. That came from not eating in the summer.

Sucking on three fingers, she twisted the corner of a handkerchief in her nose. Her room was darkened, but, zooming inaudibly, a comforting green night-light was stuck in the socket above her bed.

'Mademoiselle,' Victor said. He sat down on the edge of her bed.

'Don't act so weird. Where've you been?'

'Next door.'

'No way, you were at Stik. I can still smell, you know.'

'Have you eaten anything?'

'Plate o' strawboard.'

Instant whole-wheat porridge. She got that from Lisa.

14

Victor stood up and made a shadow theater with a lamp against the bare wall. He cast silhouettes with his hands and told stories to go with them. Then a hideous clatter interrupted them. In this house one was called to dinner by a copper cowbell their mother had brought home for some long-forgotten vacation. Today she whacked the thing with all the might which, for reasons possibly to be explained later, she had failed to put into preparing the meal. The clanging rushed out the windows, into the Hoofdstraat: the only missing element would have been to have the whole village come bellying up to the table.

'Uh-oh,' Anna said.

Victor got up, turned off the lamp and took Anna's temperature, just to be sure, first laying a hand to her cheek, then her forehead. Thirty-eight-point-five, he guessed.

'You come back after dinner?'

A wheezy little voice. She knew she was acting like a baby, but wasn't that how Lisa had conquered the world?

'I'm going next door first.'

'Why? And, Fikkie? Are you going to be a conductor? Papa says you're going to swing that noisebox around in front of an orchestra and make faces like your gut hurts, so everybody'll say: is his father really a doctor?'

'Did he say that?'

Victor left Anna's room and pulled down the ladder on the landing.

Sitting at the bar, Lisa was smoking a roll-up without inhaling. Dusty sun fell through the skylight. The attic was blazing hot and smelled of Lisa's sweat. The odor of bitter greens.

'Dinnertime,' Victor said.

He slid up onto the stool next to hers. Her shirt was hanging open. He saw her little breasts. It looked like they hurt. He saw the black stripe in her armpit too. A caterpillar that had clamped fast. The sight of his little sister filled him with a loneliness and an itching. Earlier, in Café Stik, she'd disguised herself as a little girl, but now she was the way she was: vain and aloof.

'The jug's over there,' Lisa said disdainfully, indicating a pile of boxes with a lazy wave. 'We're having beans, but we don't have to say grace 'cause they's still green.'

'It's not "they's", it's "they're".'

'Okay, Grandpa.'

She stood up, shuffled to the trapdoor and disappeared through the floor.

'Hey, your cig!' Victor shouted.

No answer. She didn't give a damn about getting caught.

Victor found the gin. His father drank from stone flasks because you couldn't see how fast they emptied. He poured himself half a glassful and watered it down with warm cola that was dead as a doornail. The fire inside, once lit, he knew would let him devour the beans like he really meant it. His mother's brilliant cooking never called for recognition, but when she'd purposely made a mess of things, as was probably the case now, she fished for compliments for all the trouble.

The kitchen was filled with oven heat. His mother stood at the counter, wearing her apron, pouring the water off the beans. Lisa was already seated. The doctor came sauntering in from the garden. Victor wondered whose sweat ran cooler, his or his father's. They both slid up to the table, both looked suspiciously at the woman with the pan in her hands, both paid no mind to Lisa, who laughed at them.

'Beer with't?' the doctor asked. Victor nodded, straight-faced.

The pan of beans came down on the table with a bang.

'No way. This boy's already had his beer f'r the afternoon . . .' The ring to the voice was corrected, the accent smoothed. '. . . Or so I've been told.'

'Well,' the doctor said with quiet mockery, 'Is that what madame's been told?'

'By the neighbor.'

A glance at Lisa.

'If the menfolk around here all pissed in the ditch, there wouldn't be a sober fish caught all summer.'

She turned to her husband.

'And a fifteen-year-old boy spending his afternoons in a bar is too ridiculous for words.'

The doctor looked at Victor and stifled a smile. All three of them saw it. Lisa and Victor grinned.

'Oh, I see,' their mother said, 'the ranks have closed.'

They ate beans with nutmeg, sausages with fried onions, potatoes boiled to a paste with gravy from yesterday or the day before. Victor and his father pulled a fast one by tucking in with a hefty bite that ruined the plate's landscape, making it look as though they'd ploughed in, then applying the strategic fork to create the illusion of continuity.

'Taste good?'

Lisa shook her head. Victor, his eyes spangling, popped one-eighth of a bean into his cheek.

'You don't have to make such a production of it, young man.'

'The boy finally shows some talent and . . .'

'Great, a wiseacre of a husband, just what I always wanted.'

'I knew that,' the doctor drawled, 'otherwise I never would have applied for the job.'

His wife tried to suppress a snort, but it didn't work.

After three bites, Lisa shoved her plate aside.

'Could I have a cigarette?'

'Are you out of your mind?' her mother answered. 'And that undershirt of yours goes in the incinerator tomorrow, you can see your whole kit and caboodle in that thing. Don't tell me you wear that out on the street?'

'There we have it,' Victor said.

'What's your problem?' Lisa snapped at him.

'Little girls who drive teachers crazy at school parties, dancing with guys like that while they try to figure out if she's wearing a bra or not . . .'

'You don't go to school dressed like that, do you?' his mother interrupted, looking Lisa up and down before losing herself in thought. 'Maybe you should start shaving yourself there.'

'Please, we're eating!' Victor shouted.

Lisa squinted at him. She blushed down to the base of her neck and looked like she wanted to pull his hair. It was a look he'd gone too long without.

'Granny on the warpath,' she mumbled.

The doctor generated a snort.

They pushed their plates back. The doctor lit a cigarette, his wife left the table to make dessert. Lisa plucked the cigarette from her father's fingers and took a drag.

'I saw that,' her mother said without seeing it.

She brought them custard with strawberries.

'Have you talked to the neighbor about that, uh, test?'

'Listen, Pops,' Lisa said to her father, pointing a long fingernail at the custard, 'try to use a clean spoon for the sugar, okay?'

The doctor glanced absentmindedly at Lisa before turning his dark, bloodshot eyes on his wife: 'Don't stand there looking at your genes so triumphantly; every adolescent whose glands are acting up has something artistic hangin' off his butt, 'n' that son a yers . . .'

'And the milkman's,' his spouse interrupted.

'Uh . . . like was I sayin', just because certain elements in this house act like they're raised by the muse of Konsalik himself doesn't mean that a boy of fifteen has even the slightest aptitude for any fine art whatsoever!'

'Is that so?' his wife bantered.

The doctor stiffened, but bounced back quickly, a family trait.

'I have a weakness for people who are too big for their britches, otherwise I never would o' founded this home' – another snort sounded, this time sardonic, from Mother – 'but I'm not going to teach my children to bake pie in the sky just because Mommy feels like she blew her artistic cookies.'

'Brilliant!' his wife ruled.

'My sentiments 'xactly,' the doctor said belligerently.

It was time for coffee, cigars and cognac.

'And what's more,' he said turning to Lisa, 'custard with strawberries is made usin' fresh yogurt, cream 'n' lemon, not with sugar, Missy, for future reference, when you take that big mouth of yours to the sideshow.'

'Oh, Daddy . . .'

A direct hit.

Lisa at a loss, mother mad, father all upset.

'Now we're talkin',' Victor said.

'Shut y'r trap, fellah,' said the doctor, who seemed more possessed of a mean drunk than an early hangover.

'Easy, easy,' his wife said.

Victor peered at Lisa. Her soft mouth hung open, her eyebrows (fused from the age of twelve) a black smudge on a deathly pale forehead.

Avoiding further escalation, she arranged her lips in a sweet little pout.

'Dickhead,' she said to the doctor, who looked up furtively. She finagled a cigarette from his pack of Camels and lit it like a princess waiting for the maid to prepare her evening toilet.

'Right, that's what comes of it,' their mother sighed.

The doctor was sitting in the garden, mother was fixing coffee, Lisa, more offended than she'd admit, had gone to change. Victor was still at the kitchen table, smoking.

'Don't pay any attention to your father,' his mother said.

'I wasn't planning to, why should I be the one to set a good example?'

'Hey! That tone of voice doesn't sound like you.'

I'm still looking for one that does, he wanted to say, but he knew the look he'd get. Accusing, as if he bought his smart-ass comments from some shady character on the wrong side of town and blew his whole allowance doing it.

'I mean, you're only fifteen, it's not like it's the end of the world.'

Silence.

'Where does he come up with this Konsalik stuff?'

'You got it from the book club, you forgot to order anything else.'

'Oh yeah?'

'It's the first thing you see when you look at the bookcase.'

'Go get it out of there, would you?'

'I wouldn't do that,' Lisa said from the doorway, wearing her black cotton dress – she'd even combed her hair. 'He'll never get off your case then.'

'Gee, how about that, at least now you look like a girl! All right, all right, I didn't say a word. So why don't you go make up with your old dad for being so nasty to you?'

And there, in the opinion of her later lover, Hille Veen, lay Lisa's beauty: like a thief in the night. As soon as more understanding was shown than her own private criteria had led her to expect, her features fell into place. She exchanged a glance with Victor – 'and you keep out of this' – and, both of them blushing, walked to the cupboard. She took out a snifter, laid it on its side and poured Rémy Martin until the cognac reached the rim. Then, warming the bottom of the glass in the palm of her hand, she strolled out into the garden. Victor got up and tagged along behind, just to keep an eye on things. The doctor was pretending to read the sports pages of *Het Nieuwsblad*. Lisa pulled his hair to make him look up and take the snifter from her. He set it on the ground next to him and, with a helplessness that chilled Victor to the bone, tried to pull his daughter down onto his lap – and sure enough, the damn newspaper was getting all flustered. Lisa, however, having driven vast herds of old farts across the steppes in a former life, pulled the paper off his lap, put an arm around his neck and plopped down, dealing the doctor – who paled visibly – the smack he'd had coming all along.

Now it was Victor's turn to snort.

They sat together without a word. The doctor was smoking a cigar. Lisa's head rested on his shoulder, her black hair mingled with his. Mother, who'd been afraid to come outside with a book, was flipping through a magazine. Their dog, a young, chronically drowsy German shepherd, lay at Victor's feet and growled in its dreams. The odor of burning leaves played tag with that of the doctor's Havana.

At seven twenty-five, Victor got up.

'Can I go with?' asked Lisa, suddenly wide awake. Fixbier, the German shepherd, arranged his limbs hopefully as well. Fix was the name of a Greek beer, one liter of which Victor and his father had consumed each and every afternoon during their gentlemen's lunches in Athens a summer ago, while the ladies were out cold in the hotel room; a beer that made you hallucinate in the burning sun. During that vacation Victor had been introduced to a life of endless evenings, evenings that did nothing but make eyes at sleep. It was the same vacation on which Victor, for the first (and also for the last) time, had a girlfriend, a French girl who took him by the hand and coaxed him along to the sea. Lisa, who often had such moods, didn't speak to him for two weeks.

When Kobus, Farmer Valk's hired man, came that summer with a pup he couldn't sell, a solid, black, somehow very German-looking animal, Victor and his father decided at a glance that they would take it. The doctor explained to his wife that having a dog would give him a reason to 'go out for walks'. That Fixbier spent prolonged stretches of the

weekend asleep under the stairs of Café Stik came as a surprise to no-one.

That evening Victor could deny Lisa nothing, so the three
of them headed down the garden path. They entered the
bank grounds from the street, along a broad gravel drive
beside the big house.

The Boss was standing in his garden, taking his after-
dinner piss on the potato patch.

He felt the dog against his leg, tucked away the family
jewels and greeted them with his Oliver Hardy imitation. A
feint, a worried look left and right, then the eyes in childish
surprise, and finally the face gliding slowly into that doubt-
ful, half-grumpy frown. The shaking head and the little
groan: 'Mmmmm-mm!'

Lisa giggled. The Boss fumbled at his tie with flapping
fingers, shook the fat comedian out of his body and walked
over to them.

Victor received the flat of his hand between the shoulders.
For Lisa he bowed.

'There was no need to dress up for my sake, mademoiselle.'

They cut through the pantry and greeted The Boss's wife,
a slender lady of indeterminate age with furious lines around
her eyes and a soft look in them, nipping at a glass of currant
gin in the back room. The room was crammed with cup-
boards, a dining table, four matching chairs, a perpetually
smoldering coal-burning stove and vases full of freshly-cut
flowers from the garden. In the long corridor that split the
house in two, and into which the fairy tale stairs came down
– a staircase made, it seemed, to accommodate a lady in

descent – Victor stopped for a moment. A corridor with seven doors, one of them leading to the billiards room, a space between the office and the stately parlor where the gentlemen farmers were once received.

(In Paris, when Victor had an attack of nerves and Simone calmed him by means of hypnosis (in babbling baby-talk into a bungled dream), the decor he chose for his depersonalization was this gigantic house, not his own house or room, let alone any later location. No later place had ever captured him so.)

The Boss opened the door and turned on the chandelier above the table. Lisa crawled up onto the window sill. She pulled up her knees and hugged them. Her hair rocked on a breath of wind in the open window. Fixbier, already dormant in a corner, sighed deeply.

The balls blew apart, thumped dully against the table's banks and found each other again in a corner. The ivory clicked like Anna's chattering teeth.

'What was ya tellin' me?' The Boss said, 'No good at math?'

Victor shook his head, laid down a double bank shot and said: 'It's Greek to me.'

'Aww!' the neighbor said, 'Supposin' I'd help ya, a couple times a week, ya gotta go to The Coast, fella. Go 'way 'n' come back again, make a man outta ya. Lookit yer pa, he's been ten kilometers from he-ah, to Town, an' has it made him a happy fella?'

'But you've always been here,' Lisa said, 'haven't you?'

'They came to me, girly.'

The Boss was referring to the war, which he never talked about.

''N' that conductor business, don't let 'em shuck ya, right?'

'Fikkie should be a writer,' Lisa said, 'he's real good at reading out loud.'

'Don't call me Fikkie!'

'All in good time, first that 'rithmetic, tell yer pa I'll give ya a hand there.'

Victor shrugged. Since the age of ten he'd wanted to be the captain of a tramp steamer, but the lure of that romantic dream had yielded to the sober demands of modern mathematics. He had one week left to put together a new curriculum. The principal had given him that much grace.

The Boss's wife brought coffee, bottles of cola, a miniature bottle of rum for Victor's tic, and pretzel sticks with which Lisa was soon playing jackstraws. They had a drink and The Boss passed out Players, to Lisa too.

'Whatever ya do, kids, always look for somethin' where ya won't be yanked up by the seat o' yer pants, but where ya have ta fight yer way up, understand?'

'Why?' Lisa asked.

'Because, Lisa my child, a man's gotta grow calluses 'n' learn ta fight if he plans to move up, 'cause once yer up there they loose the dogs on ya. When that happens, ya better know damn well why they doin' it, and ya can't know that if ya got there in yer sleep.'

'Why would they do that?' Victor asked.

'Ye'll find out in time, fellah, first jus' learn t' fight.'

Later that evening, Lisa and Victor stood under the chestnuts on their father's land and smoked.

'Fikkie?'

'Hmm?'

'Could you teach me how to inhale?'

'Some other time.'

The village was nodding off. Café Stik was barely lit.

'You going to take math?'

'Hey, I don't know.'

'Are Papa and Mama getting divorced?'

She was crying. No show this time. Big fat tears. She wasn't sobbing.

'No, come on, a course not.'

She dropped her cigarette. Looked up at him. Took a little step.   He held her tight. Real long, real tight. She smelled of the land in the last weeks of summer. She was out of breath and said: 'Goddammit all to hell!'

Nights in Paris. Not as noisy as nights in Town. Victor's window was open. The air outside was tepid, he could smell the wind. He read the letter again and sipped at mineral water.

Oude Huizen, 6 September, 1989

Ludwig,

It's my birthday, so there's no way around it.

That I cry, there's no reason for you not to know that. That I bawl, you can know that too. We're getting rid of the house. I don't want to live in town anymore. So now I'm home, with the old man. He's plastered. You too, I take it.

Okay. Here we go. That shitty postcard of yours, that really made me sick. You're a swine, but you already know that: you're even proud of it. From now on you can drop dead, in slow motion and fully lit. That postcard was too much. Sometimes you seem to think you have a sense of humor. Today I've known you for exactly twenty-seven years, but has it been a laugh? No.

(Half an hour later.) That the window of my room is open, that I'm lying on my bed, that the garden, that the . . . no, no, no remember-hows now, no more remember-hows ever (I've been at Papa's cognac, now we're all plastered again). I know that, even there, you watch *The Godfather II*. Hey? Mikey? I know you can't get enough of that scene where Diane Keaton has come to visit the children and is being sneaked out the kitchen door (what is it you compare that fucking scene to – I know there isn't a male equivalent for 'bitch', but that's what you are, a bitch! – so: what do you compare that fucking scene to, bitch!) and he sees her – this wasn't supposed to happen – and then, without saying a thing, just with that look of his, slams the door in her face, and along with the thud of the doorpost you hear that little yelp of hers, and you then, shithead, deep inside you see the goal of the century being scored (But why?). Well listen, one day I – not you, me! – will slam the kitchen door in your face, just like that. And now I'm not going to say any more, ever again.
Sissi

The paper curled in the flames. An allusive image, Victor thought. The only thing missing was a little mood music.
Just kidding.
He combed his hair in the mirror. Black and shiny, pulled back thanks to a new styling mousse that didn't start stinking in the rain. His black shirt had been ironed by Simone. His black pants were new. The gray vest old. Bought once with Anna, when she came to spend the night in Groningen. He poured himself a glass of Jack Daniel's. Nipped at it. Lit a

cigarette. Looked at his likeness. Sat down on a side table he'd bagged from the other room. Laid the cigarette in the ashtray. Folded his hands under his chin.

'Victor? *Qu'est-ce qu'il y a?*'

He turned his head. Simone, wearing glossy white underwear edged with lace. She was blonde, thin and pretty. She'd liked girls ever since she was thirteen. She sniffed loudly, tossed a glance at the ashtray and looked Victor up and down. A cautious smile crept to the corners of her mouth.

If there was anything she could do for him.

Victor shook his head. She took a step, patted his hair (goddammit all to hell, he thought) and rested her rear on the edge of the table. Was he still going out? It was five in the morning. She couldn't sleep. Smelled smoke, heard a chair sliding across the floor. Incredible, Victor thought, she must be a bundle of senses. His poise was crushed in an instant. She took his hand. Was he homesick? Was he burning his work? Photos? Letters?

He caught his balance.

He thought. Simone let him go. His hand on her shoulder. She shook it off – 'don't be so clumsy' – and fell back on his bed. He pulled the panties down off her legs – her blonde vulva, so chaste – and buried his mouth in her lap. To taste. She lay motionless on the bed. She was wet from tossing and turning, she whispered, almost apologetically. When his mouth was full of her flavor and he lifted his head for a moment, she looked at him with a tender expression. It startled him. She pulled him up next to her, patted his hair – no cursing this time – and kissed his cheek. He lay for a while with his head in her perfumed, pearly armpit. Then she crawled over him, slipped away and came back a little later, wearing a flowered dress.

'Allons-y.'

They wandered through the quiet city. For the first time since he was fifteen, Victor was walking hand-in-hand with a girl. She was cheerful, asked him nothing, only told. About Louise and the philosophers (*une liaison dangereuse*), about her studies to be a therapist (hypnosis and massage) and about her roaming girlfriend (a piteous look). He let her talk and felt the presence of Old Jack, most desolate of angels, every bit as lost on the Left Bank as Victor himself.

But even this ghost no longer took the trouble to whisper Victor's exile into adventure. Life had no script, and if it contained anything like fate – a thing Victor wanted to be convinced of; the letter was simply more evidence of that – then still one couldn't speak of a conspiracy, but of a striking coincidence impinging on one's consciousness: a sudden view of the course of your life, a detail jumping up at you from the texture of time – probably just a snapshot for the explorer with a penchant for lecturing and a weakness for showing slides.

That he had let Lisa's birthday go by unobserved, out of compassion (he thought she wanted it that way, and wanted him to have thought of it that way), had freed him from nostalgia and saved him from his heavy heart; now, after having lived in harmony for three days with the rack and ruin of his plans and pretensions, her claw seized him by the neck. Hoopla, as she'd put it.

Victor resisted by warding off the temptation to pour out his heart.

He was at a loss. He had to admit it. And he was lost.

He was almost thirty, and any faith in a concept that might put things right had been lost in the course of the years. Victor's eternal lament was: 'But why can't it all be Nothing?'

A writer of Russian origin, an exile who, to fend off madness, had reshaped the universe according to his own whims and insights, had felt that the thought that life was 'a brief crack of light between two eternities of darkness' was too lethal for the mind to embrace. And although Victor, in his paltry oeuvre, couldn't help referring to that writer at moments appropriate and otherwise (the man's brilliance was his braille), that selfsame thought was, in his view, of greater comfort than that of a before-, during- and after-life.

By going away – as he'd been urged to do so often – Victor had hoped to turn the glance over his shoulder into a glimpse of the future. But he couldn't make it without his past; he hung on to what was behind him. It was his birthright. Indelible. Inalienable.

In Paris he'd hoped to find oblivion. And inspiration, to do something with what he had. Because he knew it was weariness that made him long to return to Nothingness. And because he found weariness despicable, he didn't leave it at that. Besides, he loved *spielerei*, and he who loves playing remains in The Game. He who has glimpsed God, or one of His Boon Companions, playing peekaboo in a cathedral, or quickly turning the corner of a thought, will keep searching whether he wants to or not.

And I, Victor thought, have seen Lisa.

Simone had been silent for some time. Victor noticed her occasionally sizing him up out of the corner of her eye. A loving look. His hand in hers; it was as though he'd recovered his loneliness, without pathos, without stage directions; it had nothing to do with the lighting, or with the decor, it had to do with his wanting to be here.

'Nostalgia?' Simone whispered.

He nodded. He was homesick.

Despite The Boss's efforts, he had flunked the fourth year of secondary school. A lukewarm summer followed. Anna was sick. Victor took care of her. At the local soccer club he ran into a few boys his age. He had no friends.

His mother spent a few weeks with her sister in the West.

On the first day of school, Lisa joined him in the class without saying a word.

From that day on they went together to the middle school, twelve kilometers down the road. Their mother still wasn't back. They did their shopping outside the village.

One afternoon in that first week of boredom, they took Victor's Puch out into the exhausted countryside. The sun blared, a cloud of flies hung above their heads. They lay in the grass beside a ditch and smoked. Lisa inhaled as though her life depended on it. Victor cracked two cans of beer. They drank and were silent. They stared out over the water, leaning on their elbows. She wore her sleeveless undershirt, he'd taken off his T-shirt.

Lisa dropped onto her back and folded her hands behind her head. A waft of bitter greens reached his nostrils. He looked at her.

'Jesus, hey, is that a tick?'

He slid the tip of his finger across her pale armpit.

'Nah, 'n' dull razor.' She blushed. He peered at the horizon.

'Hey, uh, Fikkie? Did you know I'm going steady?'

'What do you mean, "steady"?'

He dragged his eyes over her body.

'Like I said, goofy, he's in our class: Pieter.'

'Pieter? I don't know any Pieter.'

'That's pretty much par for the course, isn't it?'

'Don't be so godforsaken cute, what kind of guy is it? I mean, what do you two do together?'

'So why don't you ever go with girls, huhhh?'

They'd had fights before. This was something else.

He sat up, lit another cigarette, stared at the horizon.

'Fikkie, hey, take it easy, okay?'

'Don't call me FIKKIE!'

Silence.

'God,' Lisa mumbled, 'this is exactly what I'd expected.'

Something took a long time coming. What came was a hand. At his neck. Sick of himself, he let himself be pulled down, his head on her breast, her hand in his hair.

'When we remember our former selves, there is always that little figure with its long shadow stopping like an uncertain belated visitor on a lighted threshold at the far end of an impeccably narrowing corridor' . . . that was in Victor and Lisa's favorite Gothic romance. Victor saw himself as a dreamy, perfectly normal young fellow, no memory as yet, but in its stead an empty honeycomb the bees had forgotten. That summer, though, he tripped over the brink without stopping to think, and the zooming in his head began.

Writers had talked about, fawned over and vilified memory. His memory – this was all he knew to say about it of a morning in Paris, after a majestic breakfast and a night without sleep – was shaped by the joys and vagaries of his aesthetic. How he had developed those, he didn't know, nor did he want to. The fact was that he went through life with that look over his shoulder. The present tense existed only in his recollection. Psychiatrists had warned him against this view of things. In vain. He wallowed with abandon in the story of his life. The only reason to go on – cultural baggage in his old kit sack – was to make that long ribbon on which his memories flapped, like pennants during the village festival, even longer. Memories which, he suspected, were 'artificially recolored in the lamplight of later events as revealed still later'. The gandering must have begun that summer.

After school she lay in the garden beneath the twin birches, at the edge of the vegetable patch, dressed in an off-white bikini with a golden sheen, her buns, firm buns, taunting the heavens, a calf with narrow foot raised and rocking, her head resting on one hand, her black hair a jumble, her back rolling and glowing with sweat, her breasts hidden, her eyes in a book he'd told her to read.

'Hey,' he said from the kitchen doorway, on his way to Stik for late-afternoon drinks with The Boss, 'isn't your lover waiting for you?'

She rolled onto her side. Her breasts, full and heavy now, heaved languidly. She brushed the hair out of her face.

'Wha's that?'

'Go with us to Stik?'

'Nah . . .' She turned onto her back, put her hands behind her head, squinted at him.

' "Oh," he said, looking crestfallen.'

He turned around and walked away.

'Hey! I'll go if you want. Hey! Yoo-hoo!'

Turning around without looking too crestfallen was no mean feat.

'What is this?' Lisa shouted. She sat up straight. 'God-dammit, buddy!'

If she'd been standing she could have stamped her feet.

Victor kept himself from shrugging just in the nick of time.

She waggled her finger at him. As sluggishly as he could,

he walked over to her. Tossing her hair over one shoulder, she looked at him half-angrily, half-questioningly, and slapped her hand on the grass. He sat.

'You're sitting on your butts.'

He tugged the pack out of his back pocket.

A vague smile tripped across her face and fell off. She looked furious again, cruel. He knew that look.

'You want to know something?'

He smiled. Affably, he thought.

'You drive me crazy with this crap, you know?'

He kept smiling.

'We all have our crosses to bear,' he drawled.

'That's right, exactly, and if it happens to mean anything to you' – her eyes shot away from him and sought the point of the roof – 'ever since my freshman year they've tried to touch me . . . here, and here' – she made vague but horrendous gestures – 'and I don't let them, you get it? I DON'T LET THEM! I don't put up with it! And someone else's tongue in my mouth, I don't want that either. Do you get what I'm saying?'

Her eyes black, clouded, blind.

'I'm not normal,' she said quietly.

In his chest he felt a sea rolling in.

'Satisfied, Pops?'

She fell onto her back and began to cry.

Victor saw confetti on the firmament; snow in the middle of summer.

'What's wrong with us, Fikkie?'

He bent over her, brushed the hair from her face. Her tears black with mascara. Watercolor on his fingers.

He kissed her. On her limp mouth.

And she kissed him. Her eyes opened. 'Oh God!' Lisa said then, 'Remember?'

He blushed. She looked past him.

'Victor?'

'. . .'

'I don't feel so good.'

They came to the table all dressed up.

'Are you two throwing a party?' their mother asked.

Lisa laughed nervously.

'We're going out,' Victor said quickly.

'On a weeknight?'

'Let 'em go,' the doctor said. 'School's just started.'

'That's not dealing with things,' their mother noted, 'that's talking through your hat.'

Lisa and Victor barely ate.

'Doesn't it taste good?'

'It tastes,' said the doctor, who'd come home with a pleasant buzz, 'the way your Madame Born says it should: a leg of lamb tender as the thigh of a twelve-year-old girl.'

'Goodness!' his wife cried. 'In fact, I prefer fresh thyme, don't you? Dried is a bit too penetrating.'

After three glasses of Bordeaux, their mother ticked on her glass.

'Children, listen for a second, I'm uh, I'm going to spend a few weeks with my sister in Rotterdam. That's okay, isn't it?'

Lisa looked at her father, whose face refused to cloud over.

'What the fuck is it now?'

'Lisa, dear, such language!'

Their mother forced a smile.

'I just need a little rest, that's all.'

'Sure.'

'Princess,' the doctor began, but Lisa snarled: 'Don't call me that, you prick!'

The doctor winced, let his gaze fall to his plate, reached for his glass.

'Liesje,' Victor said, 'can it, would you?'

She looked at him, confounded, fought back her tears, asked him with her eyes: 'So now what is it!'

The lamb remained untouched.

'Give us a cigarette,' Lisa snapped at Victor.

No-one objected. They smoked in silence.

'What about Anna?' Lisa asked.

'Oh, she'll be better in a day or two,' her mother said, not looking at anyone.

'Oh,' Lisa carped, 'she'll be better in a day or two.'

'Lisa, would you just shut up?' Victor shouted.

'Oh, man! Dirty prick!' She got up and ran out of the kitchen.

They heard her bedroom door slam. They even heard the key turn in the lock. They didn't hear her crying.

Victor's parents looked at him.

'So?' he said, a new and major loss welling up in him, 'what the hell is this all about?'

The doctor brought his wife to the station that same evening. Victor was sitting in the attic and listened to Anna saying goodbye to her mother.

'Okay, bye-bye.'

The front door clicked shut.

Victor drank and smoked.

When Lisa came crawling up through the trapdoor, Gershwin's 'Rhapsody in Blue' was crackling out of the speaker in the corner. In the flickering of the candlelight he saw how blurredly her hair stuck to her face, how her mascara ran, how red her nostrils were.

He took her hand and danced with her, the way they always had, until they were laughing too hard to go on.

It was a Wednesday morning. Lisa's alarm went off at seven. She made coffee in the cool kitchen and scratched herself yawningly under her old-man's undershirt. She poured half a cup of cognac, watered it down with coffee and brought it to her father, who took it from her with a look Victor could never imagine. Then she came into his room, the door slapping back on its hinges (he pretended to be asleep), sat down on the edge of his bed and tickled him awake. He could smell her bed sweat. Her breasts rocked back and forth under her shirt.

'Hoopla,' she said. She took a cigarette from the nightstand, lit it, stuck it in Victor's mouth and was gone.

In the kitchen, a deathly pale Anna was sitting at the table, her thick blonde hair combed down to her tailbone, fingers in the butter dish. The doctor came shuffling in, heavy black roll-up in one corner of his mouth, frowning, head pounding. Victor, dressed in blue jeans and a watch, pulled up a chair. Lisa slammed the plates and flatware down on the table. The telephone started ringing. Lisa ran to get it.

'Hello, Lisa Prins speaking. How was I supposed to know it was you? My name's not Liesje anymore, old cow. He has a hangover, that's right. What did you expect? Mothers who abandon their families have no right to talk. *You* watch your mouth. I don't know if the old goat wants to talk to you. Anna's dead. Then we'll have to dig her up first. Well all right, here she is.'

Lisa, eyes blacker than black, looked at Victor, grinned broadly without seeing him.

'Mama? I'm better, I'm going to school today, and I had a dream that I had to poop and then I did it in my bed. What? No, it's still in there.'

Anna screeched with laughter.

'Papa, it's your turn.'

'Oh yeah? 'S that right? Not too much, just enough. You can always go to the hoors. No money f'r that. Me too. Victor?'

'Hi, Mom. Aw, same as usual. Enough. Don't start snivelling, Mom. All right already. What? Just mind your own business, okay? What about you? That right? Oh, here we go again. Don't get all weepy on me, Mom. What? That's not like you. Bye.'

Two days later she was back again.

Lisa and Victor shared an 'electives cluster', a combination of classes seemingly designed to rule out all future prospects. In the morning they'd stand smoking together in the schoolyard. Occasionally someone greeted them, no-one stopped to talk. Only when they were apart, it seemed, did they have acquaintances. In that same schoolyard, Lisa's future lover, the budding writer Hille Veen, was turning heads with 'his little Yvonne'. The whole student body, a good fifteen hundred of them, followed the couple's ups and downs. Even the teachers got involved. Lisa had been in ninth grade with the girl; later, when surrendering to the whims of memory down in Town, she would say that Yvonne was in the habit of breaking out into hysterical tears in class, going up to the teacher and telling him that Hille, 'my boyfriend, y'know', had done 'something awful' to her that morning and she had to go to him right away because he had study hall and she was 'all choked up about it'. During breaks they'd fight, she blubbering and trying to kick him, he standing stoically with a band of cronies hawking up sputum on the sidewalk behind him: The Wild One. After school you'd find them at the bicycle racks, kissing and making out. Later, when Victor ran into Veen in Town, they didn't recognize each other. The same went for Lisa. When they saw him again, first at The Seat of Learning, later at their house (Veen came with broken heart in hand), they re-traced the paths that had crossed. Veen suffered from terminal nostalgia for those days. Victor and Lisa looked back on the schoolyard with repugnance.

Victor's former classmates, now prep-school seniors, were in the habit of drinking beer in the bar at the Hotel Parkzicht after morning exams. Before long he and Lisa were skipping classes to join them. This only increased their isolation from their classmates. They hung out at the bar with beer-drinkers and yawn-artists and toughed it out. At home they dug into their mother's writers and their father's composers, to muffle the overwhelming silence of the house and catch any echoes they might recognize.

This Indian summer is so much sadder than others, Victor thought. Sometimes he skipped late-afternoon drinks with The Boss to keep his mind clear for the writing of his first story, which he worked at after dinner in the hope of finishing it before Lisa's sixteenth birthday in early September. By the thirtieth day of the month of August, he'd written ten pages. Only the apotheosis remained.

It was a Friday afternoon, warm sun, cold wind, no school. Lisa and Victor met The Boss beneath the chestnuts.

'You're radiant, milady,' the old man said with a bow to Lisa, who was wearing her black dress with the lace collar. The heels of her faded-pink pumps gritted in the pebbles of the garden path. She had her long hair tied up in a royal knot. Her long nails were polished red, her lips were painted red, her eyelids the black-brown of her eyes. A filter cigarette was stuck between her lips. She returned the compliment with a bow.

Victor had on his bluest jeans, his whitest T-shirt, his leather jacket, his costly leather boots: the outfit he always wore at his desk.

The café was deserted. Fixbier had come inside with them to get out of the cold wind, and rubbed up against the bar before dropping to his side, yawning and taking off on a tiring dream-hunt.

The Boss took his first nip.

'How's things over at the house?'

'She's back,' Lisa said. She sipped at her glass of Oranjeboom and studied her nails.

'Your mother,' The Boss said, 'has a keg o' gunpowder up her ass, but she can't help it. It's 'cause of The Coast.'

'She was born here,' Lisa said.

'But she took her schoolin' there, girlie,' The Boss said. 'She couldn't find herself back here, not after that.'

'She puts on airs,' Lisa said.

'Just like you,' Victor said.

'An' who'd fancy bein' the big fish around these parts?' Stik asked rhetorically.

'Pa will chase her away again,' Victor said.

'Some fellahs don' get what they ask for,' The Boss said.

'And what's he asking for?' Victor asked.

''n' gun,' Stik said with a grin in The Boss's direction.

'Stik, toss us a couple o' them balls in the frier!'

Grumbling, the barkeep disappeared into the kitchen.

'Your pa,' The Boss went on, 'I've said this before an' I'm sayin' it again, your pa fancies things the way they were.'

Lisa pulverized a coaster.

'When he was young, I mean, when your father was young, eighteen, sort of like your brother here, then he was quite the lad, an' he had a steady 'n' they were the most famous couple in the village, an' that steady was your mother, she went to Amsterdam to study an' your pa went down to Town. An' between Amsterdam and Town somethin' came up, as a manner of speakin', and your mother had to come back, as it were, 'cause that's how it went back then.'

'We already knew that,' Lisa said with a glance at Victor, 'didn't we?'

He nodded.

'Your pa, sonny-boy, never made it past eighteen, he refuses.'

'Mustard, or maynase?' Stik asked.

Before dinner they were up in the attic. Lisa untied her hair and shook it free. Her big mouth a cruel stripe. Pretty was different.

'Melancholy,' she said, 'mel-an-chol-y!'

'I read somewhere . . .'

'You and your reading, can't you ever come up with something your goddamn self? Let that drunk grow up!'

The trapdoor in the floor opened with a screech.

'What's this, Tweedledum and Tweedledee?' the doctor said as he crawled up into the attic. 'Fightin' before dinner? Aren't we a little too old for that?'

Lisa stamped past him.

Victor, in the Bois de Boulogne, tried to remember every conversation he'd had with his father – there had been two or three of them. What he remembered was rage, sarcasm, bitterness. But no revulsion.

There in the attic he'd hoped to take the scales from the doctor's eyes. But, with an uncommonly penetrating look and in a sing-song voice, his father had said it was time for him to pull his head out of his books and get on with puberty. He was the right age for it. To come up with a plan and carry it out. The bloodshot eyes of his father, the man who gestured to Victor to top him up, that poker mug that said: 'Are you really too stupid to realize that you're old enough to make your own decisions? Whether your parents work things out should mean fuck-all to you. And so you're playing this little game with Lisa to save her from the claws of a worthless home life, is that it? Oh, man, that's not a plan, that's ingrown hormones. She's your sister, get it! Another year or two and she'll be out of here.'

Upon which the doctor topped up his son's glass and they fell silent. Victor thought. In the Bois de Boulogne. Shivering in a cold wind that chased the Indian summer away.

*

The morning of her birthday, his alarm went off at six. He tiptoed through the house and drank coffee in the kitchen. Then he climbed on his bike. At the greenhouse, just outside the village, he bought sixteen white roses.

'That's the first time and let 't be the last,' the farmer said, his eyes fat with sleep. ''N' take these for yer pa, will ye?' He held up a bunch of red roses, sixteen as well.

'Twenty-five guilders if you flush them down the toilet.'

'What?'

'That's what's in it for you if you don't bring them by today.'

'Are ye completely daft?'

'Okay, then make it carnations, yellow ones.'

'Well, if ye say so.'

By six-thirty he was home again. Everyone was still asleep. He showered, dressed and scented himself. At a quarter to seven he opened her door. The room was dim and as cold as ice. She slept with the windows open, even in winter. He carried in the roses and a bowl of coffee. The story, packaged in a big envelope, was pinned beneath his arm.

For a long time he stood looking at her. She slept with her arms at her sides, her fists clenched, her hair fanned out over her pillow, naked and twisted bare of the covers to her navel. A sicky-sweet tenderness took hold of him. He laid the roses on the sheet. His hands tingled. He shook his head, stepped forward and pinched the foot dangling from the bed. She opened her eyes. In the morning light he saw life flow into her pupils: amazement, a smile, a question. His face an arm's length above hers. She smelled of hair, sweat and slumber.

'Jerk!'

She took the bowl from his hand, looked at her alarm clock, graced him with a frown and slid upright. She looked at her breasts, then at him.

Victor lit a cigarette and ran his hand through his hair. Lisa pulled a blanket up over her bosom and took a few sips of coffee.

'What's this all about, Ludwig of Bavaria?'

'Your birthday, Elizabeth of Austria.'

She held out her arms. He kissed her on the cheek.

'Wha's that?'

He handed her the envelope. She tore it open, pulled out the sheets of paper and looked at his handwriting in amazement.

'A story?'

He nodded, blushed, tingled.

She flipped through it.

'Don't, don't do that, start at the first sentence.'

'Right now?'

'Whenever you feel like it.'

'Got a cig for me?'

She inhaled deeply and picked up the roses.

'Phew, what a combination at this time of the morning, I could smell you a mile downwind.'

He blushed.

'Helmut Berger, from bad to worse,' she said, looking at him a bit worriedly.

He walked over to the turntable and put on the *'Rückert Lieder'*, really quietly. *'Ich atmet' einen linden Duft'*, Kathleen Ferrier sang. Victor smiled. Lisa ruffled her hands through her hair. Her breasts billowed out of the blankets. She left them like that.

47

'Earth to Victor!' She was talking with the cigarette in one corner of her mouth. 'Sit down for a moment, would you? What exactly have you been telling the doctor? He's been looking at me rather strangely lately.'

Victor sat down on the sill of the open window and smelled the garden.

'What is there to tell?'

'That's right, what is there, do we have to start prying around in your brain?'

'What is it you want me to say?'

'What is it you want me to want you to say?'

'Our father accuses us of playing games.'

'What? What games?'

'This.'

'But it is, uh, sort of a game . . . isn't it?'

'Is that so?'

'Stop pacing around like that! Sit down.'

On the edge of her bed. She took his hand.

'What is it you want?'

'For you to read my story.'

'Don't lie to me, what do you really want?'

His scalp itched.

'Do I have to . . .' – she looked past him – 'do I really have to hide my tits from you?'

''Course not!'

Lisa shook her head like she was trying to get free of something.

'Victor, just what the hell are you up to?'

His face went blank. He ran his hand through his hair.

She looked at him, looked away, looked again. Suddenly she grabbed his head and pulled him, his neck going limp, against her breasts ... soft, no, they were hard, cold, no, cool.

'Listen, little buddy,' she hissed, 'just listen to what you hear in your head.'

He didn't go tense, not for a moment. The smell of her sweat, her hair, her smoky coffee-breath. The clutch of her claw in his neck. His head was spinning.

'Lisa, you nut! Cut it out!'

She didn't let go.

She was laughing helplessly.

'Well? Fess up! Is that what you want?'

She let him go. He straightened up and slid closer. With steady hand he pushed strands of hair from her face. She kept her eyes on him.

'It's a nice game,' he said.

'It's a game,' Lisa said.

She smiled sadly. Then she kissed him, angry and accusing, long and determined, perfectly and imbued with distance, distance conquered, that's what he thought he tasted.

In the kitchen hung the smell of morning. Outside it was drizzling. Pigeons were cooing in the trees. Victor set the table, smoked, paced. He tied his necktie, loosened it again. He read the story through Lisa's eyes, with what he thought was her fickle heart. At seven-thirty he poured himself a glass of cognac, took a Havana and went out to sit in the rain without his coat on.

A hand on his shoulder.

'Hey, buddy, you trying to give your mother a heart attack?'

The doctor took the glass out of his hand, poured the last drops into the monkshood under the birches, and said: 'Here's to you, gentlemen.'

He lingered there in his bathrobe. The smell of his heavy black roll-up drove away that of Victor's cigar.

'Your sister awake yet?'

'I gave her roses, white ones.'

'Oh?'

'You're giving her carnations, yellow ones.'

'Ummm . . . Victor?'

' . . .'

'I'm sending you to Amsterdam for a month, my treat, I have an old friend down there.'

'What's this shit? I can't go now, we've got a project week coming up in October. We're going to Münich.'

'I don't give a damn, you're going away at least until then, you've got to pull your head out of the clay, boy.'

'I suppose you're going to give me money to go to whores.'

'If that's what you'd like.'

The doctor patted him on the shoulder and shuffled off. Suddenly he stopped. Victor looked at his father.

'And until you go away, you're not drinking another drop in this house.'

Then he shuffled on.

Victor tossed his cigar away and rested his forearms on his knees. Centuries later – he was soaked and exhausted – he felt fingers tickling the back of his neck.

'What's wrong, why are you crying?'

Anna, big-eyed.

'A shitty mood, that's all.'

She crawled up onto his knee, looked at the sky, let rain fall in her face and put an arm around his neck.

'Just like Papa?'

'Hey, shouldn't you put something on? You'll catch cold like this.'

'No I won't, but what did you do?'

'Boozed it.'

'Uh-oh, dumbo.'

She rocked him.

'Come inside. Right this minute!'

His mother was at the kitchen door.

'Come on, everyone at the table before Liesje gets here! Victor, you're soaked to the skin, are you trying to make yourself ill?'

They sat down at the table. The doctor looked at him impassively. He poured the coffee and offered him a Camel. Then he stuck two fingers in the corners of his mouth and stretched his lips up into a dead-stiff grin.

Lisa came in timidly, the roses in her arms.

'Hurrah! Hurrah! Hurrah!' Anna shouted.

'Don't sing,' Lisa said, 'don't start singing.'

She got a kiss from her parents and one from Anna.

'Where did you get those?' her mother asked, pushing Lisa down into her chair.

'From him.'

Her cheeks were flushed. She stared at the floor.

'What's this, Victor, wherever did you get those so early, and take off that shirt, you're completely soaked. Liesje, you look lovely, dresses look so good on you, except your décolletage, oh, well, if you've got it, flaunt it, I guess, but if Victor would just shave in the morning, you look like an anaemic poet, but I guess you don't mind, do you? I know you. Father, just look at that son of yours, don't you think he needs to go to a sanatorium? And what's this I smell? Anna, get your fingers out of the butter dish, don't make a mess. Hey, doctor, didn't we have a present or something? Get off that fat butt of yours for once, don't sit there gawking, who wants an egg? Anna, I'm not telling you again!'

Victor tried to catch Lisa's eye. She seemed startled when their gazes crossed.

What? she asked wordlessly. He did the same. Their father sat there, following their exchange. Their mother came back with the eggs.

'Come on, Father,' she said, 'hurry up!'

The doctor got up and shuffled out of the kitchen.

'Later on, okay?' Lisa's wet eyes were saying.

'Victor's been boozin' it,' Anna whispered in Lisa's ear, 'Daddy's real mad.'

'What was that, girlie?' her mother asked with a glance at the counter.

'Nuh-thing.'

The doctor laid a present in his daughter's lap.

She unwrapped it, her eyes filling with tears. They ran down her cheeks as she flipped through the stack. Mahler, Chopin, Presley, The Doors, Waits. They dripped off the tip of her nose when she stood up, said 'Thank you,' and ran out of the kitchen. The records lay fanned out on the table.

'Huh,' her mother said, 'what was that all about?'

'Overwhelmed by emotion,' the doctor said.

*

She was standing in front of the open window in her room. It was the first time he'd ever seen her sob. Her shoulders shook. She had her arms around herself.

Victor had the feeling – *déjà vu* in reverse – that he'd already left, as if only his thoughts were still in this house.

He stood behind her without touching her.

'He's sending me to Amsterdam for a month.'

She turned around and hit him. A razor-sharp smack across the face.

Before he could get to the door, she had hold of him. She took his head in both hands and hissed: 'I thought it was nice, nice, nice . . . and nasty!'

He nodded.

She let him go and sat down on the bed.

'Close that door!'

She nodded, patted her hand on the blankets. He sat down beside her.

'It's good you're going away.'

He bowed his head: 'Oh . . . so . . .'

'*Ach so, sagt er.*'

He ran his hand through his hair.

'Knock it off!'

He shivered.

'You're a creep, you know it! I never should have told you. That I don't like it, and now you're trying to, now you're trying to . . . is that right? Is that what you're trying to do?'

'That's not what I wanted.'

'You're lying, this morning, man, I just happened to be lying here in my bare ass!'

He turned his head away.

———

The distance between them was as it had been: cruel and childlike.

'Get the hell out of here!'

At the threshold he hesitated. Something burning hit him in the back.

Standing at the kitchen door, he gestured to his father.

'Is she all right?' his mother asked.

In his office, the doctor sat him down in a chair.

'What have you been up to?'

'Nothing. I'm outta here.'

'Get your things together. I'll tell the principal you've had a nervous breakdown. What happened?'

'Nuh-thing!'

The doctor looked at him with illegible, bloodshot eyes.

His father's old friend was a scraggly chain-smoker, heir to some fortune he acted secretive about. He lived in a house-boat covered with plants, and burned candles all day in front of a statue of the Virgin Mary. 'If it doesn't help, at least it can't hurt,' he said when he caught Victor's perplexed look.

That first week, Willem, who wanted everyone to call him 'William', dragged Victor through a city he learned to hate for its bedraggled autumn looks, its cackling people, improbably big-mouthed waiters and a swathe of canals filmed beyond counting, where lingered the perpetual, melancholy sound of Toots Thielemans' harmonica. Victor felt like a character in some clumsy Dutch film. A snug backdrop like this made you loose and giggly. Here lay the cradle of Dutch irony.

Later he would hitchhike down here often from The Seat of Learning, just to prove himself right.

After that first week he began going on his own to cafés in the Jordaan neighborhood. He never called home, and no-one called him. He wandered through town, nosing in bookstores. He had money to spend and bought two boxes full. Back at the boat, an Amstel beer and Ketel I gin within arm's reach, he read his books and Willem read his, all esoteric works of obscure origin. Every once in a while the man would ask him a question. 'Do you believe in anything?' 'Ohh . . .' 'In God, or something along those lines?' 'I believe not.' Uncontrollable laughter. 'Do you know your destiny?' 'What?' 'Do you already have an idea of where your life is going?' 'Yeah, maybe a little bit.' 'To what extent?' Victor held his hands apart like a fisherman. The man cracked up. When William went to bed, he said: 'I'm turning in, will you blow out the candles? And don't be a hero, give it the sign of the cross. If it doesn't help, well . . .' With a grin, he climbed into 'the boot', as he called it. Victor pulled out the folding couch, wrapped himself in a blanket, got a stomach-ache and lay awake all night.

Ten days later a letter came, from his mother.

Dear Victor,

How are things? Everything here is fine. What happened? Lisa won't tell us. Couldn't you try to be a bit less of a cry-baby? I'm saying it for your own good. Your father is fed up with it. He could have, at least that's what I think, just come straight out and said it. But according to him even The Boss says you need to get away a little more often. I don't know, really. Well anyway, I'm not going to get involved. You understand that, don't you? It's awfully quiet at the table these days, without all your talk. But you know I don't have as much trouble with that. Your father does, in other words. He thinks you get it from my side of the family, and other nonsense like that. He wants to make a Groninger out of you. I think that's silly. But you do babble on for your age. Don't be angry, now. We miss you a lot. Especially Anna. Lisa says I'm not allowed to tell, but Anna cries about it at night. Oh, yeah. We're going to meet Liesje's Pieter before long. She said so. I think she's still real angry at you. What on earth did you say to her?

Are you having fun? I think Amsterdam is fantastic. All those houses, fantastic! If you need anything, just call. I don't know exactly what the agreement was with Father, but if you want to come home, just do it! I still have some say around here. Have a really great time and try to calm down a little. Bye.

Your mother.

Victor took pen, paper and a bottle of gin, and wrote back.

To Anna Prins (Don't let anyone else read this!)

Sweetheart,

Don't be so sad, come on, chin up. I'll be back in two weeks. I've got five books of fairy tales for you. I'll read to you every night. Don't be angry at Papa. It was my own fault. Liesje was so angry that she hit me. That has to happen sometimes. The man I'm staying with is completely nuts. He has a boat and we live on it. At night it rocks a little. When you go to sleep later on, then listen really carefully, you'll hear me tell a story on the wind. Remember how I said the sun that shines on China also shines on Oude Huizen? The very same one? The wind is like that too. And Amsterdam is real close to our house. So all you have to do is listen carefully. Tomorrow night I'll tell you the story of the prince and the chocolate pudding, the day after that the one about the little fir tree. And then you're allowed to cry. And if Mama says you're too old for that, then you just say: Granny on the warpath. So no-one can hear. You know what happened to the little fir tree. So try not to get any bigger. Just stay little. That's a lot nicer. Don't tell Lisa I wrote to you, only Mama. And she's not allowed to tell anyone else. Promise? Pay careful attention. If someone suddenly bites you in the toe tonight, that'll be me. All the way from Amsterdam. And tomorrow morning early, stick all your fingers in the butter dish, just for me. Bye. Victor. (Don't cry anymore because I'm gone, hear?)

He waited for the postman every morning for the next five days. Nothing came. He wandered through the city and drank boilermakers. He searched for books for Anna and looked around in the hope that some revelation would point him to a peace offering for Lisa. But he had enough insight into 'where his life was going' to know that it was no use waiting for a revelation. One evening he took a book out of one of his boxes and flipped through it. He'd bought it for its title and the striking dust jacket. The contents seemed oblique and unreadable – it was a translation. Still, he forged ahead. It was a grungy joke from the void: once he'd penetrated the pages and everything began to smell of honeysuckle (even the heroine, especially the heroine), he looked around suspiciously for a moment. Then the urge to wound overpowered him. He read the book in one go, threw up half a liter of gin into the toilet in the morning, put on his clothes, found a post office and mailed it, gripped by irrepressible tremors, registered mail to Lisa, with a brief note: 'Chapter Two; hoopla!' Then he drank himself under. He told William he was sick, and crawled under the blankets. The man laid his hands – burning, leeching hands – on his chest and said he was 'blocked'. Should he call his parents? Victor shook his head and asked William to leave him alone. Half an hour later, a letter came.

Dear Victor,

I didn't let anyone else see it. I don't have to cry anymore. I can't hear you, but you did bite me in the toe. Come home! Liesje never wants to read out loud. She's not angry anymore. The reason she hit you is because you always used to hit her, that's what I think. Remember when we were on vacation and you hit her and I wasn't allowed to tell from her, I thought that was stupid. She told me that, about the vacation, but I still remembered. I lied. I have to cry sometimes, but not all the time. Papa and Mama never read out loud either. They're stupid and they fight. I don't like it. Fixbier cries too. That's why the neighbors are angry. But not The Boss. Lisa goes with him to Stik. I'm not allowed to go. Will you buy a map of Amsterdam? One with all the streets on it? I want to hang it on the wall. You promised, remember, about reading out loud? I can read by myself, but then I can't see it. Only when I read *Bob and Bobette*. Bye. Anna. Please come back tomorrow.

Victor got sicker and sicker. He hallucinated and threw up.
William put his hot hands on the back of Victor's neck and
seemed to panic.

'I'll call your dad.'

''s a doctor, that's right.'

William drove him to Groningen in two hours flat.

In Town he was pushed into his father's car. Victor lay
on the back seat and heard voices in the distance.

'Young fella's one big cramp, ass to elbow.'

'He's gotta have his nose rubbed in it.'

'In what? In your shite?'

'Don't go playin' Jesus Hisself, y'hear?'

'You raise that boy by holdin' your own photo album
front of his nose?'

'I ain't got no photo album, Billy Boy.'

Victor could tell he was being carried into the parental
home, and vaguely sensed the two jabs in his arm before it
all went foggy.

He didn't sleep, but dreamed without pause. Scorching
earth across which monsters marched. He sweated, trembled.
Cramps shot through his body. There came a moment – he
couldn't tell day from night – when his father was sitting
next to his bed, dabbing at his forehead with a cold, wet
cloth. Victor looked at him, unable to speak.

'Sit up straight now, boy.'

He couldn't do it. His father put one hand behind his
head and held it up, the glass to his lips.

'Think you can keep it down?'

It was cognac, pure, sweet and burning. He took a little
sip. Fire in his throat.

'Drink it, all of it.'

The burning spread through his stomach. Peace flowed slowly out to his limbs. He let himself slide into this – almost erotic – pleasure, as into a girl's arms, and fell asleep.

Later – it had become dark for good – the doctor was there again. He dragged Victor upright against the wall and pushed a big mug into his hands. Beer.

'All at one go.'

Again that peace in his body, even though his hands were shaking so badly that he banged his lip open on the rim of the mug. Exhausted, he slid back down under the blankets. The doctor said nothing, just looked at him and dabbed his lip with a handkerchief. Then he stood up.

'This is your first,' he said, looking at his son as though he'd been careless and put his foot through the ice, 'and I hope it's your last.'

He held a mirror up in front of Victor. In the dim light he could see how his head had swollen.

Later. His window was open. Daylight was coming into his room. He'd slept. He wasn't shaking anymore, but once in a while he felt a slight cramp. A vague, familiar odor hung around him. Flowers? Next to his bed was a vase full of murky water. Green sediment on the bottom. A dying sprig was sticking out of it, leaning towards him. A sprig of linden. Victor was nauseous, screaming with thirst, but he lay there petrified, staring at the vase while a song played inside him. Then he pulled himself together. He staggered over to the window and stuck his head out. It was drizzling. The garden smelled of fall. He drank in long gulps from the tap above his sink. In one corner of the room he found a pack of Camels. He lay down on the bed and smoked, confused and excited. Horny. Inhaling made him so dizzy that he almost passed out. The door opened and Anna's blonde head peeped around the corner.

'You awake?'

He waved. She sat on the floor and looked at him.

'Get a mirror, okay?'

She looked around, then fished a compact from under a chair. He was pale, dark bags under his eyes, and thin, thinner than ever. He ran his hand over his hair and whiskers.

'Can Fixbier come in?'

The beast dove on top of him, whining softly, and crawled under the blankets; his head right on Victor's nasty stomach.

'You've got deliliums,' Anna said.

He took her hand and fought against the tears.

'From boozing it,' she said admonishingly.

Had she found her presents? She was gone in a flash. Her face red with effort when she put the box down in front of him. She took the books of fairy tales from him, enthralled. Flipped through them. There was the little fir tree. She looked up.

'Don't. Don't do that. Why are you two crying all the time?'

Lisa was still at school. She was the one who put that stick next to his bed. She was acting real weird, but she wasn't angry anymore.

'And Mama?'

'Out shopping. She was in here last night, the whole time.'

He remembered dreaming about a woman in a blue garment at his bedside, but miles away, hidden behind mosquito netting, staring into space.

'You bit me on the toe, didn't you? When you were there.

I never knew you could do that, but you can. But I couldn't hear what you said. I heard your voice, though. It wasn't scary, but it was weird. I slept real well. After you wrote that. I didn't show it to anybody. I knew you'd be home the next day. I waited for you. And then you were really, really sick. And Papa was real mad. At that man. And that man said it was his fault. Papa's fault.'

It was his own fault. He'd been homesick.

Is that why he got sick?

Victor nodded. Anna too, hesitantly.

A knock on the door. The dog appeared suddenly and jumped at the latch.

'Come in-hin,' Anna said.

Lisa was another person. Older. Thin in the face. Her mouth and nose bigger, her eyebrows heavier and blacker.

'Look,' said Anna, pointing at her books.

Lisa nodded and pushed the dog away.

Victor looked at the foot-end, then back up and saw his sisters staring blindly at each other. He felt like an uninvited guest at an old friends' reunion.

'Anna, get lost.' Even her voice was different. Dark. Fractured.

'Not if you two are going to fight.'

'We're not. Go on!'

Anna gathered up her books.

'No more punching.'

'No, silly cow, go on.'

The door closed, the dog paced and Lisa looked down at Victor.

'All right then.'

He said nothing. She began walking back and forth.

'Was this supposed to be a warning?'

'What?'

'That book, that half-baked idiot and . . . a delirium?'

He shrugged, more heartfelt than ever.

She kneeled down next to him and plucked at his blanket.

'We're going to talk this thing through, right now, I don't care what kind of shape you're in, you scared us to death.'

He ran his hand through his hair; it was like his head was going to burst. He felt cold inside.

She looked away from him.

'That story of yours, it was so pure, and you made everything filthy.'

'We can't all be saints.'

'I'm not a saint! I'm frigid, goddammit!'

'Then go to the doctor.'

'Oh, sure. So I can fuck my brother?'

'Christ!'

'Fuck! In my cunt, buddy, my cunt!' She pounded her fist on the floor and grabbed his arm before he could run his fingers through his hair. 'Would you knock that off!'

She stood up, took two steps, turned the key in the lock, tugged her blouse out of her pants and started undressing.

'Hey! Are you nuts or something?'

She didn't look at him. She pulled the blouse over her head, slid her jeans down around her hips, yanked down her panties and was naked, except for her white ankle socks.

He looked and was petrified. Her eyes squinched up, hands on her hips, her body looking like it was ready to kick out.

He turned his gaze away.

'I don't want to fuck you.'

'You sure about that?'

Victor was silent and saw the dog looking from him to her, like it was waiting for a stick someone was about to throw.

She put her clothes back on.

She unlocked the door.

She locked it again.

With a leap, she landed on his bed. The dog crept off in a corner, whining.

Victor's face was a scab that peeled and fell off.

Lisa shook her hair.

'So there.'

There was a laugh in her voice, from somewhere far away.

She slid over until she was sitting cross-legged next to his pounding head, grabbed his face with both hands, rolled a newfangled smile up into her eyes and hissed, the saliva spattering in his face: 'And I love you too . . . understand?'

He looked at her and smiled and nodded. Completely befuddled.

Victor – seeking surfeit in equation – was changing money at the Gare du Nord. The crowd was a ragbag. It looked like a European haven, some Italian director's set. Characters whose lips spoke a language different from the one you heard.

The German dubbing mania had at least uncovered one exquisite sphinx: Romy Schneider had done the voice-overs on almost all her own foreign films. So you saw her mouth moving in Italian or French, but her own timbre – the most beautiful, half-laughing, deeply sorrowful, misty timbre given to woman; the Big Bang in the alchemy of Laughter & Tragedy – dreamily belied her own lips.

He remembered, while three stations of his life were reno-vated by the stage manager of his memory into one single Gare, his banishment from the parental home long ago, his lonely arrival at the station in Amsterdam, his far-from-heroic return, his sixteen-year-old sister cruelly declaring her love, still like a child in a game picked up from watching the world at large.

On his way to Paris he had ended up in that accursed Amsterdam again and had killed time with a walk through the city. The whining of the harmonica had not been stilled.

At the flea market he had, to his fleeting amazement ('Oh yeah: hoopla!'), run into Willem. After all those years, like a man picking up the thread of an interrupted conversation, he had asked him how his sister was doing, and, with a bachelor's smile, informed him that he'd been corresponding with Lisa the whole time.

'Did she come down to see you?'

'I should say so! Before you'd even woken from your dreams. I barely got in the goddamn door myself and there she was on the gangplank, demanding an explanation. What I'd done to her brother to make him come home in a delirium. She just travelled up and back from Oude Huizen to Amsterdam.'

'I don't believe you.'

'Long black hair that she tosses over her shoulder all the time, a whole shirt full, big mouth, talks through her nose.'

'Yeah, that's right, her chest does tend to get lost in breasts. I bet you just met her at our house.'

'Do you want to see the letters?'

'So what did the two of you have to write about?'

'About the books we read! Books she said you looked down on in limitless disdain.'

'Hocus-pocus, reports from outer space, the state of the world according to Dr Heinrich Godspeak . . .'

'All right already. According to Lisa, you can only handle God if he rolls from the lips of extraterrestrial, smart-talking heroes, preferably found in the novels of mysterious American writers with a weakness for gazebos and infantile suffering.'

They sat at an outdoor café and drank boilermakers.

Victor stood up in the middle of the conversation and walked off without a word, an old itch in his scalp, an old wobble in his knees.

It was during his first, only real exile, that he'd developed the habit of looking for little sisters he could snoop on at all times. In books, but especially on television and in the movies. Romy Schneider was his favorite. When he was older, he had dreams about travelling by train through Europe on his way to her, while her voice reached him through mysterious spatial conveyance. A siren's call, until he awoke in the house in Groningen (Lisa had already gone to The Seat of Learning for her class in Dutch literature) and the day slipped by in a deep sense of loss, causing him to peruse the film pages in search of *Sissi* and swell his drunkard's tears in darkened theaters.

Victor left the station and took the metro to the center of town, pondering a film with Romy, or Kinski. In any case, a little sister *von Deutschem Blut*.

Since his nocturnal walk with Simone, he'd grown calmer. Giving in to homesickness had actually been good for his wanderlust.

He surfaced onto the pavement and saw *The Damned* in big letters across a cinema marquee. A sisterless film, but right down his alley. He looked forward to seeing his hero Helmut Berger, whose face looked more like Victor's than Victor's did. A tender Satan. Drives a child to suicide, his mother to suicide, his country to suicide. After first having slept with all of them. His swallowy eyebrows, the pencil moustache, the eyes of a violated child. European beauty, European cruelty. He was Victor's crowned kaiser of the eternal, abstract European empire, a cinematic empire of death and destruction, fascists and romantics, snobbery and decline. Victor, the descendant of Prussian nobility (they had a family tree at home with coats of arms; the emblem of their branch consisted of the tusked heads of wild swine; his father was not amused), knew evil like his own blood. All those years he'd toyed with it, teased and despised it. Went looking for it, snooped on it, wallowed in it and fled gagging, new lust building in flight like the lecher in the realm of pornographic fable.

Because he could see this film in his dreams, he lost himself in his own.

That evening they had sat together in the front room, a rare occurrence. There was a round table with four heavy old chairs arranged evenly around it. Against the wall an antique upright, on top, the glassware their mother collected. Above that a painting, 'The Hereplein with Flower Stand', that always made Victor long for Town. And later the other way around, when he stood on that Hereplein, next to that flower stand – not a horse-drawn streetcar within miles – to buy a bunch of white roses for Lisa. He wanted to go back, but he didn't know where, just back.

The heavy curtains, dull and deep red, redolent of cigar smoke, were half closed. They were drinking tea. The chandelier was on. From the little speakers behind the curtains, Mahler's First. Gentle, somber. Anna sat on a footstool between Lisa and Victor, Fixbier lay under the table. Victor was dressed and powdered, fortified with coffee and chicken broth and gagging at the mere thought of alcohol. He'd been in bed for three days and felt like the lost son in from the fields of many seasons. Anna and Lisa were sitting with their legs crossed at the knee, both bobbing one foot to the rhythm of their girlish hearts. The doctor was smoking a heavy black roll-up, his wife one of her daughter's filter cigarettes, from nervousness.

'Kids,' the doctor said, 'we're going to lay down a few rules.'

He inhaled the smoke right down to his toes and looked around with bloodshot eyes.

'Number one: that you guys smoke, all right, but I don't want you drinking here in the house. And you, Victor, not at all during the day. Not even at Stik's.'

Victor's mother looked at her son from a queer, disturbing distance, as if this were the first time she'd noticed him sitting in her room: a stranger passing through, someone leaving the next day.

'Number two. Lisa and you are leaving for project week on Monday. After that we're going to talk about schoolwork. A plan. A timetable.'

He looked at his wife, who sat smoking clumsily. The smoke drifted in front of her mouth and wafted up into her nostrils.

'And number three, just for clarity's sake. Your parents are not getting a divorce, so get that out of your heads.'

'Does anyone want more tea?' his wife asked, staring at the floor.

'And you two have to read to me when I go to bed,' Anna said. Her foot bobbed up and down.

'That too,' the doctor said. 'That too, and otherwise it's wide open. If Lisa wants to bring her boyfriend home, then, uh, then we keep our mouths shut, right?'

'You should run for political office,' Lisa mocked. 'Who's taking the minutes here this evening?'

'Okay, okay,' the doctor said. 'Pipe down.'

'I suppose this is what you call an upbringing,' Lisa said, sharply now.

'Liesje!' her mother admonished.

'Iddint tha' riiight?' Lisa badgered. 'Isn't it? Bringing up the kids! Hand in hand with Daddy, straight off the edge of the cliff.'

'Listen to me, pussycat,' said the doctor, seemingly unscathed. 'Take your accusations and write them in your little pink diary. I want peace and quiet around here. For the rest, figure it out for yourself. As far as I'm concerned you can go on the pill or whatever else you do. Victor, you can have your ivory tower. As long as the bullshit stops!'

'On the pill! How about seeing to your own body juices for once?'

'Liesje!' her mother cried.

'What is it, Granny?'

Victor thought she was adorable. Burned onto his retina was the image of her furious, naked body: pale and thin. Her flat stomach with the navel he knew like his own, her breasts, graceful and full, her neck so long and slender that she looked bigger than she was. Her whole body screaming. The pubic hair that cussed: a thin dark line fading to left and right, the deep pink of her black-speckled sex from which a blossom pouted.

'Until they set up a special court for deprived children,' the doctor said, 'you'll just have to figure it out for yourselves. Maybe I'm an asshole, but . . .'

'Could I get that in writing?'

'. . . But what I'm trying to do here is reorganize this circus, and the fact that you and your big mouth will always be the star attraction is pretty obvious to everyone.'

Lisa stood up. They were all expecting the door to slam, but she closed it circumspectly, as if putting all her feeling into it.

Father sighed. Mother looked at the floor.

'Will you read to me later on?' Anna asked timidly. Victor nodded, got up and walked to the door.

'Victor?' said the doctor, sitting up straight, 'did you hear me? Will you leave her alone?'

He bowed to his father and his mother, who was looking dazed.

She came in her bedgown to say goodnight. She left the door open a crack.

'He's taken the crock down from the attic,' Victor said.

She sat in the window and lit a cigarette.

'Is that any good?' She pointed at the book on his lap, *Maggie Cassidy*, a book that had started off promising but had slid further and further into sentimental whining.

'Aw, young love, I have more of a predilection for chaos.'

'Been flipping through the dictionary again?'

'My vocabulary came to me from a previous life.'

'What did you do, copy books in some monastery?'

'I was the Big Red Chief.'

'Did they read books?'

'Signs.'

'*Ach so.*'

'*Ach so, sagt die Magd.*'

72

'Yes indeed, there's no place like hymen.'

'Blecch, sick-o.'

'Blecch? Does that disgust you? You're a strange guy, you know that? Have you ever actually, uh, well, you know?'

'Done it, milady?'

'Christ! Keep your voice down.'

'No.'

'Oh.'

'Anyway.'

'But . . . don't you ever feel like it? I mean, you do have, uh . . .' She closed the door and went back to the window.

'You do have feeling down there and stuff, don't you?'

'And how.'

A daunting conversation.

'And what's that, uh, feeling like?'

'It's murder.'

'Why?'

'Well, it aches in your body, sometimes for days, it gets you so riled up sometimes that you could kick someone's head in.'

'But, uh . . . you can always . . .'

'Yeah, that's right, you can.'

'So what's the . . . ?'

'That only makes it worse, mostly. Jesus, Lisa, do we have to talk about this?'

'Yes. I want to know. The chicks at school talk about it all the time. I want to know.'

'Don't say "chicks". So why don't you ask them?'

'Come on, I don't want them to think I'm retarded. God,

I mean, really, it's so ridiculous that you have to make a big deal out of this.'

'Do you think you could, uh, wangle me a drink?'

'Are you nuts?'

She looked at him chidingly. He shivered with pleasure.

'Come on,' he said, 'I'm getting the shakes.'

'Well,' she wavered, 'only if you promise to tell me.'

Ten minutes later she was back.

'I gave the old fart a kiss.' She handed him a glass full of gin, a cola glass.

Victor drank. Unbridled bliss, despite the horrible taste. That burning in his deepest: the arms of a girl.

Lisa sat down in a pile of clothes, far away from him. He spoke to her of lust. After a long silence, she got up.

She tossed him a glance and lingered.

'What is it?'

'Well, um' – her brow was shining – 'should I give you a kiss?'

He nodded.

'Right, then.'

She kneeled and kissed him; her lips dry, her breath bearing the scent of toothpaste.

He wanted arms around him.

'Goodnight.'

She said it with a faint smile. A deep sigh made her veiled bosom swell.

'Yeah . . . hey, where did you get that drink?'

'From the shed.'

Another deep sigh.

'Now don't get somber on us.'

'No . . .'

Her gaze slid over him.

She left him alone.

He had forgotten to read to Anna.

Her night-light was burning reassuringly. She was asleep.
He looked at her. She opened her eyes and smiled.

'Did you forget?'

'No.'

'Yes you did.'

He sat down on the edge of the bed. She rolled onto her
side and stuck three fingers in her mouth. He tucked her in,
making a little bundle out of her. Whispering, he read her
a fairy tale, *The Elves and the Shoemaker.*

'It's a little bit childish,' Anna said when it was finished,
'but really nice. Do you have elves too?'

'What do you mean?'

'So you could bite me on the toe.'

'That was my second breath.'

'Aww . . .'

He sat there until she slept.

An hour later he was sitting there still.

They had to wait while German customs searched the whole busfull. Five minutes after the trip started, the group had split. The chaperones, history and German teachers all, sat in the front like football coaches. The boys and girls from the advanced class, ten in total, sat in the middle. The occasional wimp was tucked in between them and the teachers. The kids from the normal class – yawn artists and eternal flunk-outs – sat at the back, ruling mood and music. There were twenty of them. The only single seat in the bus, in the back, next to the emergency exit, was occupied by Victor. He kept to himself, read a book and ogled Lisa, who'd been absorbed by the group and seemed to have forgotten him. While men in uniform walked the aisle, 'We Will Rock You' pounded through the bus. The kids clapped and stamped, passed bags along and dropped terms like *Handgranate* and *Rote Armee*. The customs men became agitated and made the bus wait a full hour at the border, because, as the teachers were told, there was 'too much liquid in the tank'. The tone was set. As soon as they got into Germany, the jocks at the back forced the driver to pull over at a rest-stop, where they bought ten cases of beer.

Spirits were high and standards low, as the jocks put it. At a certain point the music stopped abruptly, and a teacher everyone called Uli Dickschädel took the mike.

'*Leute, Ruhe bitte, ich möchte gern . . .*' Lisa squatted down next to Victor. 'Are you all right? You look so somber.'

He nodded, ran his fingers through his hair, got a slap on the cheek and an encouraging smile: 'What's wrong, Ludwigchen?'

'Do you have to associate with those low-lifes?'

'God, we're back to that again, are we?'

'*Ich will kein Gebrüll mehr!*' Uli shouted.

Applause.

'I guess I just happen to have friends, mister,' Lisa said.

She left him. Someone staggered up to the front and the music began pounding again. Victor thought about home, their precarious playground, the rooms and hallways, their attic. Gone was the idyll of the last few days, when she brought him her clumsy kiss every evening, after which he'd say 'Hey, chin up.'

The evening before they left he'd finally held her, breathed in her scent like a lover, while she let it happen like a child unfamiliar with the rituals of life.

Next time the music stopped she was suddenly standing beside him, a guitar in her hand: 'Play something.'

He struck a chord and started singing: 'Beautiful People'. At first the crowd giggled, but suddenly grew quiet. When he was finished, the audience screamed and cheered. Lisa, who was still standing next to him, said quietly: 'Well, excuse me,' pulled his hair and disappeared into the back. Fresh bottles were opened. Victor was handed a half-liter by a blond jock – of the Björn Borg variety – and took it. The noise picked up, and the landscape passed everyone by.

They'd been in Germany before, the birthplace of Old Shatterhand and Winnetou. Victor was thirteen and Lisa barely twelve. The town of Gomorrah where they went to school was twinned with Heidelberg, and exchanged teams at the start of every school year. They stayed with host families. Lisa (swimming) and Victor (soccer) were placed in a prosperous household. Mercedes four-door, dishwasher, a collection of fishing rods on the wall of the ten-year-old son. A spacious guest room.

The woman of the house, Magda, took Victor's breath away with her beauty. She lay on the couch all day, like in an old movie, eating chocolates. The evening meal was served at a table set in truly stunning fashion, four, five courses long, with wine for the children as well, and the beautiful lady sat looking at Lisa and Victor with an unbearable tenderness, as if brother and sister came from a world she'd never known existed until then.

In the guest room were two single beds, made up with unfamiliar feather quilts under which you seemed to suffocate despite their fluffy weight. They didn't stick it out long that first night in the rambling house. After a minute's hesitation, Lisa, still a child and quick to be lonely, crept into bed with Victor and wanted him to curl his body around her, like he had on other vacations when the homesickness began to gnaw: her back against his stomach, his arms around her, his knees in the hollows of hers, her hair in his mouth. That's how they fell asleep, and when Magda brought them breakfast in bed that first morning she brushed away a tear at the sight of them.

It was dark by the time they reached München. The first victim of alcohol abuse, the champion of intolerance, Tjapko Tiswat (who was in the habit of shooting holes in the blackboard with an air pistol from the back row, when in class with a dorky teacher), was carried from the bus by two boys. One of the girls stuck a finger down his throat. The teachers raced into the hotel.

An old fire-trap in the center of town with a little bar in the lobby, an airshaft full of garbage and an endless staircase winding upward. Uli Dickschädel stood rattling a piece of paper and barking orders. The students split up and climbed the stairs. Lisa took the first room she came to on the second floor, along with a girlfriend. Victor took the room across the hall, stood watching in the doorway as his sister settled in with the air of a globetrotter.

'No shower? Blecch!' Lisa said, looking around. 'Probably some filthy booth at the end of the hall. With all those dirty boys!'

Girls giggling. A bed littered with clothes in no time flat.

Victor looked around his room. A double bed, a flecked mirror, a crooked old cupboard, a chair and a little table. Who would dare to share this bed with him?

He was putting his hair in a ponytail when someone came and stood in the doorway, cigarette dangling, arms folded across the chest.

'Well, Winnetou.'

Cobus B., notorious cool guy. Victor nodded and began shaving. Cobus strolled into the room and dropped onto the bed. In the mirror, Victor watched as he blew perfect rings of smoke at the ceiling.

'Puttin' dudes in a double bed. Wha' is this, the Wild West?'

'*Das Land der männlichen Kameradschaft*, the Wild East.'

Cobus grinned. 'Thing is, my kamerad, Cowboy Veen, iddn't around. He's 'n' London, but he'd 'n' loved this.'

(Cobus, as Lisa and Victor discovered years later, played a not-insignificant role in Veen's book, *The Adventures of Hillebillie Veen*, which he was working on when they got to know him again.)

Lisa knocked on the open door. Victor waved to her to come in. She sat on the window sill and lit a cigarette.

'What a surprise,' she sneered at Cobus. Cobus nodded and belched loudly.

'Imagine that, you rooming right across the hall from your girlfriend,' Lisa went on in the throes of sarcasm.

Cobus looked at her, unmoved, and blew another smoke ring.

Uli Dickschädel stuck his head in the door: 'And who do we have here, may I ask?'

'Shatterhand,' Cobus said, then pointing at Victor: 'Winnetou.'

'Come on,' Uli said.

'Take it some'ere else, fathead,' Cobus said.

'And what about you?' Uli asked Lisa. She pointed to the door across the hall.

'Prins, right? Who are you rooming with?'

'Marian.'

'Marian who?'

'That's right, Marian Who,' Cobus acceded.

Uli scribbled on his paper and moped off. Marian signalled to Lisa from the other room. She was a high-hearted East Groningen girl with a proper accent and prim gestures, a strange mate for Cobus. Lisa avoided Victor's glance in the mirror as she walked past. A glob of shaving cream did, however, spatter off his ear onto his reflection with a flick of her fingers.

Cobus looked questioningly at Victor.

'Lissun, Prins, d'ye figure there're any shops open aroun' here?'

'You're askin' me?'

A few minutes later Victor was following him down the stairs, anxious to see the tenor of his ways. Uli, his hands full of crumpled paper, saw them.

'Hé, hier bleiben, wir gehen essen!'

Cobus waved to him in passing. Outside he stopped and pointed across the street: 'Cathouse, see there? Bouncer, *Eintritt einundzwanzig*, bee-em-dubbel-ya's o' the pimp-and-Turk persuasion–'

'*Ach zo.*'

They found an underground supermarket that was still open. Victor followed Cobus through the shop and watched as he filled his cart with fifty cans of beer and ten jars of *Bismarkhering*.

'You jus' watch t'night,' Cobus said while the cashier rang up the bill. Two enormous bags under his arms, he raced out in front of Victor all the way back to the hotel. At the door they ran into the crowd that had gathered to go to dinner.

'Be right back,' Cobus said to Uli.

Amused, Victor followed him to their room. Cobus

arranged the wares in their cupboard, stood back to look proudly at his possessions and did some quick calculations: 'Two marks a can, one mark a herrin', day after amorrow we breaks even; enda the week we's rich.'

He looked at Victor and winked. For the first time in his life, Victor wasn't enraged by the gesture.

'What's your father do?'

'Little bitta everythin', snack car at the weekend, markets and stuff.'

'*Ach zo.*'

'You'd be just like yer sissy with tha' "*ach zo*" shit.'

'You know that Pieter she goes with?'

'Sure, it was him that gived ye that beer in the bus.'

'Oh, yeah.' The Björn Borg clone.

'Real decent type dude.'

'I bet.'

Cobus looked at him and shook his head in wonderment.

They joined up with the group. Lisa came over to him, a tauntingly fond look in her eye.

'Been making friends?'

He shrugged. She put her arm through his, which he found rather bizarre, and began teasing while the group headed raucously for the restaurant, Cobus, Marian, the unsteady Tjapko Tiswat and her Pieter following behind.

'Do you think it's wise to associate with low-lifes, Fikkie? Isn't that way beneath you? You might catch something!' She said it in a whisper, improperly enthused.

'Boy, aren't we cheerful.'

'We sure are, Buster Brown, no more of the doctor's bitching . . . boy, if I was ready for anything!'

Where was her homesickness?

'You can walk with your boyfriend if you want.'

'Later, maybe, for protocol's sake. But first I want to make sure you're not feeling rotten.'

'Protocol?'

'Well, uh, I mean, there's only something between us because the others think there is.'

'And what does he think of all this?'

'Oh, he *is* pretty much in love with me. Oops, I guess I shouldn't have said that.'

'Flake off.'

'Zum Befehl, Brüderchen.'

They ate disgusting cutlets at a beanery.

At around ten they broke up into cliques. A German teacher, Herr Buckel, cajoled Cobus, Marian, Tjapko, Victor and Lisa and two couples into going along to a Bavarian Bierhalle, an old cowhouse with long tables where people sat drinking steins of beer. It stank horribly of piss. An oompah band was playing in one corner. A few drunken customers were singing along.

They bellied up to a table and ordered liter mugs.

Herr Buckel was a legend. He reportedly had a problem with alcohol and pills, and he was one of the last teachers who dared to smoke in class. The way the man inhaled Caballeros was something to see: like some people slurp down oysters; a look like he was gobbling up the sex of an innocent child. His head had something sovereign to it, his hair greasy and combed back, glistening black, his eyes bloodshot with black bags beneath. He had a shiny black moustache: a bare slug traversing his upper lip. That evening they felt successively that he was in league with them, the school riffraff; that he sympathized with them, wanted to be young with them again; and, finally, that he mourned their lives out of compassion for what he saw as their lot or cross to bear: growing up just to come to no good. He was calm and mild and let the jocks rave on about the way the school was run. Lisa sat next to Pieter 'for the sake of protocol'. Brother and sister joined in the conversation, but he jeered and she blushed.

The German folk began singing more loudly. Suddenly they heard something that struck them dumb. From one corner of the cowhouse came the refrain of a Nazi song.

A chorus of about twenty men, a few women's voices. Part of the band played along halfheartedly.

'Is that what I think it is?' Lisa asked.

'*Die Unausrottbären*,' Herr Buckel said.

'Well, who's comin' with me?' Cobus asked, standing up and stepping towards the corner like a cowboy entering a hostile saloon. Tjapko Tiswat got up and followed. Herr Buckel jumped to his feet and hurried after them. He grabbed them each by an arm and hustled them back to the table. No-one seemed to notice the commotion.

'Are you out of your goddamn minds?' Herr Buckel snapped at Cobus and Tjako. 'This is Germany, they'd kill you!'

They looked around. Most of the Germans seemed to be biding their time: a blip in the drinking spree, a false note, the uncle in a nasty, drunken funk at a family reunion. Lisa and Victor exchanged a glance and shared a single thought: I want to go home!

Pieter put an arm around Lisa and whispered in her ear. Victor looked on and thought he felt endearment.

'Let's get out of here,' he said. He stood up: the group

followed. When they got to the tables where the national anthem was being raised (even more ridiculous than a Nazi song in Victor's eyes), he grabbed Cobus by the collar and pushed him out the door. Outside, Herr Buckel took a head-count. Then he looked at his students, ruminating on his thoughts, his eyes full of hate. He couldn't come up with anything to say.

They walked back to the hotel in silence. Lisa let Pieter hold her; he laid his arm around her shoulders.

The teachers stayed in the hotel bar. Cobus and Victor invited Marian and Lisa to their room. Lisa granted Victor a gaze full of pent-up homesickness. He didn't know which way to look.

Pieter and Tjapko appeared in the doorway, wavering, waiting for a welcome.

The door was open a crack, and every time Cobus saw someone go by he rushed into the hall: 'Beer here, all night long, but it's hush-hush.'

They drowned their confusion. Lisa grew calm too, even without seeming at ease. She goggled nervously at Victor. He lay on the bed and smoked and nodded to her, comfort-ingly he hoped.

For the first time in his life he felt too young for what he was experiencing. What was it he'd seen? Was it an echo, or a portent of doom? And was it confusion or excitement he felt when suddenly he remembered how, as a boy, he had sometimes thought while reading an exciting book: if only there was a war on, then I'd . . .

Meanwhile, things seemed to be picking up. Cobus and Marian were sitting on the edge of the bed, fumbling at each other. Tjapko was haranguing Lisa. Pieter listened and laughed every now and then. They were sitting on the enormous sill, the window open. Music, from the brothel across the street it seemed, droned its way into the room. Occasionally someone came to buy beer. Cobus was busy, so Victor ran the till. Suddenly Herr Buckel appeared at the door and peered around.

'Verrry cozy, you all take good care of the girls?'

Victor nodded, offered him a can, but he refused.

Cobus and Marian were lying on the bed in a drunken embrace. Tjapko was slouched on the floor, dozing. Pieter and Lisa were whispering, while Lisa made heated gestures. Victor closed the door, picked up the guitar that had remained in the vicinity for some reason and played to drown out the sounds of the *Grosstadt*.

His homesickness seemed to make way for an enormous space he'd discovered, a space that contained the possibility of longing for home. To be honest, he felt at ease. He shook his head, looked around and thought: spirits are high, standards low.

It must have been the circumstances. The hand the group had extended him. The lost vantage of his parents, which had turned the family home into a battlefield. The dubious, but nonetheless heartwarming rage of the jocks at the sight of a group of old Nazis. This cinematic gathering in an old hotel room in a large city. Finally, though, his conviction was that he had to be on his own. Lisa was the only one he tolerated next to him.

Lisa! She was still sitting there, gesturing wildly. It looked like Pieter was being served up a disquisition. He was nodding, nipping at his beer without touching her. Tjapko Tiswat was asleep on the floor. Cobus and Marian had lost articles of clothing, and Marian's breasts were glistening under Cobus' lips.

Victor tried to catch Lisa's eye. It took a while, but she saw him. She was sitting with her arms around her tucked-up knees. Her hair rocked in a breath of wind at the window. When her glance crossed his she smiled fleetingly, by way of greeting and recognition. 'You okay, man?' He raised his eyebrows. She replied with hers that she was 'on hold here for a bit, won't take long, I hope'. Pieter turned and looked at Victor, who smiled affably. Pieter's expression didn't change. He turned back to Lisa. Victor strummed at melodies that somehow seemed familiar.

A pounding at the door. Victor looked around the room. Cobus raised his head from his helpless prey and nodded. Marian covered her bosom. Tjapko mumbled something in his sleep. When Victor opened the door, a boy from the advanced class stuck his head in: 'Have you guys got beer?'

Victor sold him ten cans and a jar of herring, and asked him to take Tjapko to his room.

'I can't carry him by myself.'

Victor turned to Pieter, who was watching them. 'Maybe you should give him a hand.'

Lisa looked at her brother, startled, then said: 'Yeah, right, I do need to get some sleep.'

Pieter stood up slowly, gave Victor a dagger look – a duel of the eyes – then smiled. Tjapko was picked up and trundled out the door. Lisa waved apologetically, and a second later it was just the four of them.

'Aaaah,' Cobus said, stretching effusively, 'now we can

close up shop for the evenin', 'n' if ye sleeps in yer sissy's room, we'll be in like flint.'

'Oh right,' Lisa said, 'I was wondering when you'd get around to that.' She climbed down off the sill and glared at Marian, who made a hushing gesture.

'Cobus, if they don't want that, then it can't be.'

'Come, come,' Cobus said, '*ein bisschen Kameradschaft.*'

Victor looked at Lisa. She looked at him.

'All right,' Marian said, arranging her clothes. She signalled to Lisa and, under loud protest from Cobus, they disappeared to their room. Victor put the guitar back in the corner, pulled off his shirt, tossed Cobus a can and collapsed next to him on the bed. He would have given his right arm for a chance to talk to Lisa.

'Y'r a quiet Prins, ol' pal.'

'You're mistaken about that.'

'I guess so. 'N' I guess I'm deaf, too.'

'Could be.'

'Whadda ya think o' Marian?'

'*Schöne Brüste.*'

'Them Nazis, hey? Whaddya think o' that?'

'The nostalgia of old swine.'

'That all?'

'Let's hope so. As long as old farts hanker after the past, there's no need to worry; when young people do it, there's somethin' wrong.'

'Y'r a smarty-pants, ain't ya?'

'Pretty much, yeah.'

Cobus laughed, punched him in the arm and stood up.

'Just take a gander at the girlies.'

The door closed with a bang. Victor was touched by such a mild view of his *hauteur*. He drifted slowly off to sleep. What would it be like to have something like a comrade? Someone you hung around with every day? It seemed like a huge investment to him.

The room was dark when someone crawled in next to him. When she poked him, he smelled her hair.

'Fikkie!'

'Liesje? Christ! Did you let them talk you into this?'

'Shall I lock the door?'

'Wait a minute.'

He clicked on the bizarre night-light, white lilies painted across its shade. With burning eyes he watched as she turned the key in the lock and wriggled out of her clothes. She fell on the bed beside him, wearing black panties and a singlet, both trimmed with lace.

'Man, I'm exhausted!'

'Not me. On the contrary, my kingdom for a beer. You too?'

'Hmmm, yeah, all right.'

He brought her a can, lay down again with one hand behind his head and looked at her. She lay there squinting at him. She smelled of a whole day of life.

'That dick just kept hanging around, and I really have to sleep, otherwise I'll be dead tomorrow.'

'I doubt that.'

'What?'

'That that dick will just keep hanging around.'

'Oh boy, finally entering puberty are we?'

She giggled and slid a hand under her head. A smell like

a sea wind reached him. A new perfume from her glands.

'You need a shave,' he said, running a finger over her armpit, stealing her scent.

'Yeah, I forgot my razor, can I borrow yours tomorrow?'

'Shall I, uh, I mean I could, you wouldn't even have to get up.'

'Would you really?'

This is a neutral tone, something in her eyes in search of intimacy. Desire born of fatigue or homesickness, what difference did it make?

He was already gathering his shaving stuff. The quiver of blood. Taut muscle.

'Off with your shirt,' he said, like he was talking to Anna.

'Oh? . . . Well then . . . hoopla.'

Now don't, don't, plant a kiss there. Lather, shave, slower than slow. Linger a bit. Other armpit. Linger! Dab with warm water. Rub dry, and . . . check the results with another sly fingertip.

'We're a little drunk, aren't we?' Lisa lulled, touched but absent, nodding and sighing. Her breasts shook ever so slightly.

'So what was this speech to Pieter Pieter Pumpkineater?' He was lying next to her again, leaning on one elbow, gawking and badly in need of a drink.

'Oh . . . You know, you're a real creep, but anyway, how shall I put it . . .' She folded her hands behind her head. 'Well, that I think he's really sweet, but uh, that there's someone else, at home, somewhere . . . how do I know what I'm supposed to say?'

A smile, a glimmer of her daily desolation. He had to come up with something fast. He took a chance.

'Liesje, shall we put an end to all this?' What a thing to say!

'An end to what?'

'Well, to whatever binds you to me.'

'And what is it exactly, Your Highness, that binds me to you?'

'Mmm, love, I suppose.'

'That swashbuckling tone of yours really gives me the jeebies.'

'Don't say "jeebies", and isn't it typically female to declare your love and then become bogged down in eternal moaning?'

'And where did we read that?'

'Made it up all on my lonesome.'

'Methinks that sweeping statements about love should come from one who knows.'

'Methinks?'

'God, man, stop it, would you! Would you just hold me? Just that? Like in the movies?'

He held her tight.

She began crying, an almost calm, subdued sobbing. 'God-dammit all to hell.' Her voice soft, dark, fractured.

Even love, especially love, demands sacrifice and heroism. He rocked her a bit, his arms around her clammy back, her tears on his shoulder. He listened to her breathing slowly grow quiet. When she was asleep, and his ten-year-old sister again, he tucked a blanket around her and crept out of the room, locking the door. Bare from the waist up, he walked down the hall, up the stairs, in search of spaces where the buzzing of voices had not been stilled. Some floors of the hotel, he found, were still in pandemonium. Open doors, shrieks of laughter, screaming and the rattle of phlegm. Just when he'd reached the top floor, some fishwife from down below shouted: '*Ruhe bitte!*'

A door swung open and Victor saw a group of advanced students with drunken grins peering into the hall. He saluted.

'Heyyy, Melanie, where's your guitar?'

He gestured to accept their invitation, went in and beheld a ravage of food and drink.

'Do you guys have any schnapps?'

They set a half-full bottle in front of him. Quick, a quick drink, then another. He began babbling: 'What are you learned gentlemen doing in Germany, exactly? In terms of project week, I mean? That's what I'd know to like . . . like to know, aren't you afraid of reper- bahn, uh, -cussions? Shouldn't you be in Paris, slobbering at the Louvre, they've got John the Baptist there, shouldn't you be there waiting for the dove to alight and bless your futures?'

They burst out laughing.

'*Was soll es,*' Victor said. '*Verbrüderung in München*' – he raised his glass – '*und verflucht sei die Heimat!*'

'*Verflucht sei die Heimat!*' roared the whole crowd.

'*Ruhe bitte!*' screamed the fishwife downstairs.

Back in the room, Victor locked the door behind him. He took off his boots and trousers, crept into bed and kissed his sister on the back of the neck, causing her to shudder slightly and move against him, like in the old days: her buttocks in his lap, her back against his chest, her hair in his mouth.

The murmur of the city woke them. Lisa stretched and looked at Victor, like a girl in the movies recalling last night's misbehavior with mixed feelings. A caressing hand slid across his face.

'Pretty good arrangement, this,' she noted.

The screaming of Victor's hangover was gagged for a moment. He got up, looked at her – sure enough, she was waving at him, mocking his shyness – and stuck his head under the tap. Then, with intense enjoyment, he knocked back two cans of lukewarm beer.

'Victor, take it a little easy with that tippling, would you?'

'So why don't you tell me how the doctor looks when you bring him his drink in the morning?'

'Charming, like a little boy who's messed his pants and is afraid to say anything about it.'

'Jesus, and you put up with that?'

'You take having parents pretty seriously, don't you?'

Victor took another can of beer and a look of reprimand, a look he'd have killed for in years to come.

'When you were in Amsterdam, with that so-called home-sickness of yours, were you homesick for Pa and Ma?'

'Well, no. I was homesick for home.'

'Right, for Anna, and for me, I hope . . .'

Hope?

'. . . But you couldn't have cared less about those two?'

'Aw, I'm not so sure about that.'

'Oh, but I am. And if you'll excuse me for playing Lady Sigmunda for a moment: that's one reason why you're always on my ass all the time.'

'Hoopla!'

'Exactly, and racing right along' – she stretched again, triumphantly this time – 'I think Anna is just like you, and she's always on your ass. What a mess, huh?'

'Was this a revelation you had in some dream last night?'

'A visitation, Ludwigchen, more like a visitation.'

Victor was silent, he left it up to Lisa; he knew she couldn't stand that.

'And would the lady from the Viennese delegation like a cup of coffee?'

'Oh yeah, can you arrange that? God, but imagine if they find out what's going on here, you know?'

'When I go out, I'll look to see how busy it is. When I pound on the door, you can go take a shower or something, get dressed there. When you come back, just leave the door open a crack.'

'Hey, Victor?'

He turned around.

A look devoid of desolation.

Probably, Victor thought, only people from the same family can talk to each other with their eyes.

The hallway and stairs were deserted. He rapped on the door and, already timid and listening to his own interior croaking, went downstairs.

Herr Buckel was at the bar, drinking coffee and cognac.

'What happened? You roll over and fall out of bed?'

'Something like that,' Victor said. 'I need what you've got, but a double.'

The teacher flagged down the barman and paid for Victor.

'The girls, I take it, are sleeping most soundly?'

There was something pleading in his eyes. Victor nodded. He dawdled at his coffee and cognac. He wanted to extend this teacher a hand, a pat on the back, and he said without thinking: 'I let my sister sleep in my room because that was, uh, safer.'

The man nodded slowly and looked at Victor with shattered eyes.

'Fine by me, as long as you make sure it doesn't cause trouble when we get home. And don't let Uli or any of those other assholes find out.'

He was visibly startled by his own words.

'What I mean is, I take it that the other two weren't brother and sister.'

Victor nodded and ordered another round. They drank in silence. While he was getting ready to take a cup of coffee upstairs, Herr Buckel, his eyes roaring now, said, 'She's pretty, isn't she? Your sister.'

Victor nodded and looked at the teacher expectantly.

'Too pretty to let go.'

Victor didn't say anything. Victor got out of there fast.

Back in the room he lay down on the bed and smoked. When Lisa came in, redolent of shampoo and rouge, wearing one of her lowest-cut dresses, he saw that her dream was still burning on her lips. She slurped up the lukewarm coffee, brushed her teeth, claimed a cigarette, went to the window sill and tossed her hair over her shoulder.

'Okay,' Victor said, 'out with it.'

'What?'

A vain little laugh. Coquettishness of old, from when she was twelve and governed his life.

'I dreamed I was married to you, real weird, real serious too, with all those retarded routines like washing the dishes and cooking meals, and, here it comes, that I was pregnant and wondering how it had happened.'

'Goddamn, you really do put on saintly airs, don't you?'

'You know what I think?'

'What?'

'That it was us, I mean, you and me, from what we're doing, and that there was nothing dirty . . . hey, come on, you don't have to make a face, you know what I mean, that there was no nastiness about the whole thing.'

'I don't know what the fuck you're talking about.'

'Yes you do, I mean that I'd, uh, accepted our love, that it had come into me, um, by itself. Yeah, that's it.'

Victor looked at her, quiet, searching for words, for a gesture.

'I think that's beautiful,' he said then.

She glanced around shyly, clutched at her hair, shook her head, looked at him: 'So . . .'

She sighed deeply, but differently, different from all those other times.

'And what now?' he asked, thinking, how peculiar, that he could feel his age, like another person, rising up inside him.

'Now? Man, I don't know, I guess we go buy rings.'

She smiled, soft-eyed. Victor thought about travelling, about going on, about not going back. Lisa stood up and looked at her watch.

'Shouldn't you call Anna? You can catch her just before she leaves for school.'

'Oh yeah, shit! Forgot all about it.'

Downstairs a few students were sitting at breakfast. Lisa took a table in a dark alcove and tossed him one last pondering look before he disappeared into the little phone booth in the hall.

When he sat down beside her a little later, she was plucking at a kaiser roll and arranging the pieces on her plate.

'And?'

'Whether we can come back right now.'

'I see.'

'And the doctor asked how we were getting along, the two of us.'

A smile, first at the corners of her mouth, then in her eyes.

'So what did you tell him?'

'That we were doing well. But you know,' he whispered, 'to tell you the truth, I don't want to go back at all, I want to stay away. If we were rolling in money, we could kiss school goodbye, just thinking in nineteenth-century terms now, we could travel from hotel to hotel, uh, going to see a little art . . . sending letters to those who stayed behind.'

'Victor?'

'Hmm?'

'You're so goddamn impractical, you know that?'

'Impractical? What kind of girl-talk is that?'

'Just that. Stop wanting things you can never have.'

The day's programme included a visit to Dachau. After breakfast the hungover crew was cajoled into the bus by a cold-sober Uli. No one felt like it, but a project week is a project week, and they were all too exhausted for sabotage. During the drive, hangovers were dispersed with drink, requests played, new loves revealed. Victor sat next to Lisa in the back of the bus, amid last night's *Bierhalle* pilgrims, and cursed himself, afraid he'd trampled the morning's delicate mood. He'd have to watch what he said. He had to let it sink in that they were alone together now, with their love.

The bus stopped on a bare, misty lot. They climbed out

with the blahs. The boys found a ditch to piss in. The girls shared mascara. He got Lisa aside for a moment. Her eyes revealed her thoughts swooping down, one after the other, like gulls over a pond. Then she saw his anxiety. A mild derision moved across her features.

'Hey, everything's just fine.'

'Really?'

'Don't act so traditional.'

'What might one mean by that?'

'Well, just that, this heart-on-your-sleeve stuff.'

'Oh, well, I hope you won't hold it against me.'

'Ganz und gar nicht, mein Herr.'

They looked around and exchanged grins.

'Hey,' Victor said, the surf pounding in his chest, 'do you smell that?'

'What? Do I stink?'

'No, silly cow, the way it stinks here, don't you smell it?'

She shook her head.

The crew stumbled off after Uli, in the direction of a little guardhouse. The odor made Victor's eyes burn, the way the aroma of the coffee roaster's in Town (shopping for Sunday clothes with Pa and Ma) used to make his head hurt, his eyes water, his stomach flip. A German in a cheery uniform – droopy moustache and tourist grin – led them through the gate and to a room with a permanent exhibition about the atrocities. The East Groningen jocks turned deathly pale.

When they came out again, breathing deeply in relief, Victor was almost floored by the stench he'd had a whiff of outside the camp. A bleak field with a few rows of barracks, some of them half in ruins, others never abandoned, or so it seemed. They crossed the grounds grimacing. Tjapko and Cobus were so wound up that they wanted to go after the moustache in the guardhouse. Burning hatred overpowered the group. Victor kept his distance and tried to gulp back the smell of death that had seeped into this ground forever. Behind a collapsed barrack he bent and vomited.

Never again would he listen to a high-school history lesson.

Back in the bus they started drinking. The prevailing dismay was one many a teacher with slide projector and pointer would have given his eye-teeth to produce.

They ate *Dauerwurst und Fritten* in the hotel lounge. Around eight they went back to their rooms. No-one wanted to go out on the town.

There were ten of them in Victor and Cobus' room, drinking beer and saying little.

'Prins, buddy, play us somethin'.'

He took the guitar, struck a chord and sang:

> 'Oooooooh, to live on sugar mountain,
> With the barkers and the colored balloons.'

A boy from the advanced class cracked open a bottle of schnapps. Tjapko Tiswat fumbled furtively at a plastic bag and, to everyone's surprise, rolled a majestic joint. When there was a knock on the door, someone locked it. They smoked hash, drank themselves an ulcer and watched as Cobus' hand slid into Marian's pants. It was 1978.

Around one o'clock, the fishwife started screaming again: '*Ruhe, ruhe, verdammt noch mal!*'

Someone unlocked the door and screeched back: '*Maul haltennn!*'

Cobus and Marian disappeared into the room across the hall. The others left one by one. It was nearly two when Lisa climbed off the sill, locked the door, swept the empty cans off the bed and started undressing. Victor lay down on the bed and smoked and watched her. She pulled her singlet over her head and began washing herself. Her face, her armpits, her breasts. She dried herself, threw the towel in a corner, leaned on the sink to look at her reflection and said: 'I'm starting to get pretty sick of this place.'

He nodded.

'First those filthy Nazis last night, and then today ... the hatred you guys gave off, I don't want that, I can't do that!'

He said nothing.

'You were ready to kill that poor museum guard.'

'Never before,' Victor said calmly, 'have I felt so at home with this crowd. It's the first time in my life I've ever been completely content to play cowboy.'

'Don't be so awful.' This softly.

'And who are you to decide when people are allowed to hate?'

'It's misguided, it's too easy, it's not like us.'

'Bullshit, you just can't let yourself go. Even if you wanted to hate the krauts, that old grandma in your head wouldn't let you.'

She looked at him in bewilderment.

'Is that so, asshole?'

He bowed his head.

She stepped, breasts thrashing, to the other side of the bed, tossed back the blankets and crawled in. Victor got up, found half a bottle of schnapps, poured a tumbler full, toasted

Lisa – who pretended to be staring at the ceiling – and took a big slug. Pacing, a long time since he'd done that. He lit another cigarette and walked around the room, drinking and smoking. Lisa was right, but still, this hatred was tasty as a double shot on an empty stomach.

'We were sincere, if you ask me.'

'Huh!'

'At least, considering we're a dense and simple band of provincials, we were sincere.'

'Don't try to act so heroic! You're not dense, you don't believe that yourself!'

'Okay, all right, I just feel like hating.'

'Pretty damned sorry. It's a kind of stupidity that doesn't suit you!'

He stood next to her, then sat down on the edge of the bed, put the glass on the night table, leaned over and kissed her right on her astonished lips. She turned away angrily: 'Knock it off, creep!'

Face buried in her hair, she whispered: 'I wish you'd start acting normal again: musty, arrogant, snooty . . .' A snorting laugh. '. . . Just listen to me . . .'

'Yeah, listen to you.'

She grabbed his hand: 'I want you to just stand and watch, and talk gibberish, like before.'

'Why?'

'Just because, I want to see things through your eyes too, I guess.'

'Aha . . . may I, uh, may I presume, I mean, just a guess of course, but is this your way of saying in, uh, songwriter talk that you need me?'

Soft but urgent, almost guiltily: 'Yes.'

They looked at each other without a word. Then she patted the blankets.

'Come on.'

He emptied his glass. Undressed. Crawled in next to her. Clicked off the lamp.

She slid over to him, wormed an arm under his neck, kissed him on the cheek and sighed. He started to sing an old Elvis Presley song, very quietly:

> 'Don't, don't, that's what you say,
> Each time that I hold you this way.
> When I feel like this,
> And I want to kiss you baby,
> Don't say don't.'

She giggled, squeezed his arm and said: 'Okay then, do.'

BOOK TWO

Kräftig bewegt, doch nicht zu schnell

In the early morning hours of her sixteenth birthday, Elisabeth Maria Prins had a dream that was not so much predictive as depictive. She was lying on her back in a newly mown field, in searing, ominous heat. In the distance, the field hands were leaning against a combine, listening to The Boss and waiting for the hay to dry. Lisa stared up at the bleary blanket of clouds, which suddenly became gray and thick and downy and were then ripped open by an angry fist. And out of the rip came a voice, like a bungling black whirlwind, a voice familiar and a thunderous comfort. This was God, and God roared: 'Enough is enough!'

She immediately felt the urge to nod, to agree with the voice, although she had no idea what was enough, let alone whether the voice was even waiting for a sign of assent from her. She awoke with a start, in the panic of the dreamer searching for words.

She wiped the sweat from her forehead, noted that it was five o'clock and that she smelled far from fresh, though familiar enough, to say nothing of homey. Then, after these reflections, she again sought the state of slumber that would return her to that landscape above which God existed. She wanted to find out what could be 'done about it', for once awake she knew right away what was 'enough', though she would never have been able to explain it to a soul. She tried to form an image of the excess that had roused God's wrath: the universe a vacuum about to burst from the accumulation of what, in earthly terms, could be called filth, and which generated itself like gas in a rubbish heap. But she was already fading into a watercolor of her dream's final image, returning to the mowing field where the combine now pursued her, about to chop her to pieces if she didn't run faster and faster – then she awoke for the second time with a start, and decided to leave well enough alone.

She crawled out of bed, went to the cupboard, pulled a pack of heavy black tobacco from beneath a pile of underwear, rolled a bomber and sat down in the open window to smoke. It was getting light, drizzling a bit. Spatters of rain reached her naked body. She looked at her lap, at the little fan of pubic hair, frowned and shouted to herself: 'Yoo-hoo!', but her pelvis gave no reply. She didn't know what would happen if things ever did liven up down there, but it was about time something happened. She was turning sixteen and still hadn't awakened to the erotic. Sometimes she imagined being tested by a doctor – not *the* doctor – who would poke around inside her with white gloves and announce that she wasn't 'all connected up'. Invasionary procedures would be needed to force the link with the nervous system. She shuddered, tossed the butt out the window and lay down on her bed again. Dizzy from inhaling, she drifted off. When a tickling, penetrating odor made her open her eyes again, she saw her brother standing there with an envelope under his arm, looking befuddled. Was she dreaming?

*

It was that morning Lisa remembered so often, second by second, frame by frame, when she woke up in the house on the canal in Town. She was twenty-one, dead for all time, had never been born in a certain sense, and lonely in a way that belonged in books. But who was writing her? A nineteenth-century female neurasthenic, Victor would say. Lisa, quite simply, ascribed authorship to her own life. She was demonstrably lonely on a daily basis, but when she made the effort (and a reader with her), she could poke through the tear in the sky.

'My sister sort of has her head in the clouds,' Victor would tell the odd person he brought home after extensive prying into references and motives. If she happened to be present, he would raise his glass in her direction.

It was a Saturday morning. She shook God's fist from her mind, jumped out of bed, lit a Caballero and slapped herself on the buttocks to measure the 'jiggle quotient'. She lifted one breast and let it drop. Two bounces. Nice, very nice. Naked, she crawled onto the window sill. Waved to imaginary onlookers in the row of houses across the canal. It was drizzling. The rotting smell (Veen) of the water made her sad.

After showering she put on a faded pink dress (décolleté to the nipples), black fishnet stockings and high-heeled pumps, completing her toilet with a necklace of inestimable value, of plastic and glass, won at the carnival in Oude Huizen, 1972. She breakfasted alone in the kitchen, the only hygienically secure space in the house, and lit her second cigarette. She was allowed forty a day. She cleared the table, poured a bowlful of coffee, filled a tumbler half-full with Jack Daniel's, diluted the stinking concoction with lukewarm water, put it all on a tray and went back upstairs. The door she kicked open.

'Get up. Anna will be here in an hour.'

Moans, a cough. Victor rolled over and looked at her. Somber morning eyes. Sorrowful you might say, if you didn't know better.

Sometimes she felt the urge to sit on the edge of his bed and tickle him awake, kiss his stinking head and laugh at him until bowl and tumbler were empty, his smell changed and he began fishing sentimentally for touches. But lovers, or at least boys who considered themselves such, took a finger and were soon clawing at your soul. Ravenous swine. Veen was sweet, though. But distrait, so terribly distrait. And that boy on the island, last summer, who'd tried to seduce her (what did he know, poor guy?) with drinks and joint after joint, and had worked his hand into her pants after all that mushy kissing (which she enjoyed sometimes, but which mostly cracked her up), only to find drought. He'd rolled onto his side, given her a confounded look and, without a trace of the usual disappointment, came up with the classic remark: 'Whoops, looks like I took a wrong turn there somewhere.'

So sweet that she'd cried with laughter for fifteen minutes and spent the rest of the vacation with him, walking hand in hand. Which she never did otherwise.

In her living room, she plucked her brows and painted lids and lips. No rouge, this was no day for a blush. She heard Victor going to the toilet, entering his living room and throwing open the windows. Then the blaring of The Residents, 'The Third Reich 'n' Roll', one of the records she hated most, an LP on which the sweet songs of the sixties were rendered by the devil himself. Music for cave people. When Victor dreamed of songs, she'd heard him say, this was what they sounded like.

The telephone rang. Anna.

'Hey listen, I'm at the station and it's raining. Can someone come and pick me up?'

'God, milksop, can't you take a bus?'

'I hate buses, people stink in buses.'

'Victooor!'

He stumbled out into the hall, half-dressed. The stumbling was demonstrative. She didn't look at him.

'Little Bo-Peep wants you to pick her up at the station.'

Without a word, he turned and walked back into his room.

'He's on his way, teenybops.'

Victor would never drive into a brick wall. She was sure of that.

Half an hour later they made their entrance in a cloud of cadaverous decay, blown through with Anna's stinkingly expensive perfume. Pecks on the cheek. Brother and sister were having a grand old time.

'Goddammit, Lisa, do you always have to parade your tits around like that?'

Anna combed her long blonde hair at the mirror in the hall, checked her eyes, which were painted blacker than fashionable, and beat her flat chest: 'Nothing, absolutely nothing. Thanks a million, Granny.'

Victor stood there grinning like the shy brother in some hokey family film: the scene in which a good scrubbing and her first party dress transform the unattractive sister into a princess. Disgusting, but also really sweet. Sometimes she could hack those two to pieces for their utter normalcy. 'To get to my little sister you have to come through me,' and that kind of nonsense. She hated it, she loved to see it. Anna, of course, thought her brother was a genius. He'd dropped out of school out of pure disgust (a real reason was never given), wrote endless stories that only she was allowed to read, sent letters to the editor that were actually printed, and smiled constantly around her. Anna was sixteen, downright pretty, and so vigorous, with her smooth pink complexion, airs like the czar's lost daughter and that improbably filthy language: 'Yeah, well, listen, I've had more pricks in me this week than a second-hand dartboard, don't you have something I could kind of grease it up with?'

'Jesus Christ, Anna, please!'

Victor snorting with laughter, not knowing which way to look.

'Breakfast?' he asked. 'Alley-oop, let's tie on the feed bag. We have miles to go before we sleep.'

'Make it brunch then, I've already had breakfast,' Anna said. 'But shall I open the envelope first?'

She counted the hundred-guilder notes out onto the kitchen table.

'Seven, with lots of love from the folks.'

Victor served shrimp in a homemade whisky sauce, warm French bread with garlic butter, and a muscadet. He himself drank only half a glass, to defend his taste buds against 'the violence of fish'. Lisa got up to fetch the mail. A card from Hille Veen, her part-time sweetheart, Victor's comrade.

GREETINGS FROM GRONINGEN: 'Can I come by, or is there a war on?'

She walked to the phone and dialled his number, then stood ticking her nails on the telephone stand.

'Yeehaw-well-helloo.' Doing his J. R. Ewings.

'It's Lisa.'

'Well, well . . . howdy.'

'How's our cowboy?'

'Uh . . . what about tonight?'

'Yeah, all right, sure, okay.'

Groningers on the phone: completely hopeless.

Back in the kitchen she found Victor and Anna making plans, skimming film pages, looking for concerts.

By all means, make yourself at home, Anna.

Lisa recalled how the doctor had brought her to this house three years earlier, suitcases, boxes and all. It was Victor's house. He'd been living here for six months, attending The Seat of Learning where Lisa would go too. Of course she'd visited him during that time, like a girl from the provinces going to stay with her boyfriend, with all attendant risks. She smiled when she thought about it, and felt a painful stab of something almost like homesickness. When Anna's here, I love him. Then he's a brother again. Hers. Pretty face. I want one too. Tough luck. Sometimes it's exactly what I don't want. He's a handsome guy. A guy.

'Hille's coming by tonight.'

'People who invite themselves over should be shot.'

'I asked him.'

'Sure you did.'

'Your boyfriend?' Anna asked. Incapable of a loving look, her little sister.

'Kind of.'

There went Victor's eyebrows.

*

Veen was what she called 'rock & roll', unlike Victor, who was 'classical'. Veen played guitar, Victor no longer. Veen wore worn-out jeans, smelled of sweat and didn't wash his hair often enough. On the street he was always looking around, in the hope, as she knew and he didn't, that a voice from his past would ring out and call his name. Sometimes he thought he actually heard it, stopped in his tracks and looked over his shoulder across the square. It broke her heart, these boys, eternal children it seemed, clinging so desperately to what lay behind them. It almost made her cry. Barbara Cartland, right up to the hilt. But sometimes, when she was in a nasty mood, she'd say – regret catching up to her words: 'God, baby, but Yvonne doesn't even live around here.' Which made him look confused as if caught red-handed.

Goddamn prick! Grab *me*, if need be. But carefully. Oh, forget it.

From him she'd learned how to hold one of those things, and how to move it. God, how cute, God, what a mess.

'We're going to see The Gun Club,' Anna decided. 'You going with us? The two of you?'

'The singer's a lush, and he can't sing,' Lisa snapped.

'A perfect combination,' Victor said.

'Shouldn't you call one of your barmaids first to wangle some tickets?' Lisa said even more snappishly.

'Certainly, Your *Hoheit*.'

'And go wash yourself.'

Victor bowed and disappeared.

'How's it going at school?' Anna wheedled, inspecting her long nails.

'Okay,' Lisa said.

'Why are you ticked off?'

'I'm not ticked off.'

'What you need is a good hard d—'

'Shut your face or I'll shut it for you!'

They laughed.

'You still don't want it?'

'No.'

'Dame Freezerstein.'

'That's me.'

'What about this Hille?'

'He's not angry, but it makes him sad.'

They giggled.

'Would you want to with him?'

'My insides don't want to, Anna.'

'What a waste of tits.'

Lisa swung. Anna ducked.

'This Hille, is he that cute one?'

'Not your type.'

But she was his: sixteen, blonde, flat-chested and completely debauched.

'I wouldn't dream of it.'

'Don't lie.'

Victor, reeking of aftershave and *eau de toilette* and dressed in his Anna's-here outfit (black Levis, burgundy shirt, silver-gray vest, priceless boots, brick-red Levis jeans jacket) had gone into Town with his sister. They'd prised two hundreds off Lisa. To buy presents. For each other.

Lisa was trying to analyze a novel for her course in post-war prose. Her room was next to Victor's, but was half the size. The books were in Victor's room. Hers was filled with two old couches, plants and side tables. She was smoking her tenth cigarette.

'Which characters in Part One are reflected in the characters in Part Two?'

She could hear Victor say: 'Who gives a fuck!'

She'd fallen in love with Veen in class, when he got into an argument with the professor about the role of God in literature.

'How about this!' Veen had waved a novel. 'God depicted as an Italian pimp! What are we to think of this?!'

'Hille, that character reflects . . .'

'No way! Forget it! A vampire, sir!'

Clacking his gum and pounding his fist on the table, Veen had disagreed with each and every one of them. He was like Victor, but Hille's rage was real. Victor would have pretended not to give a shit.

After class she'd walked right up to him, bought him a cup of coffee in the cafeteria and asked if he 'wrote too, or something'.

He'd looked right through her.

'It sort of radiates off me, doesn't it?'

What a sweetheart.

He'd excused himself ('to the can') and came back with eyelids red and hash on his breath. Then Victor suddenly pulled up a chair: 'So, I see you've met young Willy Meister.'

She hadn't seen him again, not even in class, until one evening when she stomped angrily into Victor's room to ask him to turn down the music and found Hille there, listening to some cock-and-bull story from her brother, who was in his second phase – seemingly sober, sardonically drunk.

Lisa turned a page, threw the novel in a corner (don't let

Victor see that: throwing books was something done only with Kosinski), sighed deeply and went to her room. She tossed herself on the bed, laid her arms alongside her body and clenched her fists. Granny's meditating. She called it her 'flight to reality'.

It took a long time for her to relax. Then she let loose and was released. Her body was wrung by soundless forces, like in a centrifuge. It reduced her to what, when conscious, she referred to as 'a Softenon flipper'. Unbearable! Still she went on, her body finally tearing free of who she was and billowing and blossoming and expanding until it hung somewhere around her. Now she floated, there where she was and had to be, far beyond death, in the Nothingness and the Everything, and that Everything was her. The silence was eternal and absolute.

Someone put a thumping seven-league boot in her repose. Heart pounding, she opened her eyes. Victor next to her on the edge of the bed, a bunch of white roses at her feet. He looked at her and smiled. Almost pure, but his jaws contorted with the effort it cost. He put his hand out, brushed the hair from her face, caressed her cheek, leaned over – no booze on his breath – and kissed her on the lips.

'Knock it off.'

His eyes turned cheerful. She saw him fighting the urge to tickle her. He wanted to purloin a laugh. He needed a laugh so bad. She didn't want to give in.

'Where's Anna?'

'Tending to her crotch.'

She feigned revulsion. He rummaged for words.

'Everything all right, missy?'

She shrugged. Okay then. She loathed this fiddling in her

sentimental registers, but when he tried to be sweet, he was, right away.

'Where's the cash?'

'She wanted patent-leather boots. A mere hundred florins, and tonight we're eating tenderloin. We can ask Veen if you like.'

'Do you think Hille will fall for, uh, for our puss-in-boots?'

A real smile now. Ten points for wordplay.

'He's not doing any more falling, try to get that into your head . . .' A pause, she knew what was coming and wouldn't have missed it for the world.

'. . . Just look at me.'

She turned up her nose. He became his old self. Hoopla: it was love. Precisely because Anna could come chattering through the door any moment, she stuck her arms out. He didn't think twice. His need outstripped his fear. His perfumed embrace, his guilt-ridden kiss, penance, penance, with the tip of his tongue against hers, like a greeting from outer space. Hairs tingling with the fear of discovery. Ponderous romantics. Sublime kitsch. Letter to *Cosmo* (a publication banned from this household): 'Sure, my brother and I live together, and we're very happy and we think it's ridiculous that . . .'

If he kept this up, tonight, just because Anna was staying over, she'd sleep next to him. We tempt the gods, that we might . . .

In Victor's room, a record came on. Prince. Victor tried to pull away, but Lisa wouldn't let go. This was her scene, she hadn't let herself go for nothing.

Anna came running up the stairs, into the room and saw them wrestling.

'Awww, gee, isn't that cute.'

She dove on top of them.

'Anna, holy shit, did you wash your hands?'

Lisa and Victor felt their veins itching with something for which there were no words.

The roses bit it.

At the table, that evening. Veen sat there ogling Anna. Victor flambéed shallots and made Stroganoff. They ate their boeuf, drank red wine and listened to Victor, who drank little and talked much. Lisa suspected that the gentlemen had been sniffing. If that was true (she barely got the chance to examine Victor's pupils), then he could forget it tonight, and Veen would be raked over the coals later on.

Around eleven they went into Town, wormed their way into Rock Palace Bella and dived into the crowd being warmed up with brain-searing music. The sisters wore miniskirts and sleeveless blouses, their hair ratted wildly at the boys' request. Anna had refused to shave under her arms and Veen was looking, Lisa noticed, at the blonde hair in her armpits. But Anna behaved in exemplary fashion, and soon left them behind at the bar. Victor drank only beer, leaving the firewater to Veen. Lisa was willing to forgive him that one line, as long as it remained at that. She grabbed him by the back of the neck (Veen quickly turned the other way) and forced him to look her in the eye (he knew what she sought), only to find his old tired and familiar gaze. He received a flawless smile and considered himself warned. He was so much on the ball, in fact, that he walked over to the corner of the bar where his favorite bartenderess was working, just to leave Lisa and Hille alone.

'Did you bring coke?' Lisa roared in Veen's ringed ear.

He looked at her for a moment, apparently wondering what damage he might do by confessing, then nodded, the jerk, in the assumption that he was doing her a favor by being honest. She put on her nasty nit-picker face.

'I had rehearsals two nights in a row, I was dead.'

'Having a reason for it is twice as dumb.'

He looked chastised. She softened again. He saw it and went for the kiss. But it wasn't happening. One pair of lips a day.

She saw Victor bending over the bar to kiss his post-modern punkette, who tried to slip him a free drink. When Lisa saw him refuse, it was settled. The sweetheart. Precisely because he didn't know she was watching, precisely because she saw how touched he was by the bargirl, who was at least six years younger than him. That he sometimes stayed away for days and did all the slimy things she didn't know about, and didn't want to, made little difference to her now. That young girls, her sister in their vanguard, submitted to such things, that was a fact, and as such it left her cold. But in those rare dreams driven by nostalgic need she saw her brother cleansed of such cravings. Not like a prince on a white horse, but like an androgynous snob with a penchant for tenderness. No more than that.

'It's a fairy tale . . .'

Okay, Grandad, that's enough.

The four of them were up in front when the band started playing, pressed against the stage with a bouncing legion at their backs. Veen evaluated guitars, amps and music, was in short a crashing bore (although Anna pretended to listen with interest to his bawling), and Victor was clearly out of control. She threw an arm around his neck – what the hell did she care? – and kissed him on the cheek, to his alarm.

Alarm and gratitude. She had him where she wanted him. Herself too. I should be having my period, she thought, but that was bullshit: it was only her third week.

After the concert they stood outside, ears ringing, in conclave. Veen asked Lisa with his eyes if she would go with him. No way.

'Anna has to get to bed, it's already one-thirty.'

'What the hell is this?' Anna said. 'Are we turning senile?'

The girls shivered in the cold September air. The verdict was that they would have one for the road at a bar on the way home. This, too, was a test. Victor had a single shot. Big deal. Veen guzzled himself into a slur and was brushed off at the door with four kisses on the cheek from Anna and Lisa and a ceremonious handshake from Victor. Lisa felt guilty for a moment.

Home at last. Anna went KO on Lisa's bed: succumbed to the influence of hash and beer. Together they undressed her, silently, almost docilely, like children imitating a grown-up ritual. It was a lovely girl, it was theirs. Independently of each other, but sharing the selfsame thought, they heard Anna deny this claim. This skinny child with her slight curve of breast, the down covering her spine, the blonde pubic hair sticking out of her panties, the pouting face that looked like it would start whining for a story any moment. They tucked in their sister and looked at her. Then Lisa followed Victor, closing the door behind them. In his room she dropped down into an old armchair. They played records, most quietly, smoked cigarettes (the count lost) and said nothing; for the first time in weeks, content enough with each other's company to remind them of how things used to be.

'A drink?'

Lisa nodded and looked at him questioningly. Victor's eyes said he'd remain sober if she felt like getting tipsy for once. She took ice-cold Campari in a long-drink glass. He drank a beer. She felt like crawling onto his lap, but she'd never done that. He might find it unseemly. But in whose eyes? Well, in The Eyes. When she finished her drink and felt the right tearfulness coming on, she swore loudly. Victor looked up, smiled and looked away again. She went over to the turntable, put on her Bowie, and just did it: she crawled onto his lap, the way she'd done with her father until the day she left home. No, no, no analysis, even though she missed her father more than she'd ever dared to imagine.

Victor didn't look surprised.

'Hey, are these tears I see?'

They should have seen them like this. But who? Them. They. Them there people.

Victor had his arms around her waist. And now no remember-how's, Lisa thought, but one popped out anyway.

Remember how? At home, back then. Miles back.

'Remember how you gave me a story? On my birthday? I was thinking about it this morning, with that fuddled face of yours, you remember?'

' . . . '

'Victor?'

' . . . '

'Can't we take Anna home tomorrow?'

'Do we have to?'

'Yeah.'

She kissed him on the cheek. It made him shy. She felt him shiver, and loved him. To keep things in perspective, she fetched another glass of Campari and sat down in another chair. Victor filled the hash pipe. She decided not to nag him about the coke. She took the pipe, drew the smoke into her grating lungs and handed it back to him.

'I'm going to bed,' he said.

She nodded and let him go. She stayed there dozing a while, then turned off the lights, climbed the stairs and slipped into his room. He was lying in the glow of his night-light – a light like the one Anna still had in her room – staring into space, and more surprised than she'd expected.

'*Darf ich?*'

He nodded, tensed. She undressed, bare naked, and shimmied up against him. She didn't want to smother him, but still she whispered: 'Okay then, do.'

It was their languid, sweating embrace, 'Eternal Summer' (or: 'Everything Was Better Then'): first his head real long against her breasts and her hand in his hair, then an occasional kiss with the tips of their tongues (hello there), his hand on her left breast (always the left one), his hand on her buttock, his fingers slowly scratching her back and scalp, sometimes for an eternity, making her sigh and turn moist, his hand between her legs, almost motionless, her hand on his sex, majestically immobile, out of tenderness (that slow pulse and throb beneath her fingers), then a long kiss in which he beheaded something in himself that always left them awake when light came and exhaustion overtook them. After that they would fall asleep by degrees, swaddled in the childlike limberness of love and without unravelling senses, making their dreams hysterical but never dismal or dreary, always bright and promising, and their waking poignant, as though sleep were the *intermezzo* in an everlasting prologue. Until she jumped out of bed blushing, granting him the look born of a morning in Munich, and left him alone to calm down, which was, as she knew, a question of thought bridled, for he never wanted to complete what she'd aroused and didn't experience herself.

It was almost six by the time they felt sleep approaching. Victor held her soaked crotch captive, moving his fingers lightly over her sex. It relaxed her, that slithering. Even the smell of her body she could tolerate, she liked it, or rather, found it fitting. She smelled of grass growing along the banks of a ditch. She saw the summer and the land, and stretched without moving. Only her muscles tightened.

'Go to sleep, Miss Persnickety,' Victor said softly, and his breath smelled of him, of the nest, of rolled up and tucked in. She let herself drift and tumbled into a dream. There was a house, there was land and a horizon, and where was everyone? She went into the house, it was her house, and she decided the kitchen was much too big; next to the front door, the garden, the stairs came out into it – and what are all these people doing at the table? Fuck off, would you? and presto, they were gone. She made some food for the doctor, yoo-hoo, Daddy, oh no, drunk again, oh no he's not. They were eating at the table and Mama came in and gave her a little slap on the cheek because you should learn to dress properly. And when Lisa opened her eyes for a moment and realized she was awake, she said out loud: 'It's really weird, but I never dream about you anymore.'

An alarm went off. Or no, someone was shaking her. She smacked her lips, smelled her sweat and felt her clammy back being tickled.

'Wake up, it's ten o'clock. Anna's here, remember?'

She disentangled herself and saw his eyes drifting over her in poetic hunger. Then she realized what he'd said. She jumped straight out of bed, saw his naked body, blushed deeply and began picking her clothes off the floor, chattering nervously all the while.

'Oh my God, stick out your can, here comes the garbage man, oh God, do you think she's awake?'

She flew out of his room, taking only Victor's truly loving eyes (she imagined) with her on the retina, and dressed, tripping and moaning softly. She opened the door to her own room, saw Anna still asleep, sighed in relief and ran, after closing the door quietly again, down the stairs to the kitchen. She made coffee, boiled eggs, fixed toast, squeezed oranges and sang softly to herself, the blush still burning on her cheeks. She heard the shower and turned on the classical music station, lit her first cigarette as a Chopin *étude*, so sad it made her grin, came trickling into the kitchen.

She found Victor, dressed and aromatic, on the bed in her room, looking at Anna, who had tossed herself bare and lay there snoring.

'Wake her up,' Lisa said, clumsy and blatant, drinking of his shyness like a thirsty woman at a well. He poked Anna in the ribs. The child murmured and rolled over angrily.

'Hey, bimbo, wake up!'

Anna saw her brother, her sister rummaging in a cupboard, and said: 'Oh, Aspirin, go away, I stink, please, get the hell out!'

'Breakfast's ready,' Victor said, rising with the movements of an old man. Sometimes, Lisa thought, it's like he can't wait for his bones to start creaking so he can complain about his rheumatism.

The two of them, in the kitchen. They stared at each other over bowls of coffee, through cigarette smoke.

'So can we be friends again for a week or so?'

'That sounded like it came straight off the TV.'

'What do you mean?'

'You playing the gracious paramour.'

'Nicht doch, ich habe dir zu danken.'

'Gern geschehen.'

'Is that so?'

He bowed his head.

Anna came in wearing a towel, with clean hair and a morning mood she'd borrowed from Lisa.

'What's on the agenda today?'

They ate breakfast. Victor, who was clearly having trouble knowing what to do with himself, elected to mix Anna his own hair of the dog. She drank the lukewarm, watered-down Jack Daniel's like a kid tasting its first Suicide, eyes big, smacking her lips demonstratively.

That afternoon he took her to the soccer match (Groningen–Volendam). Lisa stayed home alone and wandered through the house. She tried to think of a way to keep Victor at home this week. He usually disappeared after a night like this, showing up again only days later like a dog run off after bitches in heat, having explored the countryside, slept in dry ditches and gnawed on his own hunger in the interests of adventure. Then he'd come stumbling into the house of an evening, stinking and exhausted, drunk and inconsolable, aggressive and unapproachable, with half a gram in his pocket and countless wild plans, all having to do with

Heading Out into 'Deepest Europe'. So impractical that she felt like kicking him: you're too old to dream like a child.

In her room she dug up a folder containing a few letters from back when he lived in Town and she was still at home.

> Most Gracious Empress,
>
> I toss my hat out of the ring, I am giving up. I'm quitting this school, they're all a bunch of left-wing partisan idiots and students with the IQ of pigs. I'm going to subsidize a composer and drown myself in the canal. And I'm not coming home.
>
> Ludwig

Every letter the same old song and dance: I'm quitting school and I'm not coming home.

Beneath the letters lay the big envelope with the story he'd written for her sixteenth birthday. She pulled it out and flipped through the pages. She remembered that day the way she remembered the night in the boathouse when she'd heard God speak for the first time: with the shock of recognition at a symbolic turning-point passed. Victor had been without a home ever since, but when she tried to talk to him about it he waved her away, pretended she was acting like 'the lady from the Viennese delegation', and changed the subject. Of his hatred towards his parental home, she was authorized to know no more than that it was there. While it was precisely the story which spoke of love for the family he'd grown up in. She read it, whimpering quietly, a handkerchief to her nose.

Dizzy Spells

As soon as you heard the first pigeons coo, you also smelled the leaves and the wet moss. Woods, I thought then, I'm in the woods. And I kept my eyes closed a little longer to hold on to the secret of sleep gradually drifting away from me, which somehow never worked. Holiday homes always smelled of fresh air in the morning; in the evening they smelled of people. People smelled of meat that had been lying around for a long time.

I stretched, shivering. It was great to shiver on a summer morning: not because you were cold, but because of the coolness, the smells and the holiday feeling. My sisters were still asleep. Liesje lay on her back in the top bunk, stretched out like a corpse. She was dreaming. You could tell by her fluttering eyelids and the frown on her face. Little Anna, down below, was invisible. All you could see was her hair on the pillow. She herself lay beneath the sheets, undoubtedly sucking on four fingers at once. I snuck down from my bunk, pulled on my short pants and T-shirt and tiptoed outside. The little lawn was gleaming wetly in the morning sun. It was surrounded by tall trees, like the clearings in fairy-tale forests where pixies held their parties at night. The cottage next to ours seemed deserted, but I knew people were in there, sleeping. A little girl with curls was among them. Trembling, I crossed the lawn. The dew chilled my bare feet, it gave me goosebumps. At the edge of the woods I stopped. It was a real forest's edge: a gentle slope covered in grass that petered out among the trees. Countless times I'd rolled down it. You rolled right into the woods, and when you opened your eyes you could see the trees spinning for a moment and falling pieces of sky that were blue and white and red. I couldn't get enough of those dizzy spells, the first of which each morning produced an especially strange tearing sensation in my head, and left a tickling on my lower back that went on for ages.

Hoopla, there I went. Round–and–round–and–round we go. And then I lay still. Everything spun and fell away. And a fine morning to you, I said, laughing in my head. A little later I skipped into the woods. Skipping felt a lot nicer than walking.

At breakfast my mother said to my father: 'Headache again, I suppose? Well, if you go out fishing at night, you have to dry your nets in the morning.'

She always said that, even though I'd never seen my father with a fishing pole. He didn't say anything, just grimaced. I burped loudly. My sisters laughed shrilly, but stopped quickly when the blow from my father failed to arrive.

That afternoon I stalked my sisters. They were sitting with the curly-haired girl in the wigwam in front of the cottage. I bellied over the ground like an Indian, a knife clenched between my teeth. I'd painted my face with mud. When I heard their voices I lay absolutely still, waiting for the right moment to slit their throats and scalp them. Next year at school I'd wear the little girl's curls on my belt. 'Is that your grandma and grandpa you're with?' I heard Liesje ask her. 'No,' the little girl said, 'they're my father and mother.'

It was quiet for a moment. 'But why are they so old?' Liesje asked. 'They're not that old,' the girl said, 'I have a brother too; I was an afterthought.'

An afterthought?

'So where is he?' Liesje asked. 'On the farm,' the girl said. 'We have a farm too,' Anna said. 'No we don't!' said Liesje. 'Do too,' Anna said. 'No we don't, silly cow,' Liesje said angrily, then asked: 'Didn't your brother want to come?' 'He's not allowed, he has to keep an eye on the land.' 'What do you mean?' 'Well,' the little girl said, 'my brother is as old as your father.' It was quiet again for a moment. 'And he gets drunk all the time too.' 'Really?' Liesje asked testily. 'What's drunk?' Anna asked. 'He gets drunk all the time,' the little girl repeated, 'and then he came into my bedroom, and one time he peed on my bed, and then my mother locked my door after that whenever I went to bed.'

What?

'Whatever,' Liesje said. 'What's drunk?' Anna asked again. 'That's when Papa says goddammit all the time,' Liesje said with a sigh. She was right. Sometimes my father swore about everything. For example, he'd say: 'Goddammit, the weather sure is nice.' But I didn't care about that now. Was that little girl being locked up? Then I'd come to her rescue! As carefully as ever, I crept back into the woods. An Indian had to be ready for anything.

My father was sitting in front of the cottage, waiting for night to fall. He was smoking roll-ups and drinking beer out of one of those swing-stopper bottles. Whenever his hands were empty, he rubbed his eyes. I sat down next to him and started staring at the edge of the woods, just like him.

'Nothin' ta do?' he asked. 'Shall we take 'n' walk?'

'No,' I said. 'Too hot.' Then I said: 'Pop, what's an afterthought?' 'What?' 'An afterthought,' I said. 'That girl from over there says she's an afterthought.' 'Oh, like that yessay,' he said.

'That means she shouldn't really a' been there, but she still is.'
He laughed. I realized he wasn't in the mood to explain. 'Where's
Mama?' 'In town,' he said. 'Hot, innit? Goddamn hot t'day.'
'Mm,' I said, and we both went back to staring at the woods.

It was getting dark. My father was poking up the fire we
used to roast potatoes on the grass. My mother was making
sandwiches. Filled with a strange mood – a kind of homesickness
– I scraped the charred skin off my potato and tried not to let
the burnt smell ruin my appetite. A house on our street had
once gone up in flames in the middle of the night, and ever
since, the smell of fire made me panic: I'd crawled out of bed
so many times at night because of flickering behind the curtains,
but it always turned out to be headlights. 'Mom, can I have
some more cola?' I asked, feeling my stomach churn. 'You
shouldn't drink so much,' she said, handing me the bottle.
'You'll have to go all night again.' 'I have to pee,' Anna whined.
'Not while we're at the table,' my mother said sternly. 'Well,
okay, but make it quick.' 'Silly cow,' Liesje said with a pensive
look before wiping the hair from her face and adding another
black smudge to her pale cheeks.

And suddenly it was evening. You could tell from the colors
in the air.

Liesje and Anna were standing in their bare butts at the
counter in the little kitchen, washing themselves and, when my
mother acted like she wasn't looking, throwing wet cotton balls
at me. Liesje had really pretty buns, they were rounder than
boys' and they shivered when she moved suddenly. It made
you feel like pinching them, or giving them a slap. I aimed and
threw a cotton wad at her butt. It hit her on the right bun and
stuck there for a moment before falling on the floor.

'Ooooh, blecch, dirty pig!'

'Come come,' mother said, 'Liesje!'

I grinned and saw that neither Liesje nor my mother were really able to get mad. That's how it was when you were on holiday.

My father was lying on his back on the lawn, acting like he was asleep. My sisters, draped in white nightgowns now and smelling so strongly of soap that he had to know they were coming, snuck up barefoot and jumped on him just as he opened his eyes. He wrestled with them briefly, tickled them until the clearing filled with laughter, then tossed them off. 'Two squeaky-clean little angels,' he said, and then, his gaze resting on me: 'and one stinking Indian.' I grinned proudly. Then I saw his eyes veer off to a point behind my back. I turned around. The little curly-haired girl was staring at us with big eyes. 'And another little angel,' my father said amiably, 'but I think this one still needs a bath.' The girl looked at him as if she'd seen a ghost, and didn't move a muscle. 'Papa?' Liesje started whining, 'can we play for a little bit? I told her we would, we won't get dirty, really.' A smart one she was, my sister; we all knew she was lying, and because of that we were too embarrassed to say anything.

They disappeared into the woods, two little ghosts and a shadowy little girl. My father pushed his tobacco tin over to me and was emphatically silent. I rolled him a cigarette. Sometimes, when my father didn't speak for a long time, the silence turned heavy and oppressive, as if the whole world was waiting for him to finally say something. I knew even then that there was something in his head that just wouldn't go away, something huge and mysterious, something only big people knew about. Now there was something in my head too, and that made the silence light and exciting.

'What say we take 'n' little walk?' my father asked.

'No,' I said, 'not anymore.'

My mother came out. 'Has your father let them go away again?' She shook her head. My father grinned. 'Come on,' she said to him, 'let's sit inside.' She winked at him and turned to me: 'In fifteen minutes, you send your sisters in.' Then I was alone in the evening air.

I found them at last: two white patches, accompanied by the colorless form of the little girl. It was dark and hot, and I discovered that the smell of evening came up out of the ground. The loam I was lying on was dry and crumbly, cool and relaxing. If I didn't watch out, I'd fall asleep and lose sight of my prey. The three of them were standing together dreamily, impaling leaves on sticks. I wondered what the point of that was. Probably complete nonsense, like most things girls did. That alone was reason enough for me to drive my knife into their bodies and watch as the blood turned their nightgowns into wet, red rags. At home once, I'd dropped a brick on a boy's head from the roof of an old shed. His plain white T-shirt had turned into a cartoon, but because I was up so high I couldn't really see the coloring of the cloth.

They started walking, threw away the sticks – all that fuss for nothing – and left the place they'd been standing. I rolled onto my back and felt the cola slosh around in my stomach. My legs were asleep. I stayed there for a long time. When I got up, the girls had disappeared.

Coming to the edge of the woods, I looked out over the dark cornfields. It was awfully quiet. It seemed like the darkness muffled the noises; there *were* noises, but they didn't sound, they moved, the way they did in books. In books you could see noises.

I knew where they were, they were over at the fen. I slipped back into the woods. What a wonderful thing, to hunt! I knew these little woods the way Indians knew their hunting grounds. At a cluster of young birches I squatted, then crept along on hands and knees. As always, the smell of water was suddenly hanging in the air, even though the wind was blowing. I approached the fen noiselessly, and before long I saw a white patch amid the dark fringe of reeds. Anna. I could tell from the long hank of hair dangling halfway down her back. Liesje and the little girl were nowhere in sight. I bellied past a thicket and lay still. Anna barely moved. Maybe she was looking at something. Again the waiting made me drowsy, but a constant pressure in my bladder kept me awake. Something made me think of fairy tales, of a hill in a story from some book, a dark, green hill you climbed at the beginning of the story, with a beautiful forest behind it, a forest full of stately trees hung with huge, unfamiliar fruit that looked better than the real thing. Strange, I couldn't remember whether the book had pictures. But that view of the forest was so clear to me. It was light and dark there at the same time, it was warm, you fell asleep right under the open sky and . . . something was tickling my neck.

'Ahaaa,' Liesje screamed, 'got you!'

She grabbed my hair with both hands and pulled.

'Dirty little shit,' I said before throwing her off. My heart was pounding wildly. Liesje stood there laughing at me. 'You can come out now!' she called to Anna. She gave me one more disparaging look and walked away. A little later all three of us stood staring wearily at the black water of the fen. 'Where's that girl?' I asked. 'Who wants to know?' Liesje snapped. I glanced at her and she was startled, because she changed her expression and said: 'She went home.' 'You two have to go in too,' I said, 'but first you better wash those mitts.' 'I have to pee,' Anna said. She pulled up her nightgown and squatted down. When I heard her say that, I almost did it in my pants. I unbuttoned my fly as fast as I could. Liesje didn't say a thing, just squatted down gravely. Together we peed. A little pond formed at our feet. We always peed together when we were outside. At home, on the street where we lived, we would sneak into people's gardens on hot days when they were on vacation and pee on the stepping stones under the dry conifers, which caused a lovely odor to rise up and gave use this strange sensation. After we were finished, we went to where you could walk into the water a ways. Liesje stopped a few times to shiver and wipe a drop from her thigh. When we got to the mossy beach, she walked into the water to her knees, her nightgown pulled up above her butt. She stood there like that for a long time, deep in thought, probably feeling sad about nothing. I kept a close eye on her. It was dangerous to walk into a fen that far. But I didn't dare say anything about it to her when she was like that, even though I was almost two years older. My father didn't even dare when she was like that.

Later, in our bedroom, there was this strange smell and it was too hot to sleep. I'd been lying awake for hours. Liesje tossed and mumbled unintelligibly. Little Anna didn't move at all. The boredom made me itch. I'd thrown the sheet back ages ago, but I still didn't feel any of the fresh air that should have been coming through the open window. I decided to do something about it. I snuck out of bed. The empty bottom bunk creaked loudly when I stepped on it, but Anna and Liesje didn't wake up. Even the linoleum on the floor was hot. I walked to the window and pushed the curtain aside. Warm, sweet-smelling air brushed against my stomach and my face; it only made me hotter. 'Are you awake?' Anna asked in an anxious little voice. 'Sshh,' I hissed over my shoulder, 'shut your mouth!' 'Will you tell me a story?' she asked, suddenly sounding chipper. She couldn't have been awake for more than a minute, I was sure of that. 'I can't sleep,' she said. Liesje tossed and mumbled something. 'Would you shut your mouth!' I snapped at Anna. She was quiet. I walked over to her bed and sat down. 'Once upon a time,' I started whispering, 'there was a big green hill and, uh, you had to climb over it to get to the enchanted forest, and on that hill lived a witch who locked up little girls, and there was this boy who climbed that hill to get to the forest and he stabbed the witch to death and scalped her, you know, cut off her hair with a piece of her head still on it . . .' Anna looked at me with big vacant eyes, Liesje tossed so hard that her bed creaked. '. . . and then he frees the locked-up girls and takes them to the forest and, uh . . .' 'Mama,' Liesje said, loud and clear. 'She's sick,' Anna said, 'from the water.' I got up, put a foot on the edge of Anna's bed and pulled myself up. Liesje was lying tangled in her black hair, still asleep. I laid a hand on her face, it was cold and wet. What do I do now? I thought, suddenly nervous. 'Wake her up,' Anna said. I started shaking Liesje. She opened her eyes, looked at me and closed them again. 'You're sick,' I said. She didn't respond. I poked her in the ribs. 'Ow!' She sat straight up, looked at me in amazement and was suddenly out of breath. 'Dickhead,' she said, panting and gulping. 'Are you sick?' I asked. 'Are you sick in the head?' she said angrily. Then she threw up. A black wave gushed out of her mouth onto her lap. We looked dazedly at the spot spreading across her nightgown. 'Jesus,' I said, 'go get Mama!' Anna crawled out of bed and was gone. 'There's something in my stomach,' Liesje said, staring into space. She wasn't crying, which was the worst. 'Mashed potatoes,' I said, 'and now they're here.' She smiled faintly. She was real brave, and that made my pity just that much more huge. My mother came in, followed by Anna. 'Did you throw up?' she asked without shock or amazement, even without interest it seemed. Liesje said nothing. I got a smack on the back of the head. 'Get away from there, you.' Anna pointed triumphantly at Liesje and said: 'She went wading in the fen.'

It was a little cooler in the room. My mother had left the curtains open. Liesje was lying in the bunk below mine, wearing a pair of my pajamas. There was a bucket on the floor next to her head, but she didn't throw up again. She drank two glasses of water before she lay down, and hadn't moved since. I was exhausted and felt myself sinking into the mattress. A few more minutes and I'd be asleep. But suddenly there was this churning around down below me. 'My stomach hurts,' Liesje said. It took a moment to sink in. 'Hm,' I said, waking at the sound of my own voice. 'Come lie down here,' she told me; she wasn't asking. I thought about it for a moment, then crawled out of bed, easing my foot down onto her mattress. 'I'm cold,' she said, rolling away from the wall as I climbed over her. I crawled under the sheet and we both turned onto our sides at the same time. Liesje pressed her back against my stomach and pulled her knees up. She put my hand on her bare stomach. 'Jesus,' I said, 'it's all swollen up.' 'It's full of wet cotton.' The way I was lying wasn't too comfortable, but I decided not to move until she was asleep. Liesje was quiet, she just pressed my hand against her stomach. For a long time I lay there listening to her breathe.

Something woke me later on and I saw my father looking at us, still wearing his clothes, even though it was almost morning.

Peering with one eye past Liesje's ear I smelled the odor of medicine, which was from the beer. When he saw me looking, he nodded. Then he saluted loosely, the way tired soldiers do, and disappeared.

I woke up with my hand on Liesje's stomach and my mouth full of salty black hair. The pigeons were cooing. The clear smell of morning filled the room. Carefully I pulled my hand back, even more carefully I crawled out of bed, but as soon as I was up and stretching on the cool linoleum, Liesje rolled onto her back with a sigh and looked at me with swollen eyes. 'Did you get any sleep?' she asked. She knew I couldn't sleep on my side, but strangely enough I'd slept tight without stirring. I nodded. 'You're lying.' She did her best to give me an admonishing look. I pulled on my shorts and got her a glass of water. She gulped it down and fell back onto the pillow. 'How's your stomach?' She tossed back the sheet and pulled up the pajama tops. Her belly was strangely swollen below the navel. She looked at it in horror. A sob started at the back of her throat. 'Aw,' I said quickly, 'it's not so bad.' Suddenly what I wanted most was for her not to start crying. Her puffy eyes looked away offendedly. I was ashamed. Sitting down on the edge of her bed, I pulled the sheet over her again. 'It'll go away,' I said in embarrassment. She turned to face the wall, pouting like a little kid. It made me feel weird. Then, to my amazement, I bent over and kissed her on her soft cheek. She wasn't even surprised. She turned to me and smiled shyly. 'Goofball,' she said. I stood up, grabbed my T-shirt and got out of there fast.

It was lovely outside. Elated, I skipped across the dewy grass to the edge of the woods. There I went: round-and-round-and-round. This time the dizziness was overwhelming.

I went to the fen and stood on a rock and let the morning

sun dry my clothes. I was an Indian, so I could act like the sun was a god. Occasionally I spoke to it, not out loud, but in my head; that was mysterious *and* completely safe. Then I heard her scream.

I was already flying through the woods. The air was thick and heavy, like in a nightmare. She screamed again: 'Mamaaa!' A desperate howl. I reached the grass, the cottage, the hall, the room. Anna and the little girl were standing in the doorway. My father was there, staring at Liesje, and didn't look up when I rushed in. 'Anna,' he said in a strange voice, 'take that little girl outside.' Liesje was sitting straight up in bed, gawking at her lap. The door closed behind me, and I walked over to Liesje and looked at her lap and saw the blood on her bare thighs. The pajama pants were down around her ankles. We both looked at the blood and the spot on the sheet. The blood was coming out of her belly. 'What's going on here?' my father asked me in a real peculiar voice, and when I looked at him I saw panic in his eyes. I'd never seen that before. 'What?' I said, looking at Liesje. What was going on? Why was he asking me? Liesje's eyes were bigger than ever and her cheeks were deathly white. 'Oh hey, wait a minute, you don't let any grass grow under your feet, do you?!' His voice had suddenly returned to normal. He laid a hand on my head – Liesje just sat there looking at her lap – and I saw a shiver run behind his eyes. Then he smiled. Oh great! There was Liesje, bleeding to death, and he was laughing. 'Get outta here, boy,' he said, 'there's noth'n to worry about.' I watched in confusion as he made Liesje lie down and pulled the sheet up over her raised knees, stroking her hair clumsily and avoiding her glassy look. 'Get out, boy!' he said. I left the room and stood in the hallway, crying.

When my mother came back from shopping in the village, she stayed with Liesje for a long time. When she came out again, she gave me a funny look. 'Are you still here? What are you crying for? Everything's okay, it's fine. Why don't you and your father go take a nice long walk?' A tap to the back of the head and there I was, walking through the woods with my father. My shock was complete. My father smoked and said nothing. He must have been broken up about it inside, but it seemed like any moment he'd say: 'Goddammit, sure is fine weather we're havin'.' 'What Liesje's got, is it a serious disease?' I asked. My father started coughing. It took a while before he looked at me again. There were tears in his eyes. 'Boy,' he said, 'it's notta disease, it's somethin' girls get. Anna will too, later on.' Not a disease? But blood was coming out of her, just like that. On TV I'd seen people who were shot to death, and they bled just that much, only out of their mouths. Something happened. My body tingled, the sky spun like at the edge of the woods and I was lying on the ground with my father bending over me.

I woke with a start. It was still afternoon. What had happened? Oh yeah! I leaned over the edge of the bed and looked into my sister's eyes. 'Hi!' she said, like nothing had happened. I pulled my head back fast. 'What's wrong with you?' she asked. I said nothing. Then I heard rustling and creaking. Startled, I leaned back over the edge: 'Don't get up, nutcase!' But she jumped out of bed anyway, and when her head popped up she looked at me questioningly, then past me in embarrassment. 'Stupid guy, who goes and faints?' she said in a strange voice. I looked away. 'You have to stay in bed,' I said weakly. 'No I don't, I'm not sick,' she said excitedly. She lowered her eyes: 'It's for having babies.' 'What?' 'For having babies.' She looked at me shyly. 'That blood, that comes out when there's no baby growing in there, you get it?' Liesje? A baby? 'And . . .' she went on, 'that's going to happen every month now.' She laughed shrilly and her eyes darted back and forth. 'Can you imagine that?' She pulled herself up to sit on the edge of my bed. Then, looking distracted, she started plucking at the buttons on the pajama tops. She tried to say something, gulped it down, then said: 'Dumb, isn't it?' I nodded, trying to fathom what she'd told me.

The sky was changing color from dark red to dark blue, as if the clouds had been sucking on a jawbreaker. For hours there'd been the smell of fires in the distance, so my father had built one of his own, a fire that gradually died down and was smoldering now like a coal heater, spreading the smell of roasted potatoes. The dusk gave Liesje's pale cheeks a black sheen. She was wearing her nightgown again, sitting with her arms around her knees and staring into space. She didn't eat anything, just drank countless glasses of water that Anna, looking bewildered, had to fetch for her. My mother never stopped talking. My father poked at the fire and said nothing. It was all strange, but not really what you'd call frightening. It was just that everything seemed so full of Liesje, like she'd suddenly become extremely important, more important than all the rest of us. And it was like she knew this and thought it was completely normal. She looked sad and proud at the same time, so you didn't dare to say anything to her.

'Bring your sister to bed,' my mother said later, 'and Anna, go play with that little girl next door, but not in the woods.' She wanted to be alone with my father. 'Mama, I'm not going to bed yet,' Liesje said, 'because I don't happen to be sick.' But my mother would not be moved. She stuck her finger in the air admonishingly and said: 'Now!' I shuffled along behind Liesje, who slammed doors in anger and threw herself on the bed. 'Are you going next door too?' she asked, turning onto her back. She was going to act mean, I could tell from her eyes. 'Aw,' I said, 'I dunno, I think I'm going to the woods.' 'You're in love with that girlie, aren't you?' she shot back, 'I see what's going on, just in case you think I don't!' 'Aw,' I said again. She was scary, with her eyebrows clenched in a frown and her angry eyes and her big distorted mouth. 'Dirty bitch,' was the only thing I knew to say. I turned around and walked away. But before I could close the door behind me, I heard her crying. She was making a scene, that was obvious, but I stopped anyway: it was hard for me to take and, besides, when she cried you could make her laugh; then she'd laugh through her tears. I went back into the room. Liesje gave me a murderous look before rolling onto her side and staring at the wall. She sobbed quietly and rubbed her hair in her face like a little kid. I was overcome by a weird mixture of rage and pity. I went over to the bed and pulled her onto her back, so she had to look at me. 'Knock it off, goddammit,' I said. 'You're acting like a baby.' She was startled, and there you had it: laughter through the tears. 'I'm going to tell Mama that you said goddammit.' I thought about how scared I'd been and how she was just lying there making fun of me, and how all this made my stomach flutter. I sat down on the edge of the bed and thought about hitting her. Instead, I started tickling her. I poked my fingers in her ribs until she shrieked and roared with laughter and begged me to stop. When I finally did, she lay there panting. Her hair was sticking to her face and there was a glistening under her arms. She smelled like water. I stood up and went to the window. My stomach was still fluttering, but I also felt a shame that made my ears ring. I scrambled out the window. A few yards into the woods I heard her shout: 'Hey, where you going?' She caught up to me on the path, but I walked along, not looking at her, not saying a word. 'What's wrong?' she asked. It was getting dark, and something strange was happening to the woods. This is an adventure, I thought, I'm not afraid. But the silence had something heavy and oppressive about it, and I hoped Liesje would say something soon. But Liesje was pouting – I could feel it at my back. I had to come up with something myself. 'If Papa finds out, he'll paddle your bare bottom!' I said without turning around. 'Oh, no he won't!' 'Yes he will.' 'No he won't!' '"Yes he will, no he won't"; what are you, still in kindergarten?' I heard her jump at me and felt her arm around my neck. She pulled my hair and tried to strangle me. Then she let go and started walking along beside me. Without saying a word, we walked straight to the fen. There was the strong smell of water. A cloud of mosquitoes hung still, but still moving, above our heads. Liesje sat down on a rock and stared into space. 'You tell me a story?' she asked suddenly. 'Do I have to?' I asked, but I could tell from her face that I did. 'Uh, once upon a time there was this big mountain range, and behind it was a forest, you know, where the happy hunting grounds are, where the Indians go when they're dead, but if you could cross those mountains and get to that forest, you could enter the happy hunting grounds without dying first. But on that mountain lived this guy, and he didn't just let you cross, you know what I mean, you had to beat him first, cause he scalped girls, right, cut off your hair with a piece of your head still on it, and he used a rock to beat the boys' head in, only I had a tomahawk, right, and the girl who was with me was pretty scared, like girls are . . .' 'Huh!' Liesje said. 'So the boy snuck into the mountains first and left this trail of buffalo droppings . . .' 'Ha!' Liesje said, 'how charming.' 'And the boy creeps up to the guy's log cabin and climbs onto the roof, and he makes a noise so the guy comes outside. Then he drops a rock on his head so the blood spurts out, and then he jumps on him and slits his throat so he's all covered with blood too . . .' 'Uh-huh, sure.' 'And then he does this bird call, like he agreed with the girl, so she can follow his trail, and she comes up to him and, uh, then they kiss . . . the way they do that . . .' I stopped. 'Is that all?' 'Well, can you think of anything else?' I snapped. 'Pretty dumb,' Liesje said. We were quiet for a long time. 'It's still hot, isn't it?' she said then, and sighed deeply, 'I think I'm going into the fen.' She stood up and walked to the little beach. 'Hey!' I said, stomping along until I caught up with her. I grabbed her by the back of the neck and spun her around. 'Ow, ow, ow!' she screamed, twisting around. 'You're not going in anywhere!' I shouted. 'You get it!?' But she yanked herself free and walked on. 'Okay,' I said, suddenly calm, 'go ahead and drown.' And I walked away from her, straight into the woods. My heart was pounding, my skin tingled in annoyance. I plopped down on the ground next to a big tree, crossed my legs Indian-style and tried to collect my thoughts. There were so many feelings going on inside me, but every time I tried to feel one of them, another one jumped in the way. And I still felt that fluttering in my stomach the whole time. Was it because of the little curly-haired girl? No, I'd lost interest in her. When I tried to think about her I saw this hazy face with Liesje's big cruel mouth on it, and I felt this painful stabbing somewhere in my body.

When I climbed back in through the window, Liesje was lying on the bottom bunk again. Her hair was stuck to her back and she was wearing a pair of panties. She'd tossed her night-gown in a corner. 'So,' I said, staring at her back. She didn't move a muscle. I kept walking, right out of the room, and slammed the door behind me. 'What in the world are you up to?' my mother asked as I thumped down on the grass. 'Noth-ing,' I said gruffly. My father looked at me and seemed to look right out the other side. The fire had gone out. A lukewarm breath of wind swirled the ashes and blew them on my legs. The evening smelled of grass now. 'All right,' my mother said, 'it's about time I got started.' She disappeared with the dishes and silverware. My father slid his tobacco box over to me. Moving slowly, I rolled a cigarette for him. 'Keep it,' he said. He rolled one for himself and, while the smoke poured out from deep inside, he asked: 'So how's Liesje?' 'A pain,' I said, tasting the smoke. 'A pain in the butt.' My father smiled. 'That's the way she'll be more often from now on,' he said with an uneasy glance in my direction. 'You oughta leave her alone 'n' bit . . . women, fellah' . . .' Again he looked at me uneasily. 'And you two should stop sleepin' in the same bed, I bet she doesn't like that anymore, you're both too grown-up for that now, wouldn' ya say?' He tried to grin confidentially, but his smile was faint and embarrassed. I nodded and looked the other way. The edge of the woods had wrapped itself in darkness. 'Liesje says it's because there's no baby growing inside her.' My father burst out laughing. 'It's so she can have babies later on.' He suddenly seemed relieved.

'How 'bout 'n' little walk?'

'Okay,' I said.

The heat in the bedroom was unbearable. Anna was already asleep, buried under her hair, curled up like a young cat. Liesje was washing herself in the kitchen. When I tried to look in on her, my mother sent me to bed. Everything was changing, but what it was and why it was changing I didn't know. When I thought about it my body hurt like I was sick, so I started thinking about an adventure real quick, to forget the rest. When Liesje came in I acted like I was asleep, but I was looking down on her through my lashes. She stopped in the middle of the room, sighed deeply and said: 'Christ, it's so hot.' Then she pulled her nightgown over her head and threw it in a corner. She looked awfully brown in the dark, especially with those white panties on. She scratched herself, yawned and walked over to the open window. 'Hey, dumbo, you asleep?' I didn't answer. I hated it when she talked to me like that. 'Hey, Big Chief.' She put a foot on the bottom bunk and her head appeared. She saw my open eyes, laughed and climbed onto my bed. 'Just as I thought,' she said. She shook her hair and kneeled on the mattress. 'You with your stupid navel,' she said, pointing and smiling. 'You with your stupid nipples,' I said, 'like someone's been pinching them.' She laughed: 'That's how it feels too, sometimes.' Her gaze drifted for a moment. 'Papa says,' she went on, 'that you fainted because of me.' I lowered my eyes and said nothing. 'Fainted,' came Anna's mumbling voice. 'Aw, go to sleep, candy-butt!' Liesje snapped. She twisted her mouth so meanly that a shiver ran down my back. 'So?' She was looking at me again. Her face lost its angry lines. I shrugged and clasped my hands behind my neck. I didn't want to talk about it. But Liesje jumped on me and put her knee on my legs and started fighting before I could even move. 'Fess up!' she said, breathing heavily and with one arm so tight around my neck that I almost suffocated. 'Yeah, okay,' I said with difficulty. She sat up straight, leaning her butt on my stomach, and looked down on me in triumph. Then she smiled, a weird smile that startled me and, to my surprise, made my hand shoot out and give her a loud, ringing slap across the face. The silence after that was enormous. I watched my hand drop, saw Liesje's baffled look, saw how her glassy gaze turned on me and how her eyes filled with tears, and she began crying without a sound. Something tore in my chest. Blood was dripping out of the corner of her mouth. I sat up straight, so she almost fell over backwards and hit her head, but I put my arms around her and caught her in the nick of time. She started sobbing. 'Dirty bastard,' she said, 'dirty rotten bastard.' 'That's right,' I said, pressing her against me. I didn't want to say I was sorry. 'I'm going to tell Mama,' came Anna's voice, 'that you two fight while I'm sleeping.' 'Shut your face,' Liesje said, gulping back a sob. I lifted her head from my shoulder and looked at her. 'Why did you do that?' she asked, then her tongue slid to the corner of her mouth and tasted the blood and she started sobbing again. 'You were making fun of me,' I said. 'Oh, no, I wasn't,' she said. 'Yes you were.' 'No, really, not at all.' I looked at her doubtfully. 'Well, that's what I thought,' I said. 'Well, that wasn't it at all,' she said, crying audibly now and giving me a hurt look that made my stomach growl in pity. I didn't know what to do. Carefully, I kissed her soft, wet cheek. 'I didn't want to,' I said, 'hit you, I mean.' She looked at me from the corner of her eye, then smiled wanly through her tears, making my stomach flip again. 'No, of course not, that's why you did it.' She dabbed her lip with the tip of her finger. 'Hey, I'm bleeding.' That hurt look again, and I couldn't help myself. I leaned over to her, saw her eyes coming up close and felt how my mouth touched hers, and how I sucked ever so lightly on her bloody lip before straightening up and seeing her whole face again. 'Now we're blood brothers,' I said dizzily. There was a fluttering inside me, and suddenly I felt cold. Liesje looked at me in astonishment. 'Now you'd better lie down,' I said. She crawled off me, deep in thought. I lay down next to her, leaning on one elbow, and looked at her. I felt calm and flustered, all at the same time, I felt the heat but I had goosebumps, I smelled water and tasted rusty metal. Liesje stared at the ceiling and brushed the hair out of her sweaty face. A new drop of blood welled up in the corner of her mouth. 'Again?' I asked. 'Huh?' She seemed preoccupied. 'You know,' I said. I leaned over and kissed her on the mouth and sucked the drop from her lip.

'Nut,' she said with an anxious look in my direction.

We were quiet for a long time. 'Again?' I asked then. She didn't say a word. I kissed her on the mouth and felt her lips move. Then I looked at her again. She smiled shyly. 'Again?' 'All right,' she said, 'go ahead.' She laid a hand clumsily on my shoulder. Then she closed her eyes.

'I'm still going to tell, that you two fight,' Anna said.

*

Because Lisa saw loneliness in all people, especially in those she loved, she tried to bear her own like a morning mood, though she was of the opinion that her loneliness was unique. Peculiar to herself, at the very least. But for fear of being blatantly self-indulgent, she tried, each time she fell prey to this loneliness, to place this singular burden in perspective by moving among others of her own kind, in the vain hope of finding a comparable form of misery.

After reading the story – her nose red, her lungs aching – she spent some time in a classic bewailing of her lost youth. Then she decided to pay a surprise visit to Veen. Veen absolutely wallowed in self-indulgent misery. When Victor called him Broken Heart, he even seemed flattered.

She followed the canal to the Indische Buurt (missing Fixbier at her side), and rang the bell at the house Hille mockingly referred to as 'the walk-in youth center'. He had a room there, a telephone, and shared a common space with an assortment of characters, the precise configuration of which remained unclear to this very day. A beautiful girl opened the door and, before Lisa could speak, said: 'Hille's here, come on in.'

She climbed the stairs, suffered a wave of nausea at the penetrating cat fumes and saw the pigeon-gray tom, Pipo Caligula Ndugu, one of the nine beasts, peering at her from the hallway. The girl piloted her into a room, then remained standing next to a bookcase, leaving Lisa to fend for herself. A group of boys was sitting listening to music and smoking the Two Foot Chillum. The thing was passed around with the ritual gestures of the ancient hippie, the smoke was thick enough to cut. Hille was sitting in an enormous brown armchair and didn't see her. A boy kneeling at the turntable (before a wall of LPs; it looked like thousands) noticed her and gave her a television smile: fake, but charming. He tapped Hille's foot, and Hille looked up and saw her standing there. The others looked up too, gaping. Not a face betrayed whether she was welcome or had come at a bad time, not Hille's either. He beckoned to her, almost sternly. Feeling awkward, she walked over. He tapped the arm of his old chair – she sat down on it, completely at a loss – and said: 'This is Lisa, Lisa, this is Johan, German cosmopolite on his way through, momentarily occupying the apartment above

Black Bombay, this's Jimmy, of the old Holy Spirit Hospital squat, and the others you've met.'

She nodded shyly. The boy on the floor, the only one who had smiled, said in a voice sweet as honey: 'Hille, you make this sound like a gathering of the like-minded.'

The German began packing the chillum again. The girl brought Lisa a beer, then curled up on the floor with a book. Another record came on. Zappa. Heads began moving rhythmically, even though Lisa didn't hear any rhythm.

Hille squeezed her arm: 'Everything okay?'

They were looking at her.

'Ohhhh, okay . . . ,' she said to everyone in general.

Someone held a flame to the bowl of the chillum and the German sucked his lungs full. A dragon cloud rolled towards the ceiling. The chillum went around the room and came to her.

'Jesus, how are you supposed to do this?'

Hille showed her. She took a little hit, got a kick like a mule's and took a quick slug of beer. The volume went up. The boy on the floor raised his finger. People nodded.

'From America, a total fuckin' mind-bender at the border, man, these bootlegs, it's got Billy Boop on the cover! Where'd they come up with that, I mean, I guess it beats Donald Duck . . .'

'Or Greggery Peccary,' Hille said.

The boy looked up, disgruntled.

'But they weren't going for it, Paris eighty-seven, fan-fucking-tastic concert, but the sound, *merde à la mode*, got five more of them in . . .'

What was this all about?

'By the way, anybody want to do some acid? Hey,

Cuntsey, get the hits, would you? In the back of the fridge.'

Cuntsey?

The girl put down the book and left the room, only to return right away: 'He's doing it again!'

Hille jumped up, and the boy on the floor did too. After a few seconds they came back, the pigeon-gray tom dangling by his legs between them. Lisa saw a red cat-weenie.

'You trying to fuck your mommy again?' Hille said tenderly, then explained: 'Ndugu always jumps his mother, and she's not fixed yet. If we weren't quick about it we'd have another litter, a nest full of mongoloids.'

They tossed the tomcat all the way across the room. The animal landed on its feet and came running back to them. The girl appeared with a roll of colored paper.

'Come on,' Hille said, taking Lisa by the arm, 'I hate watching, and I don't like chemical humor.'

Lisa, glad to get away, followed Hille up the stairs to the next floor, which was painted in candy colors. Light pastels, pinks, blues and greens. It was supposed to look cheery, but it frightened the hell out of her. Hille's room was old and dirty. It was full of phonograph records, books, guitars and all kinds of equipment. The floor was littered with cables, little brightly-colored gadgets and microphones. The curtains were closed and the room smelled of him, a dash of sweat, his hair and wet clothes. He tried to hug her. She ducked under his arm.

'Unseasonably cool, isn't it? Have a seat.'

He turned on the light.

'Sorry about that,' she said. She sat on his bed, the bed she'd shared with him back when he lived alone in his condemned hovel on The Heights. Hille messed with a tape player. Then there was music, distorted, dizzyish, extraterrestrial.

'Recorded this yesterday.'

'Oh, wow, great.'

'Right.'

He dropped down beside her.

'So what's up?'

'Nothing, well, you know.'

'Oh . . . sure.'

'How, uh, how's your writing coming along?'

'It isn't writing at all, it's typing, as Capote once said.'

'Aww.'

'Really, bull-fucking-shit, but it'll do, as long as the author himself presides over it, snivelling, because the love-interest in question has to . . . aw, you know how it is, never mind.'

They sighed.

'So you gave him another night, huh?' He wasn't jealous, just surprised, time after time. It kept him from feeling at ease. He was content to watch the drama unfold, but from the standpoint of the suspicious reader, willing to surrender disbelief only at the last page, at the end, the punch-line, if there was one.

'Could you turn off the music? It's making me nauseous; sorry about that.'

'Never mind. That's a true compliment. Can I quote you on that?'

She smiled. Now there was noise from downstairs.

'I don't mean to get personal or anything, but what's the reason for this visit?'

'Nothing, I have to get going anyway.'

He rocked his head back and forth in mock exasperation: 'Come on, my God! What's eating you?'

'You know that, uh, that yearning of yours, for uh, old times and stuff? How abnormal is that?'

'Abnormal? We don't use that word around here, but anyway. I've said this before, you know, I'm snagged on this fantasy about my sweet sixteen in my old home town.'

'Well, don't get angry, but doesn't that mean you're acting like an incredible baby?'

'That's right, sugar pie, in-cred-uh-ble. So what is this, a pilgrimage to the Sentimental Oracle?'

She'd forgotten what it was she wanted to ask.

'I've told you a thousand times,' he said angrily, 'go live by yourself, cut the horseshit, become my girlfriend if need be, we can fake it, a marriage of convenience for those psychologically unfit for service; one day it will all go away, when we're grown-ups. That's what happens, at least that's what the starry-eyed youth downstairs try to tell me.'

'Are we completely Barbara Cartland?'

'Completely and absolutely.'

'Are we ashamed of that?'

'In no way, shape or form.'

'Good, then I'll be going.'

He'd let her out and watched her go. Another melancholy face. Victor had once stated that the television generation (*'Excusez l'expression!'*) was the most susceptible to sentimentality in the history of mankind. They thought and recalled in dramatic rushes.

At the time, Hille had added that this generation unconsciously accumulated pet mythologies, which then, using the emotive eye trained to such heights by television, they held up to their own primal accounts (the wish often being father to the comparison), thereby compiling an ever-expanding anthology of 'stories of my life' to flip through like a collector in search of new renditions. Lisa thought they were right, and she longed for a simple but balanced nineteenth-century existence on some remote estate, far from pathetic rituals and cravings.

At home she found Victor and Anna in the kitchen. Victor was having a drink, and looked right past her.

'Hey-ho, hey-ho, deep six the fish-guts,' Anna crowed. 'Victor, do that guy in the stands again, listen to this, Lisa, this guy was screaming at the line judge: "Coom on, buy a dog 'n' a stick, then ya'll ha' something' better ta do come Sundays,"' Victor chimed in, but woodenly, and a bit tipsy.

'Cute,' Lisa said.

'Christ, you two are loads of fun,' Anna said, looking back and forth between her brother and her sister. 'Listen, that you sickos sleep together is one thing . . .'

Victor's eyes shot open, Lisa immediately blushed and gasped for breath.

'But that it makes you grumpy is the part I don't understand.'

Anna looked triumphantly from one to the other. 'Gee, take it easy, I won't tell anyone.'

Silence. Red alert.

'Well, there's nothing to tell, is there?' Victor said. Method Acting.

'Is that right?' Anna grinned.

'It's just,' Lisa mumbled, 'otherwise you might have barfed on me during the night.'

'How cute,' Anna said. 'And then lying about it. Lisa finally enters puberty.'

Lisa dropped down on a chair, felt like punching, telling all, but saw her brother straightening his lapels, recalling a scene, adopting a pose. 'Anna, dear child . . .'

'Yessss?' She made you feel like wringing her neck, but, Lisa figured, this *was* invigorating.

'Do you remember? Once upon a time there was this prince, and he was looking for a princess to marry, but goddammit all to hell, he couldn't find one. Until one day he discovered a rain-soaked maiden standing at the draw-bridge, eh, about three years ago, right?' He looked at Lisa, poking fun, what a nerve! 'And the prince thought: she looks like a princess, but her personal hygiene is nothing to write home about ('Ha,' Lisa said.), yet still he let her in (Anna breathed a bored sigh), and because the maiden had asked to spend the night he placed a lumpy mattress on her bed and, lo! the next morning she arose black and blue, thereby proving herself a princess. To celebrate that, the prince let her sleep in his own bed, for he pitied her blackness and blueness and certainly wasn't planning to sleep on that lumpy bed himself, and that is how they came to live decidedly happy ever after . . .'

'What kind of horseshit is this?' Anna said.

'In fact, Miss Prissy,' Victor said, 'it's none of your fucking business.'

'Wait a minute, do you two sad sacks think I'm stupid?'

Lisa lit a cigarette, halfway into the giggles, and didn't know which way to look. Victor put on his Helmut Berger face and made his eyebrows dip in flight. With maddening deliberateness, he said: 'And what does Anna herself think of all this?'

'Hell if I know, you guys do whatever you want, and if you have a spastic litter together I'll even drown them in a bucket myself, but don't go lying to me!'

Lisa slapped as hard as she could. Anna's head rocked on her shoulders. All three were shocked. Anna was the first to recover, raising a hand to her reddening cheek.

'Retarded bitch! Are you off your rocker?'

'Well then, keep your nose out of it,' Victor said. 'You're a guest in this house.' He walked over to the cupboard for a refill.

Don't do that.

'So you think I care? Can't I even ask what's going on here?'

'No,' Victor said, knocking back his drink and taking another.

Stop that now.

He grabbed Anna by the back of her neck – a rare outburst – and said calmly: 'And now you're going to stop whining about it.'

'Bunch a plebs!' Anna said, yanking herself loose. 'I haven't forgotten how it was at home. Don't you think everyone could see what you were up to? I just want to hear you admit it!'

'We sleep together,' Lisa said, 'sometimes.'

'And then?'

Victor walked out of the kitchen with glass and bottle.

'Anna, goddammit all to hell, stop acting so pubertal!' Lisa shouted, watching her brother go, relieved, greatly relieved.

'I want to know!'

'He holds me.'

'Jesus Christ, blecch, mushy cow! "He Holds Me!" Right, just fuck off, would ya!'

'He holds me,' Lisa repeated. That's what he happened to do.

Anna shook her head and feigned disgust.

'You mean you foist your fear of sticky fingers on him!'

'Oh, uh-huh, sure, well sod off.'

Anna walked off after Victor. 'I'll ask him myself.'

'Please do that, dearie.'

Lisa stayed in the kitchen, blushing deeply, enjoying the moment intensely. She felt like clapping her hands. Goody, goody, goody! And then: I have to find a way to keep him home, this time.

Victor drove wildly, but not recklessly. There wasn't much traffic. They'd taken the freeway, the gash in the landscape. The Scar. In their youth, the old road along the Winschoter Canal had been one of adventure. The factories at the waterside, the shipyards, the naval boneyard close to Kolham, and hamlets along the road that reminded them of the prints in their old school primer. But Victor had refused to take that route now. He wanted to race. Anna sat beside him and glanced at him every once in a while, not without shyness; he'd never been angry with her before. Lisa lay in the back seat and stared at the sky to the east, painted in black and red: the native land. East Groningen. The peat colonies. The mudded acres, as Veen liked to say. The Chilling Fields, Victor called it. Just past Hoogezand they turned left, towards Oude Huizen. Lisa would have liked to keep on down the Hoofdweg, all the way to the Woudbloemlaan, and then back through Woudbloem, but she didn't dare ask Victor to do that. She saw familiar ditches, roadsides, farms, landscapes, there and there and there. Valk's farmstead surrounded by tall trees, just outside the village, where she'd once taken shelter in the boathouse down by the fen, because her father – she remembered (not now, not now!) how she and Victor had followed her father one dusky evening (*maman* probably gone errant), because he'd been so secretive about the plans muttered over the kitchen table with The Boss and Farmer Valk's hired man, while she, wearing her old sleeveless undershirt (my old shirt, see if I can find that thing later), had poured coffee and eavesdropped. That evening her father had been uncharacteristically skittish, had asked if they'd mind if he went out for a walk by himself, and if they'd be sure to go to bed on time. They followed him, crawling through dry ditches all the way to the swamp and crazy Luppo's land, his ramshackle house, the barn where krauts had once slept (and where the barn still smelled of krauts, Mama said), and saw their father greet a few other men outside. The Boss's hat was clear to see. The men stood talking and smoking for a while as they passed something around, something of grave import. You could tell.

A long time they'd lain and watched. When it grew dark they could see only silhouettes and the fire-light of cigarettes. Then the men set out. They were heading into the swamp. One of them had an animal on a rope. A billy goat or a nanny, Victor said. In the swamp lay a pasture surrounded by birches, the grass there easily a yard high. They saw the men pass a bottle, light new cigarettes, then shoo the animal away. Lisa and Victor lay on boggy mud, watching and waiting, and Lisa felt a tear slide down her throat like a clot of cold yogurt. She wanted to go home. She was ten and she had to go to bed. Stop whining, Victor said, wait a little bit. They heard a shot, they saw the grass move. They heard another shot and saw one of the men firing a pistol into the tall grass, then someone else did, then someone else, and then The Boss and then her father, who she recognized by the way he tucked his head between his shoulders. They were shooting at the animal they'd let go. She was paralyzed, she forgot to breathe. She got up and ran away. Victor stayed.

Later that night she was sitting in the boathouse, shivering and smoking cigarettes. It was already getting light. She drank water from the fen, pooped in one corner of the wooden shed and later it got dark again. She wasn't hungry, but she was thirsty and kept drinking from the fen. It had started stinking in the boathouse, stinking of piss and shit, she was becoming quite fond of that smell. When it grew light again she went swimming in the fen (mortally dangerous, Mama said). She knew she wouldn't drown, because a lot still had to happen to her. That was for sure. She saw men out in the field and hid herself again. She threw up. Drinking and shivering and vomiting. She was shaking so hard that everything started to hurt. She felt hot, took off her clothes and lay down naked on the planks. There was a murmuring outside. She clenched her fists and squeezed as hard as she could. That calmed her. She got up again and found a storm lamp, a wall socket too. When it got dark again, the darkness and the sound it made scared her for the first time in her life. She plugged the lamp into the socket and the thing exploded in her hands. She didn't feel any shock. She lay down on the planks again. A warm, dry hand had come out of nowhere and laid itself on her forehead. Calm down, she heard, in great big words, and she collapsed in tears. The next morning Victor found her, naked in a puddle of vomit. He shook her. She didn't want to wake up – never leave this peace again – until he dragged her to the fen and dipped her feet in the water. She opened her eyes, saw his pale face and felt so sorry for him that she moved. She felt splinters in her buttocks. He'd wept and cursed for a long time.

It was a hermaphrodite, her father told her, a useless animal. Lisa hadn't spoken to him for a year, even though her mouth said things once in a while.

Victor stopped at the edge of Oude Huizen.

'Do you want to go in?'

'Yeah.'

Anna said nothing, just looked at Victor, who touched the gas and pulled into the drive beside the bank. He turned off the engine, rolled down the window, laid his arm on the sill and looked at The Boss's house. There was a light burning in the billiard room.

He didn't look at his parents' house.

Lisa sat up and ran a hand through his hair. She petted his cheek.

'Aw, come on, man.'

Anna jumped out of the car, ran around the back and slammed the kitchen door behind her with a crash. Victor lit a cigarette.

'I'll be there in a minute.'

Lisa sighed and got out.

Her father was at the kitchen table, and he got up when he saw her. She let him hug her.

'Where's Fixbier? Where's Mama?'

'Out for 'n' walk.'

There was mail for her. In her room. What was wrong with Anna? Wasn't Victor coming in? She left her father in the kitchen, climbed the stairs, sniffed the odor of their house and ran into Anna on the landing. They stared at each other.

'Come on, out with it,' Lisa said.

'I bet now you won't want me to come anymore.'

'Stop acting like a baby,' Lisa said, and walked into her own room. She heard Anna blubbering. She couldn't care less. There was a letter for her, from Amsterdam. She threw open the windows and tossed herself on the bed. The worst thing, she decided, was that when you got older you could only sleep over at your parents' house. She heard her father out on the gravel. She moved over to the window sill and listened.

'Well, captain.'

'Pa.'

Now hands were being shaken through the car window.

'Where's the dog?'

'Out for 'n' walk with your mother.'

Silence. A cigarette being proffered. Victor to father.

'Aren't you comin' in?'

'In a minute, just getting acclimatized; so how's the old fellah?'

'Good, wife's goin' downhill though.'

'I'm going to pop in on 'em.'

'Do that. So ha' thick's your blood?'

'Thick enough.'

'I'll leave 'n' for you on the side table when you get back.'

Her father walked back into the kitchen. She heard Victor get out and go over to the bank. Lisa left her room and went into Anna's. Her sister was fixing her make-up in the mirror. Anna's room was a chamber of horrors; a strange, guarded keep within the house. The walls were hung with posters of American movie heroes, there was a TV spitting out video-clips, a dressing table buried under expensive junk from Yves Saint-Laurent, a rack with countless earrings, a shop's worth of clothes hanging on iron bars that ran right across the room, a four-poster bed built by Pa with a night-light above it just like Victor's, a silver-painted nightstand with a strip of pills on top, and then the crowning glory, an old mirror ball on the ceiling that spun and reflected the light like crystal.

Lisa laid a hand on Anna's shoulder.

'You're a complete degenerate, you know that? How can you sleep in here?'

No reply.

'Well? What did Victor say?'

Anna, who was doing her lashes, looked past Lisa in the mirror, shook the hand off her shoulder and said, less coolly than she'd hoped: 'That I should learn to read more carefully.'

'*Ach zo.*'

Lisa sat down on the four-poster bed.

'Do you think I, uh, could I look at a few of those stories sometime?'

'First you slap me around,' Anna said, painting away, 'and then you ask me to betray someone's trust?'

'I don't go for those little jokes of yours and you know it!'

'The world, Granny, is what it is. When girls I know miss their period, they "go off for the weekend". When hard guys have a mongoloid, they stomp them to death. When . . .'

'Knock it off! Don't act like that, like some dumb blonde, that doesn't suit you.'

'So we're back to that again, are we?'

'Anyway, go on, what else did he say?'

'God, I mean, I can't even talk about it!'

'Come on.'

'You're not only completely fucked-up, you're also totally tiring, you know that?'

Lisa bowed her head, the way Victor would.

'Get the hell out of here,' Anna said. 'I think I came down with something nasty at your place. I'm going to lie down, so why don't you go downstairs and sit with the old fart?'

Lisa walked over to her sister, stroked her long blonde hair and lingered until Anna turned. Lisa got a shove, then a big wet kiss on the cheek: 'Grow up, old biddy, what difference does it make to me? It's just that he's so gloomy, it makes me wonder what kind of goddamn fun the two of you could possibly have together.'

'He's unhappy,' Lisa said, 'by nature.'

'Don't lie. He may be your . . . "sweetheart", but he's my comrade. If you hurt him with your exalted persona, I'll come down there and personally punch you in that big mouth of yours.'

'Huh!'

'Now get out of here!'

Lisa went downstairs, poked her head around the corner

of the front room, then walked into the kitchen. She sat down at the table with her father.

'Well? How are you?'

The doctor took her hand, looked at her nails. 'Good. Real good.'

'Is that right?' She asked it quietly, but pointedly.

'And how 'bout you two? What's he do all day?'

'Oh,' Lisa said, surprised to find she didn't know herself, 'waits around, I think.'

'Waits around?'

She shrugged.

'Ya gonna stay for a couple a days?'

'No.' She recovered. 'Maybe next weekend.'

Anna came in. She was wearing a see-through blouse. She was half-naked.

'Hey, old fart, any calls for me?'

'Don't refer to your father that way,' Lisa said.

'Go back to your wuthering heights, would you?'

The doctor loved it.

'That fellah' yours called. I told him yu'd be home 'roun nine. Should be here any minute.'

'With a rise in his Levis,' Anna said. 'Too bad for him, but I'm still black and blue.'

'Christ Almighty, Anna,' Lisa said. And to her father: 'Are you doing anything to bring this child up properly?'

'I've been ruled unfit,' the doctor said.

Victor was standing in the doorway, pale, with sunken eyes, behind him a boy. A pair of Levis, yes indeed, and a whole fly-full. Jesus, Lisa thought. She shook her head.

'Found him,' Victor said. 'Sniffing around the bushes.'

Anna threw her arms around her boyfriend's neck. Victor

sat down at the table, looked at his father and said: 'Have you already given him a blood test?'

'He has a clean bill of health.'

The boy was dragged upstairs. A bit later music pounded through the house and you could hear Anna shrieking and laughing. Hysterical, gushy. More wild pretension followed. Fixbier barged into the kitchen, barking, and jumped up on Victor. Hi dog, Lisa said. The animal ran outside again, then came back, growling and pulling their mother by the sleeve of her vagabond's jacket. She stopped in the doorway for a moment, then ran her fingers through her children's hair.

'Are you two staying?'

'No,' Lisa said. 'We're going in a minute.'

The doctor poured four glasses of cognac and they sat together for fifteen minutes, Victor silent, Lisa chattering, mother nodding, father dreaming. When Lisa saw that it was becoming too much for Victor, she stood up, 'an early class tomorrow', and ran upstairs to get her letter.

He drove out of the village like he was saying farewell for good (for the umpteenth time), with angry jerks of the wheel and jaws aquiver, his glance icy and roaming, as though looking for something in the darkness being devoured by the headlights.

'That's that,' Lisa said, lighting a cigarette (only her tenth). She laid a hand on the back of her brother's neck.

'Das kann man wohl sagen.'

He came back to earth. She stuck her cigarette between his lips and took another.

'You going to stay home tonight?'

'And then what?'

'And then what? What kind of a question is that, do you have to go out on a spree again?'

Oh no, she thought, and said with a nervous giggle in her voice: 'All right, I'll try not to be so traditional.'

'Please, help yourself, it's rather gratifying.'

They looked at each other. Lisa blushed right down to her breasts, her skin tingled with shame and excitement. What I'm going to say now, get what I'm going to say now.

'I have a proposal.'

Victor looked over at her, took the cigarette out of his mouth, shifted into fourth and leaned back. 'What're we going to do, dance around the house?'

'Uh, no, I want to, uh . . . could you slow down a little, please?'

Victor sighed, but let up on the gas.

Lisa punched the radio, looking for a station with noise, then turned off the blaring right away.

'I want you to, I mean, if you want to . . .'

She gulped, thought: get on with it!, and took a hard drag on her cigarette.

'I want you to de-flower me.'

Brakes slammed. Just like Victor: always glance in the mirror first.

He looked at her, blinking.

'I want you to, I want it for myself, and uh, I'd like to give it to you . . . if you want it.'

He hopped out. Lisa climbed out too. Onto the shoulder, the land dead and dark. The smell of ditches. She looked at him across the roof of the car.

'If you want.'

'Get in . . .'

'What?'

'GET IN!'

Victor's face had gone red, his lips clenched tight. Lisa turned on the radio again. Uh-oh, it echoed in her head, uh-oh.

She didn't dare to say anything the rest of the way home. She didn't want to believe she'd made an enormous blunder, but how she ever came up with a request like that was a mystery to her too.

Victor waited in the car until she was inside. She went to the toilet, roamed through the house and found him in his room. He was pulling on his jacket, slapping aftershave on his cheeks, taking a quick drink and acting like he was deep in thought.

She refused to start crying.

'Are you going out?'

'Looks like it, yeah.'

She walked along behind him.

'Hey . . . man.'

The front door slammed hard. Lisa made the classic gesture of impotence: she clenched her fists and went: grrr.

In his room she poured herself a straight Jack Daniel's. Burning and a familiar flavor: fizzy soda pop. OLD NO. 7, it said on the label. Aha. The aged trapper in the hippie series *Grizzly Adams* had a donkey named Old Number Seven. Victor liked to imitate that trapper: 'Me and Old Number Seven . . .'

Boy. Where had she come up with this? She was twenty-one and didn't want to be a virgin anymore. Why not? Did she feel handicapped, incomplete, or too complete? Now that she thought about it, she decided it was merely a need, a need for the ritual. A need to seal the bond. She knew it would hurt her, she knew it would hurt him. And she wanted to see what he was like after an orgasm. She wanted to see him, even if it was only once. The thought of his seed inside her moved her, the way she used to be moved by the thought of coming across a fledgling fallen from the nest. (She'd never found one.) In other words, it seemed fascinating and compelling, and more-than-a-little grisly. And had he ever told her he loved her? Boys said things like that after the release, bastards that they were.

He stayed away for three days. When she heard the front door open, she flew to the hallway. He looked like an actor who'd been made up for *Night of the Living Dead*. Overdone, but riveting nonetheless. His eyes bulging from their sockets, cheeks whiskery and sunken, an effluvium of sweat-, booze- and cheap-girl smells clinging to his wrinkled clothing. His pant legs were half tucked into his boots. He had the shakes.

'Tagjen.'

He staggered over to her, kissed her on the neck, took a step back and looked her over from head to toe. '*Entzückend*, baby.'

She pushed him away, would much rather have held him, but decided to gratify him by acting traditional. He walked into his room, pulled off jacket and boots, poured himself a drink, put on The Birthday Party (cover of The Stooges' 'I'm Loose', a terrible barrage of noise) and grinned at her.

'Do your homework?' he shouted, glass raised in a toast.

She stomped into his room.

'These displays of yours are starting to make me pretty sick.'

'Ah, tell me about it, sweetheart.'

She just stood there.

The music paused for a moment.

'I hope you'll excuse me,' she began, choking up a lump in her throat, 'for destroying your aplomb with my, uh, proposal.'

'Present,' he corrected her.

'We can stop talking about it and never start again . . . if that's what you want.'

'You take a hand grenade, pull out the pin, toss it to me and then, studying your nail polish, you say: hey, you can give it back if you want.'

'Well, mister hoity-toity, how clever of you.'

She took the bottle, poured herself a drink and knocked it back.

'So where've you been, you and your donkey, for the last couple of days? You know, one of these days I'm going to call the police and report you missed.'

'Missing, mademoiselle.'

'Aw, man.'

She did it. A dramatic tear trickled down along her nose. Victor didn't seem impressed.

'Have you done your homework?' he asked again.

'What are you talking about?'

'About coitus *an sich*, the penetration and the spattering, the gnashing and grinding, the blood, *Liebchen*, the blood, the risks of pregnancy and disease, and . . .' His grin broke.

'The not-inconsiderable risk of desired repetition of the deed.'

'So that's what's bothering you.'

She turned up her nose, sat down, lit a cigarette.

'Don't be so incredibly obtuse, sissy, you're the one who wants to give me something. Regardless, of course, of whether or not I want it.'

'Don't you want it?'

'To muck around with you?'

'Muck around?'

His pose was crumbling.

'Whatever made you come up with this idea?'

Lisa produced another tear. She couldn't say. He sighed. She saw the desire to touch her rising in him.

'Ever hear this one?' he asked. 'Two little boys at the door at Hallowe'en in England. The man waits there while his wife gets the candy. The man, a little embarrassed, asks: "So . . . do you boys like football then?" The boys nod. The man asks hopefully: "Do you fancy Arsenal?" No, the one little boy shakes his head, and the other one says: "I rather fancy my sister, though."'

Lisa burst out laughing.

'Where'd you get that from?'

'Saw it on TV at someone's house.'

She started crying through the laughter.

'That's enough,' Victor said, finally getting up, walking over to her, pulling her up and holding her tight. Wordlessly, as always.

He'd showered, set a case of beer at his feet and was watching *Paris, Texas* for the hundredth time. Lisa watched along, her thoughts elsewhere.

Should she go off and live by herself? Should she 'get a

life', as the Americans so cynically put it? The fact that she and Victor were nurturing their suffering was suddenly shameful to her. Like Victor, she longed for style, and style, she decided, was the last thing they had. Their aversion to people who desperately sought out relationships in order not to be alone was a part of that style, she'd always thought. But that was easy for them to say: they'd had each other since early childhood, and sometimes their lives seemed governed by that self-same despair.

Lisa wanted to be pure and full of compassion, clutching humanity – in most of its manifestations – to her breast. She felt that purity, purity of soul, was her aim, so her life was a lonely struggle, an honorable struggle, although she expected no ovation, let alone a monument in her honor. In deepest slumber, when she put her body through the wringer to become the brief splash of light she was, there were no arguments about purity, in fact there was nothing but purity itself. It was probably the reverberation of that splash of Lisa-light that forced her, once she'd abandoned slumber and had come to herself again, to link that purity to the cares of human existence, but she wasn't completely sure about that. It seemed preposterous that the creature she was, and which she had come to know by disappearing in herself, gave her faith, simple faith in God and the Hereafter, and at the same time a feeling for norms and values that bore a suspicious resemblance to Christian mnemonics. She looked for a gap between her bond with the All-being and her practical quest for noble motives. She trusted no link between one and the other. A link like that, after all, would attest to the existence of a being-above-being (bad enough as it was), and in religious terms to a boss-above-boss, the way some writers cast their religious ideas in the musty and patently ridiculous framework of a supreme boss (The Old Wazoo, Victor would say) who tended to botch things rather badly, as though the show were being run by a director slipping into senility. It was all just evolution, although that term didn't entirely cover it, seeing as how it denoted development, the perceptible development of matter. In Lisa's view, the All-being was a shell that closed slowly, imperceptibly, and the moment which could be embraced by her finite understanding, the moment at which everything would change to All, probably didn't even exist. But she wasn't sure why not.

Everything was development.

'Compulsive development,' Victor would add. 'And who, pray tell, called for any of this?'

The call of the homeless, the call of those who will not and cannot understand that one has to go away before being able to come back. Who, in being driven out, curse their homes for good and refurbish them in the light of future events, causing Home to become deformed and disturbing, and the cry 'Come Back!' to become lost, buried beneath the accusations of the wanderer who is at home nowhere and blames life itself for that.

It occurred to Lisa that Victor had only one form of home left, and she was it. And with her usual feel for heartrending conclusions, she went pale, her eyes brimmed over and her throat seized up painfully.

She stood up and, for the second time that week, plopped down hard on the lap of her brother, who felt a dull jab of pain (as she remembered too late) but didn't show it. He pressed her head against his chest and tugged on her hair, his oldest sign of affection.

'Shall we go out and buy rings?' she asked. An almost unpleasant itching, of shame, of surrender, tickled her belly-button.

'So that one night you can set fire to me and I'll have to run all the way to Mexico to live with the Indians . . .' He put on his Albert-Finney-as-Consul voice. '. . . Like William Blackstone?' His two favorite personal myths of the moment: *Paris, Texas* and *Under the Volcano.*

'You and your stupid fucking movies!'

She let the evening take its course. She hung on Victor until the movie had given him his lump in the throat, let him go on drinking beer until he started 'playing tunes', which meant he was looking for songs of kindred theme, kept an eye on him when he excused himself and looked him in the eye when he returned, so that around midnight he pulled the Lilliputian packet from his pocket and said, looking guilty: 'Flush this, would you?', which she did without comment or word of commendation. At around one, when Victor began peering at the bottle out of the corner of his eye, she even played the role of consul's wife and said with a Jacqueline Bisset laugh: 'Go on, Geoffrey, take your drink.'

Which caused him just the kind of embarrassment she'd hoped for. After the drink they danced, like they used to. They even got the giggles. She let him go to bed, without word or gesture, and wandered around the house a bit. She turned off the lights, took a cold shower and walked into his room, naked. He was lying there thinking, with the night-light on. Or was he waiting? Seeing her didn't surprise him, but it did make him nervous.

She crawled into bed with him, wormed one arm behind his neck and laid her head on his chest.

'Do you want to sleep with me? Do you want to?'

He reached up and pulled the plug from the wall.

After a few whispered words about being afraid of this and afraid of that, she told him she'd be having her period in three days and would tell him what she felt. They had plenty of time. She let herself be caressed till dawn, her head, her back, her buttocks. She lay on her stomach and thought about before. She saw the land, the summer and the clouds on the horizon. She felt tense and happy. When Victor laid his head on her back for a moment, she rolled over carefully. He didn't seem scared anymore, only very curious. 'Come,' she said and let him lie on top of her. She spread her legs and her slippery sex (it was the first time her fingers had felt this: what a weird kind of wetness) and let him push softly. He waited for minutes in between, and she could feel his blood pounding, the way they said in books. Then he broke her very slowly. The pain was a pang in her head and back, nothing like what she'd expected. He lay still in her, sought her eyes. She smiled.

'Go on,' she said.

She held him tight, loosely, her hands on his shoulder blades. He moved and kissed her on the neck. It was soft and slow and tender (Barbara Cartland, here we go) and she thought about boys who played Indian and how they became this. No pleasure grew in her belly, nothing grew at all. What she really felt was his body around her, his tensed muscles, his attentiveness.

'Hey, go on,' she said again.

A moment came when he stiffened and she thought: oh, wow, here it comes, but she felt only warmth up as far as her navel, then realized that was it and thought: oh God, oh God, it's done. He slipped away from her and she grasped him and let him breathe against her neck, and she wanted to say something but waited until he – then she felt a tear. From him.

'No, no,' she said, 'don't do that, don't.'

She squeezed him till he cracked. He squeezed her.

So this was an embrace.

She ran her fingers through his hair and said: 'Now we're blood brothers, for life, and I, buddy, I love you.'

He couldn't get the words out of his mouth, but he didn't have to anymore. She knew now. For sure.

Lisa was in dreamland and knew it. She knew this dream like the back of her hand, and thought about the horrors that awaited. This was the swamp, a backdrop from life, not from her imagination – I'm not Lisa now. The swamp was weeping softly. If she awoke, she knew she would think: in dreams you don't smell anything. Now she had to go on. The slimy trees and vines parted. This was the path and that was the place. The white spots spattered across her vision. Two children, rotting in the muck. The swamp was green and brown, the children white, but befouled. Lisa was too late, always much too late, and the crying in her screamed everything full. She screamed herself awake.

That dream again. She opened her eyes and remembered that other dream in which she and two children were being held prisoner in a bamboo cage, half under water. The cage was full of rats, and Lisa, who was someone else, held the children's heads above water as long as she could and kicked at the rats. Images from a former life, she'd known that for a long time, and she knew it for certain. She sat up in bed, but the crying in her chest wouldn't stop. She gnashed her teeth. Oh, those children. She'd died in that cage herself, she hadn't been able to save them.

Lisa grabbed a cigarette. The Town knew no more silent nights, the roaring never stopped. It was as though the Holland–Germany match, a year earlier, had induced a never-ending euphoria. But there was more to it. According to Veen, the junkies no longer let themselves be driven to the outlying neighborhoods, but crept through the center of town at night. And, according to a girl he knew at the paper, the clubs along Peperstraat downtown were run by a gang which, just like on television, provided them with protection; bouncers who claimed new victims each week. All that racket still seemed diluted by sweet-sounding collegiate fun. But, Hille said, it was only a matter of time until the Grote Markt had earned the status of the OK Corral, and shootings would no longer be a laughing matter.

She'd committed herself to waking by six. It was six. She crawled out of bed in a dirty fog of looming catastrophe and exhausting torpor, and dressed. A few minutes later she was out on the street and saw the blood. Tom Severed Thumb, she thought deliriously, making tracks on his way home. She followed the spoor to a doorway, afraid of finding a corpse there, but it was empty. One street down she tossed open the door to the bar, looked around, but no Victor. She wavered, felt panic rise and decided to go home straight away. There were two boys on the bridge in front of her house. One of them was pissing in the canal, the other one throwing up. 'Hey, sweet cheeks,' the pissing boy called to Lisa, flashing the stream in her direction, 'want a drink?'

Lisa exhibited her middle finger. She went back into the house, turned on all the lights and put on some coffee. After two bowls full and three cigarettes, she walked to the bed-room, look a Lilliputian envelope from under her pile of underwear, chopped up two lines and snorted them through an empty ballpoint, raging and sweating, despising herself in a way that was starting to seem familiar. Fifteen minutes later she was at the kitchen table, flipping with imperious clarity through her thesis on 'Conflux of Circumstance; a Date with Fate as Plot in Dutch Literature'.

By the time Lisa finally heard the front door open, her whole being was packed in ice. Victor came into the kitchen, *'Tagjen,'* took a half-liter of Alfa out of the fridge and sat down beside her at the table.

'At it again, are we?'

She said nothing, didn't look up, didn't move – oh wait, she was tapping her pen on the table, knock that off! This was a dull, thudding standoff. This was a day in a life that was starting to drag on. When she was finished with school – another week or a couple of days – she'd make a plan and carry it out. On the spot. Hoopla! What plan? Not the foggiest.

Victor opened the fridge again and walked out of the kitchen with three half-litres under his arm. She heard him rummaging in his room. Deep cursing, a thump, then music. Screaming negroes, the sound of machine guns, a shrieking beat. Hip hop. She saw the music sweating. She saw a baseball bat beating a body to a pulp. Did this still fall under 'Cowboys and Indians'?

She poured herself a glass – of what? Oh yeah, Old Number Seven, walked into Victor's room and plopped down in the chair across from him.

'I imitated you,' she said tonelessly. The music sounded like late-night pile driving.

He looked at her.

'For the first time in my life, I went out looking for you, to see where you were.'

'And? Where was I?'

She felt cruelty sneaking into the corners of her mouth.

'I just wanted to see where that need comes from, I mean, I wondered why, whenever I'm only a half-hour late, you start hanging out the window with the telephone clenched between your knees, and then go out in the streets in a panic. I thought, is this what being worried is all about?'

He just sat there. Listless. Drunk.

She was on him before he could change that taunting expression. She hit him with fists balled. Kick, she thought, and she kicked. The whole room pounded in shock.

She stood looking at him in exhaustion. He was still sitting in his chair. One eyebrow was torn. His hair was smeared with blood. What came out of his nose dripped into the corners of his mouth.

His expression was unchanged.

'Have I,' he said, 'ever mentioned why I quit school?'

He took a slug of blood beer. Lisa sat down. She came to rest on the edge of the table. She saw her bloody knuckles, felt the ache in her wrists, looked at him, at his head, his legs, his trousers changing color. She saw how calm he was. Calm and beaten. She started throwing up. It gushed over her knees and splattered on the table.

Amazed, she looked at the puddle.

Then she ran away.

Dressed in a T-shirt and gym shorts, he was standing beside her bed. It was daytime. She stared into space and didn't know whether she dared to look at him. He pulled back the sheets, took her hand and pulled her to her feet. One arm behind her head, one arm under her knees. There was no way he could pick her up, she was way too heavy for him. But she was picked up, ferried out the door, through the hall, down the steps, into his room. Her head was against his chest, and if she hadn't expected his back to break any moment she wouldn't have let herself drop into a chair. He brushed the hair out of her face and smiled. He went away, came back again and poured a big glass full of beer right in front of her eyes. Bottoms up. Beer had never tasted so good. She wanted another glass, but didn't dare, or didn't know if she dared, to ask. She got another glass. He seemed so young. It was the shorts. Ten years ago was the last time she'd seen him in those, out on the soccer field, sprinting, shooting hard, making jokes, flushed with an excitement she hadn't seen in him since. Ten years ago. She'd been sixteen then, and nice to look at.

'Well then . . .' Victor said. He sat down across from her and lit a cigarette. 'There's something I have to tell you. Our loving parents have officially invited us out to dinner, at a really expensive place. Tomorrow evening, to be exact. I didn't tell you about it yesterday because I didn't know whether I could tolerate such an invasion of our private life, but I promised Anna we'd come, so she wouldn't be alone.'

A cigarette came tumbling at Lisa. Victor, pretty much in a daze, came over to give her a light. She took his hand and pulled him down on his knees in front of her. One of her fingertips brushed over his eyebrow. He was smiling again.

She didn't dare to, but she did anyway: she let her glass and cigarette fall, just like that, pressed his head down on her lap, laid her head on his and cried for the first time in years.

In the kitchen, they killed the bottle of Old Number Seven. Lisa had no stomach left, only a hole scalding deep inside. The radio was spitting pile-driver music. Fuck this and fuck that. And than an Uzi: ratatatatat! This, Lisa thought, isn't even funny anymore. Victor's favorite films: *Scarface, The Godfather; Say hello to my little friend: ratatatatat!*

She could look at him again now. What was going on in his head? He just kept smiling. It didn't seem like silent laughter, more like fond recollections. Lisa's head was filled with lukewarm mud. Her whole form felt sullied.

'Hey, man, dreaming about one of your barmaids?' What a question, Lisa thought, and what kind of tone is that? What is this? Sound. The sound of voices.

'Aww! No . . .'

What then? What then? What did it matter?

The way he knocked back those drinks. Hoopla!

The radio: 'Don't fuck with me!'

'What is it that appeals to you about this noise?'

He looked at her from beneath his eyebrow-and-a-half, weighing, reckoning.

'This, dearest, is fucking, ruthless fucking.'

Lisa shook her head.

'A thing knocked to the ground and fucked brutally from behind!'

'Hey, all right already.'

'In a pool of sweat.'

'Aaw!'

'Up the ass! Know what I'm saying? Up the ass!'

His language didn't match his look, but she knew the look that went with it all too well. That gleam in his eye when she caught him at the TV with one of his new personal myths in the video. She shrugged her shoulders: 'Are you finished?'

They hadn't slept together for at least six months. It seemed to suit Victor. As though it gave him room to trot out the ghosts that occupied his world. And what about Lisa? She'd never thought about it. They had a whole life behind them.

'Somewhere,' Victor said solemnly, 'there's an incredible amount of violence.'

'Somewhere?'

'Somewhere.'

'So?'

'So that violence is hurdling through th'air.' His tongue was growing thick.

'Okay, so what?' For the first time in a long time, she could smile at his drunkenness.

'So no-buddy knows where's gonna land.'

'And when it does?'

'Awrightt!' This spoken with the inflection of East Groningen, the word completely savaged.

'All right.'

'Yup, and all the boys who ever read Sergeant Fury get to sign up 'n' shoot as much as they want.'

'Don't you think it's about time you went to bed, Chief?'

'Hell no, we won't go!' A ditty from their childhood. Lisa giggled.

'We fuck 'em up!'

'Sure, baby, I'll wake you when we get there.'

'We cut them in pieces and, uh . . .' There was the Consul again.

'*Entzückend*, love,' Lisa said, 'but you're 4-F, so you're not allowed to play.'

'Precisely,' Victor said, index finger raised. 'Precisely I and others of my sort, the certifiably mad, will be in the field! We, uh . . . fuck 'em up!'

'Right, you said that.'

'Yup . . . I told that psychologist, I told him: 's nuthin; personal, y'understan', but if some sergeant starts flippin' me shit, I pump him full o' lead . . . mind you: 's nuthin' against the army, nuthin' at all, but fuck wi' me and I blow you away . . .'

'Hm.'

'He knew what I meant, you could see him thinkin': this is a good one, we save him for later, if the shit really hits the fan.'

'Oh right, sure, that must have been it.'

'For God marred, uh . . .' – Victor raised his fist – '. . . God made the earth and came to see if it was good, and he chose to visit the land of East Groningen, and met there 'n' farmer in His field, and God asked the farmer: "Is it good?" And the farmer pointed his rifle and roared: "Ge' off'n muh land!!"'

Lisa burst out laughing. Victor raised his glass and Lisa clinked hers against it.

'Skol!'

'Cheers, preacher!'

She got up, came around the table and pulled him out of his chair.

'We gonna dance?' he asked.

'No, sleep.'

'Ahaa, indeed, indeedy-do!'

She dragged him up the stairs and made sure that, when he fell, he landed on the bed. She closed the curtains and plugged in the night-light. He was already asleep. For a long time she sat beside his bed.

Could it be she felt cleaner, or was she just drunk? She knew she was being polished by life, but it wasn't clear to her whether the side being worked on now was already smooth or still jagged. Tomorrow she'd start thinking again. She undressed and crawled in next to him.

It was evening or night when she woke up. Her whole body hurt, and she felt a strange itch in her belly. She rolled onto her back. Victor growled and snored on. She had this screaming thirst. Carefully, she crept out of bed. She felt her panties sticking to her crotch. Wow, she thought. She hurried downstairs and remembered a dream in which the head of someone she didn't recognize was lingering between her thighs. Jesus, she thought, definitely distasteful, these guys. She opened an ice-cold bottle of beer and drank it down. Then she lit a cigarette. It was ten o'clock. Tomorrow dinner with Dad and Mom. She didn't even want to think about it. She took two more bottles, opened them and went back upstairs. In her own room she opened the windows. She finished a second bottle. Lovely, lovely. The beer cooled and warmed her stomach. The second cigarette made her dizzy, like she was smoking hash. She lay down on her bed and pulled a sheet over herself. The cigarette she left burning on the ashtray. Her hand was lying on her belly. Mmm, let's feel that. She let her fingers glide down into her hair, and further, and when they disappeared into the thick, warm wetness she thought: holy cow! She let her fingers slither around a little. No, not like that. She pulled her hand away and squeezed her thighs together. That was more like it. She squeezed and relaxed and squeezed and relaxed and the itching in her belly moved to her back. What's going on here, are we actually getting horny? She almost laughed out loud. She kept squeezing her thighs together. We'd better find out what this is. After a few blowzy thoughts, she slid her hand back into her panties. Well, how does one go about this? She pushed one fingertip inside, just a little ways, but didn't find what she was looking for. It was roomy and pretty elusive in there. She pushed two whole fingers deep inside. She roiled a bit and thought about how Victor made love to her. Somehow she almost had the giggles, somehow she was drunk and somehow something was on its way. She moved her fingers the way Victor would move inside her: slow, heavy and close. She tried to concentrate on the itch creeping to her flanks and nipples, then to her neck. It was like she had to bear down, somewhere in her head. She clamped down on her thoughts and, oops, it was squishing. But there was no one to hear her, and now she was reeling something in. She felt the muscles in her buttocks and clamped her thighs around her hand. She pushed her body in around her fingers. A cramp came from a long way away, and heat flashed in the hair on the back of her neck. She pulled up tight and held her breath. A wave ran through her body. A little tickling wave. She mashed her hand to a pulp. She had to get that butt up in the air now, absolutely, up with that butt. The sheet disappeared, and with a yank of the hand squeezing her buttock she tore the panties off and away. It was sopping, and that was nice too, and slowly another wave came rolling in. She gasped for air and felt her cheeks burn. Then it ebbed away again.

She saw herself lying there: hips hovering above the mattress, fingers lost in her cunt, her knees laughably far apart. She moved her hand again. Christ Almighty, if they could see her like this. She dropped down, squeezed her thighs one last time and turned onto her stomach, her breath lodged in her throat. The waves rolled from her toes to her shoulders and, blushing to her tailbone, she wormed around on her hand. Out of breath, she lay still. Then she rolled onto her back again and pulled her fingers out of her throbbing vulva. She held her sticky hand just above her breasts, like a trophy glistening in the nocturnal light from the window. She caught the smell of sulphur. God-damn, she thought, goddamn. Then she felt alone. In a little-kid way.

She crawled in quietly beside Victor and laid her sticky hand on his sex. He grew in his sleep. Without waking, he rolled towards her. When he opened his eyes, she pulled him on top and he slid right in. He may have thought he was dreaming, because his head lay motionless next to hers. Her hands on his buttocks, she moved him to his climax and he was back asleep by the time he slid out of her. Lisa smiled and folded her hands behind her head. She was proud of herself. But she suspected that this was the first and last time her body would lure her in. She knew now that what she'd reached in her disembodied slumber could not be surpassed.

Victor took the old road. He drove carefully and his eyes were smiling again. What in the world was he up to? Lisa felt the need to apologize for punching him, but that seemed to be the last thing on his mind. His face still looked awfully damaged. She wondered how he would explain that to the family.

She hadn't washed herself, on purpose. She smelled the sharp odor of sex right through her dress. The thought of sitting down at the table like this excited her, not sexually, but maliciously. What was happening to her? And when she thought about her fingering, a shiver ran down her spine. Not of shame, but disbelief. It felt like she'd been dreaming for days and was only now slowly starting to awaken.

Before Victor reached the turnoff to Oude Huizen, he pulled over to the side. He turned off the radio. She expected consultation about the tactics to be employed should things become too much for Victor, for if he tried to run away while the soup was still being served.

'There's something else I have to tell you. Do you remember those Parisian girls in Greece, the ones I sort of flirted with?'

Lisa nodded.

'Well, I've been corresponding with one of them ever since.'

She looked at him in surprise.

'Care of the Oude Huizen Bank.'

Lisa couldn't believe it. Fifteen years.

'Fact is, I've been invited to go down there.'

She shook her head. He was lying. He was delirious.

'And I'm going to. I can stay for at least a month or so.'

He started the car and spun away from the hard shoulder.

'A month?'

'Or longer.'

'And then?'

'Never ask the hero heading into the sunset on his old paint, cigarette dangling from the corner of his mouth, et-cetera, exactly what his plans are . . .'

'You're pulling my leg . . . aren't you?'

Tyres screeching, they turned into the driveway next to the bank. The car bucked once and they were standing still.

'And hoopla!' Victor said.

When Lisa appeared in the kitchen doorway, Anna was hanging around her brother's neck and Fixbier was barking wildly. Father and Mother were sitting at the kitchen table. Uncomfortably. Unusually, undisguisably uncomfortable.

'Hi, hello,' the doctor said. Lisa didn't let herself be hugged. She grabbed Victor by the back of the neck and dragged him, before the eyes of the embarrassed audience, out of the kitchen. She pushed him – he was almost pissing with laughter, goddammit! – up the stairs, into her bedroom.

'*Déjà vu*,' Victor said, 'hit me, hit me again.'

He was giggling!

Lisa kicked him. Limp with laughter, he fell onto her bed.

'Listen,' she hissed, 'pull yourself together, idiot. If you don't tell me what this is all about, I'm going to scream so loud they'll hear me at the other end of the road!'

His face softened. He patted the mattress. Shivering, she sat down next to him.

'You're going to hear a lot more than that today,' he said. 'So save the screaming for later.'

'What *is* this?'

The door swung open. Anna.

'Time to go.'

'We'll talk about it later,' Lisa said. 'This evening, deal?'
Victor smiled. 'Girl-talk,' he said.

The five of them went in Victor's car. The perplexed silence
that hung between them kept trying to slip away. They
drove out past Woudbloem, following the lines of the trees in
half-light. At the edge of a hamlet was a famous restaurant.
   A waitress led them to a burning hearth. Couples were
eating at two little tables. Muzak sounded from hidden
speakers. The dining room was done in blue and yellow,
color coordinates for the tasteless. There were big bouquets
of flowers. The fire crackled. Lisa dove into one corner of a
huge sofa and pulled Victor down next to her. Anna dropped
down beside him, their parents took the sofa that was left.
Their mother blushed again at the sight of her son's battered
face and her oldest daughter's despond. She looked at the
matter practically, and was therefore at a complete loss. Lisa
was taking things further than ever, with that smell emanat-
ing from her crotch and her hand clenching her brother's.
Anna thought: this is the end. When the doctor called for
them to name their poison, Lisa turned to the waitress and
asked if the house had ever heard of Jack Daniel's. The house
had, and the glasses proved well-filled. Anna and mother
drank juice. A tray of herring was laid before them by way
of an appetizer, but Victor kept his mouth shut. He squeezed
Lisa's hand. Menus were brought and Victor grinned briefly.
They studied the menu, hand in hand. The doctor had
finished his drink, and the first family clamor consisted of
waving. Yoo-hoo, we need a refill over here! You there,
Sweda-lips! The refills were punctual and lavish. Anna took
a herring from the tray, held it up, looked at it in disgust

and let it fall. Splat! The waitress started sweating. They never saw her again. An older woman appeared instead. She bowed to the family: 'I have a table for you by the window.' Victor didn't say: 'Methinks you have full twenty for us.' He squeezed Lisa's hand again and the lady, still stuck in her bow, nodded to him.

'Is there a preferred seating arrangement? I could put you and your girlfriend next to each other, and the same for you' – a nod to Pa and Ma, who did their best to cover up a few involuntary quivers of limb – 'which means, young lady, that you will be at the head of table. How does that sound?'

'It sounds fantastic,' Victor said. Mother snorted nervously with laughter. Father snapped at his second drink.

'Goodness,' said the lady, risking serious back injury now, 'You two could be brother and sister, you look so much alike, but I'm sure you must hear that all the time.'

'I've mentioned it to them on numerous occasions,' the doctor said, 'but they don't seem to listen.'

'Oh, well, the resemblance *is* noticeable. Have you been able to make a choice?'

'Several,' Victor said, 'and we're going to run through them in a little bit.'

'Excellent,' the lady said, 'can I get you anything else from the bar?'

'Would it inconvenience you terribly,' – Victor as sweet as could be – 'if we requested the bottle in its entirety?'

'No, of course not, shall I bring you a bucket of ice?'

The lady turned and choked in her first firm tread when Victor said: 'By the way, ma'am, resemblances are *always* noticeable, aren't they?'

She turned back to the party, saw how the doctor snapped at his drink, how Mother rose and sat again and how the young lady kissed her lover loudly on the cheek; the smacking noise made the other diners look up.

'And now,' Victor said to his parents, 'it's your turn.'

'Well,' the doctor said, 'once they catch a whiffa the feed-bag, there's no holdin' 'em, is there?'

'My sentiments exactly,' Victor said, 'come on, out with it.'

'Liesje, dearest,' Mother said with a blush, the grooves visible in her powdered face, 'could we tone it down just a bit?'

'I wouldn't think of it,' Lisa said. 'It says somewhere that we get used to everything, in the end.'

She slung an arm around the neck of her brother, who hadn't been expecting it and blushed now as well. Anna grinned. They drank their glasses to the very last drop and studied the menu. The bottle arrived, and the silence still trying to sneak out of the party had its feet tickled by the tingling of ice.

'So,' Victor asked, 'who's going where and why?'

Mother slid to the corner of the two-seater and looked at her children. 'Liesje,' she said, begging with her eyes for that arm to be removed, 'how's it going to go next week?'

'Like it always does. I turn in my thesis and then, a month later, I get my diploma.'

'So you already know you're going to pass?'

'Yes,' Lisa said, 'and Victor's leaving.'

Black rings appeared beneath her big, incredulous eyes, like a child waking from fever dreams to the memory of hellish hallucinations, before seeing the light of day and daring to greet it.

'What do you mean?' Anna asked. 'What is this?'

All eyes turned to Victor.

'I'm just going to stay with someone in Paris for a while,' he spoke.

'Oh,' said Mother, who wanted to weigh her words but now thought everything came out brassy, 'well, that doesn't matter.'

'Naw, Granny,' Lisa said, 'that doesn't matter at all. Hey, but tell us, why are we here, anyway? What are we celebrating?'

The doctor topped up his glass and swung visibly plumb with the planet: 'Maybe your mother can catch a lift, now that one horse has already bolted.'

'Oh, is it time for that again?' Lisa asked. Victor grinned. Anna looked at him and, for the first time in her life, got angry with him. 'Hey, dickhead!' She jabbed her elbow into his side. 'Put another twist on that rubber mug of yours!'

'Oomph,' Victor said, 'a low blow.'

'I'm still waiting,' Lisa said.

'I,' said their mother, longing for her vagabond jacket, 'am leaving your father.'

The doctor gestured with his hands: hoopla. Mother looked away. Anna let her tears flow.

The lady stuck her head out of a blue and yellow floral hedge: 'Have you decided yet?'

'You've hit the nail on the head, madam,' Victor said, 'we'd all like the tenderloin, but then as follows: raw on the inside and blackened on the outside.'

The lady nodded and looked at Anna's tears.

'Or would the young lady prefer something else?'

'Akiddyburgerandfrenchfries,' Anna said, 'and a sundae for dessert.'

Victor nodded: 'Is that within the realm of possibility?'

The lady walked away, shaking her head.

'So that's what you've decided?' Lisa snapped at her mother.

'Sweetheart, we've talked about this at length, and it's the only way.'

The doctor hooked back his fourth glass and nodded.

'This is what you call the fruit of thorough deliberation and, uh, what I'm going to say now is the most . . . horrific thing I've ever said or ever will say . . .' He looked at his wife with love and aversion. 'We're parting as friends.'

'Are you getting a divorce?' Lisa asked, thinking of sleep, of sleeping nicely later on.

'No-o,' Victor said.

Father and Mother shook their heads.

'So are you fucking someone else?' Lisa asked her mother.

Mother got up and walked away. Anna flew after her. Victor topped up their glasses.

'Well?' Lisa asked.

'No,' said father and son in unison. And father: 'She wouldn't do that.'

Victor leaned over to his father and hissed: 'You're doing it all wrong, old man. You should leave, and let her stay there by herself.'

The doctor, bowled over by his son for the first time in his life: 'Hey, that's no way to talk to your father, this isn't America.'

Victor stared at him.

'I'm not going anywhere, not on your life.'

'Aha,' Victor said, and knocked his back.

'I think I have to throw up,' Lisa mumbled.

'What you have to do is keep drinking,' Victor said.

The doctor forgot his suffering, his lot and his life, and said to his daughter: 'Honey, please, calm down an' stop guzzling that stuff.' He looked at his son. 'An' you ... what're you pullin' on me?'

'Your table is ready.'

When their mother drove them back to Oude Huizen after dinner, there was music in every meter slipping by. An orchestra that never stopped tuning. This family dragged cacophony behind it, whichever corner she took, whatever turn she made. She decided to drive on to Town, to keep Victor from killing himself and his sister. She took the old road, gnawing her memories to shreds. Four parents they'd had between them. All wiped out by cancer in five years. It had been like living in the churchyard, that's how much time they'd spent there. Their fathers gentleman farmers, their mothers proud and magisterial. God, the love there'd been, even though it had seemed like fighting at the time. But they hadn't fought for love, they'd fought with love, for the land and for their lives. That whole life had had a covetable simplicity and directness, though she knew she was being romantic about it. But what else could you do with life besides romanticize it?

At the house on the canal, Anna expressed a desire to stay. It was fine with her. When she slid back into the car beside her husband, he was snoring in his seat. She drove back, along The Scar this time, and thought: I can cry all I want, but no-one's getting my tears anymore. Especially not this land, this wasteland where nothing will ever grow again.

When Anna awoke with a start that night at three and found herself in Lisa's bed, she missed her night-light and was frightened by the roaring outside the windows. She tossed, stared into the darkness. She clicked on a light and found a torn pair of black lace panties that were hard in the crotch, crusted white with girl-juice. For the first time in her life, she blushed. A painful dizziness swept through her skull. Then she felt the loneliness of the house. A ghost, she also thought she heard a ghost. She shot out of bed and ran from the room, shoulderblades prickling. In the hall, she calmed down. She listened at Victor's door and heard nothing. She opened it and looked inside. In the soft-green glow of the night-light she saw her brother and sister, lying there asleep. When she paused at the foot of the bed and saw how Lisa lay with her head on Victor's chest, sucking her thumb, she wished she'd never been born. Never before had she seen anything so mournful, so much din in so much calm, so much doggedness in such deep sleep.

'Hey,' she said.

Lisa raised her eyelids. Smiled. Lifted her head carefully. Only then pulled her thumb out of her mouth.

'What is it?'

Anna shrugged. Lisa sat up straight, and Victor opened his eyes.

'Can't you sleep?'

Anna shook her head.

Lisa tossed the blankets aside and beckoned to her. Lisa was naked.

'May I?' Anna asked.

'Come on,' Victor said. He took a cigarette and lit it. In the light of the flame, she saw his soft eyes. From back then. Anna, who'd forgotten she didn't smell of perfume and spring water, peeled off her singlet and panties and crawled in quick beside Lisa. Then she rolled over her sister and nestled in between them. An arm slid behind her neck and Victor laid her head on his chest. He handed the cigarette to Lisa. She took a drag and crushed it out. Under the blankets he sought Anna's hand.

'Time for a story then?' Victor said.

BOOK THREE

Feierlich und gemessen,
ohne zu schleppen

BOOK THREE

Gomorrah, January 1990

Alter Knabe,

You still there? Lisa tracked me down, and asked me to do the same to you. Not that she doesn't know where you are, but she entertains the ridiculous thought that you might be susceptible to my Reason. And, while we're on the subject, isn't it ridiculous that little boys who try to get lost are found by means of the first shot in the dark? (As a young spud, I was wont to run away from home in just this fashion, knowing they knew exactly where I ran to – which meant no-one ever came looking for me, but that's another story.) Anyway, old fellah, brace yourself, although the situational heading above has, without a doubt – at least if you're not too trashed yet – caused you to guess: I have Gone Back. Please feel free to throw up or throw in the towel.

Completed masterpiece under one arm, having nailed shut all hovels in Town and taken a taxi, of the American eight-cylinder variety, I have Cut My Losses. No, She hasn't Come Back to me, but she *is* here. My mother says it's not right to interfere in someone else's marriage; after all, we've entered the nineties and adultery as such is no longer 'in', but for the time being I have no such intentions. By the way, are you still able, as we (your sister and I) are, to file yesterday away under The Past? Gomorrah hasn't changed, you know what I'm saying? Unchanged. Are you still fond of anecdotes? Or have you doddered off after Joyce & Ko(rsakov) for good? Here comes one anyway, for old times' sake. I had my first story published, rife with allusions to my masterpiece, *Not Available*. The rag in question was in all the shops in Town, but not in Gomorrah. So what else is new? The masterpiece I secreted away in my hotel room, the magazine I folded under my arm. After all, when one visits one's Old Home Town, probably to stay after a decade's absence, it's essential to come rolling in with a pose that immediately establishes the right tenor. Agreed? After two days of walking around like Scott Fitz without running into anyone (a miracle in a hole where no one ever Goes Away), I decided to spur my despond to a lather by visiting the new library (the first mark of decay). And coming around the corner of the Kerkstraat – the high stake takes the cake – who should I run into but Yvonne! She, as though eight years had never passed, smiles shyly, a little startled (But not too much: if anyone remains unruffled under the antics of destiny, it is she.), but not a day older – I swear to God – and says, in that singsong voice of hers: 'Heeey, hi.'

And what do you think? She's pregnant!

'Well well,' I say.

After all, I do read the occasional book, and I swear by Godfried Bomans. So then I add: 'Well I'll be, talk about a twist of fate.'

Whereupon she nods, looks around (after ten years of pondering over it, still an enigma, that) and, in perfect unison with me, asks: 'So how you doing?'

Then, in enthusiastic chorus: 'Oh, reaaaal good.'

The smoke lifts and I lay a hand on her belly (in retrospect, my reflexes make me want to cry) and ask: 'Baby?'

I want to underscore this, old boy: I haven't seen her for eight years, and within two seconds I'm touching her in a manner too filmic for words.

And she concurs: 'Baby.'

A silence follows. Then she raises a hand to her left breast – a breast heavier than I'd ever dared to imagine – and makes a fist and goes: 'Pitter-patter pitter-patter, oh God, man, say something!'

She turns around. And then, by the way, I see that there's some girl standing next to her, watching the whole thing. She looks at me again: 'I don't know what to say, you know?'

Know. Know. Know.

But I do, I feel like screaming, but instead I say: 'Hey, it's okay.'

Now if that isn't decadent. Isn't it, Prins? I mean, isn't it? The rest I will now summarize. Ten seconds later, her mind's wandering while I spout words.

Well then. Your hair on end, your toes curl. Will you, foul *Versager*, listen to me for a change?

What the hell kind of quasi-artistic flight have you undertaken? (For what it's worth, I've dealt at length with a Banal Banishment in my own masterpiece.) Everyone knows where you are. Everyone knows what you're doing there. And everyone has better things to do than sit around and Mull Over Victor. Lisa's not mulling either. Top up that tumbler and take a snort. She was here with me, here in Gomorrah, she took a room next to mine at my own expense, and she asked me to write to you. The rest of the time we spent taking strolls in the winter rain, visiting old school-yards (deadly, schoolyards devoid of children, the buildings deserted, Gomorrah, if I may quote from my own work, robbed of life once and for all; all this being a second mark of decay) and walking through the park that's in my book. I showed her Places. (The pain of homesickness does not differ from that of melancholy, if you know what I'm trying to say with regard to Times & Spaces and, aw, forget it.) After that I dined with her at a gourmet joint out beyond Woudbloem (she seemed to know the place and was afflicted by a giggle at the back of the throat), for, as the third mark of decay, I now possess a car of my own. In Woudbloem itself we spent a while mourning at canalside, in the rain, with a view of the old factory where our fore-fathers, etc. After staying with me for four days, she returned to her island. She's down, just so you know, to barely fifty kilos. We kissed each other chastely on the cheek by way of farewell and she tried to leave a message for you, which I refused to take, so we got into a fight there at the end. I told her: he ain't my brother and he is too heavy, upon which she, as you can surely guess, burst into tears, tossed her locks and fired up a cigarette. Beautiful and gripping, to be sure, but my muse has a higher Fiddle-Dee-Dee quotient.

In other words, there's something you should know, but the ayes have it that it's your move. At least that's how I understood it.

Enclosed, please find my publication. I told Lisa that if anything could draw you out of your carapace, it would be prose from my hand. So fire at will. Be well.
Cowboy Veen
Veenlust, Gomorrah, the Peat Colonies, Holland

*

Paris, February 1990
(Postcard showing the Hoofdstraat in Oude Huizen. Caption: GREETINGS FROM OUDE HUIZEN)

Dear Gawdsby,
The weather here is lovely. We're enjoying the beautiful surroundings. The city is fascinating. The museums are gorgeous. The food could be better, the hotel's pretty lousy, the people are filthy, and everything's ridiculously expensive. Fond regards from,
Victor

*

Gomorrah, February 1990

Old Boy,

Do I have to use force? All right then. I've spent each Friday, Saturday and Sunday evening of the past two weeks Waiting, in the tunnel café, (Burned down and reconstructed; decay, decay!) just as I did from early 1977 deep into 1980 (that's not true: it was only the last two years, but memory, etc.) Of yet she has failed to appear as she used to, deep in the night, when the odor of potato starch causes the little town to hallucinate in its sleep, flapping out onto the dance floor with a new Henry in her wake. Where are the cunthounds of yesteryear?

Hereby: the word 'cunt' will no longer appear in my writing; I've spent fifteen long years trying to get accustomed to the word: I have not succeeded.

So I'm sitting at the bar, waiting. No candidate for the role of Carraway has yet appeared. Where, by the way, does one organize a tea party in the Peat Colonies? My mother doesn't own a gazebo, and besides, if she knew what I was up to, she'd kill me slowly. But, to the point. Brace yourself. Each evening I stagger whiningly back to the hotel. I've been pining for just this proper, upright brand of snivelling for the last eight years. Genuine Sorrow is a phenomenon that requires nurturing in this day and age. (My new band's called Cultivated Emotions, our first gig is planned for the day of labor, a superannuated holiday, in the Bella concert hall, and I swear I'll dedicate our first number – 'The Embryo' by P. Floyd – to you. *This one goes out to V.P., who's living in Paris and is a missing person!* Lisa attended a rehearsal yesterday. She came over from Oude Huizen, where she was visiting your father and the matter in question. We kissed goodbye, a little less chastely this time.)

When we met that time on the Kerkstraat, I told Yvonne about my book.

She: 'Oh, I don't know if I like that, you know, you writing about me.'

Where is the vanity of yesteryear? Or did she only say that because some girl was standing there listening? Must this phenomenon – vanity, that is – be reanimated? I didn't tell her that I Came Back to force my book on her. She has to beg for it first!

I know where she lives, who her man is . . . Her man? A mere boy! Boys we are and boys we shall remain! Apropos of which, I culled the following for you from the pages of *Het Nieuwsblad*: 'Young man, slight mental handicap, aged 61, occasional migraines, hobby: going for drives, seeks girlfriend of approx. 77 yrs.' I shit you not!

Who her man is, therefore, and even why. Does he allow her to go out alone? I know this guy only by looks and limb, and at the moment there's no-one who can provide me with any information. *I'm just a stranger in my old home town.* Ridiculous when you consider that I once knew everyone around here, and they all knew me. Or rather, Us: her & me. I'm not out to impress him with my Return, but I am her. Lie awake and toss and dream and remember she shall! Even if I have to grab her by the scruff of the neck and drag her through the book. After all, what kind of idiot would write a worthy tome for a girl, then refuse to show it to anyone but her? I pride myself on being such an idiot. Over.

Veen

*

Paris, February 1990

Trapsby,

Enough! Uncle! Have mercy! If you don't knock it off, I'll tell your mommy! I can't believe it. Is this all some terrible but good joke, or are you really planning to besiege that girl?! I refuse to believe it. Extramarital affairs, however you look at it, are *passé*. And if you're so bent on ending up in a pond with a bullet in your noggin, then commit your own suicide, goddammit!

And what's this shit about a matter in question? What's my family to you? Worry about your own petty, wetty little life!

Your publication was not bad. Thank God no Brat hunt-and-Pack, although I'm quite aware you idolize such folk. Are you a writer now? Do other people think so too?

Well, come on, write and tell me what's going on, and not a whisper to the wicked witch concerning my reply. What I want to know is: where's Anna these days? Has she already moved to Amsterdam? Be creative, and ferchrissakes, be a man for once!

V

*

Gomorrah, March 1990

Ouwe jongen,

We're sitting here in the lounge at Veenlust, hitting the Jesse James bourbon in remembrance of you. My table companion is using her long nails to scoop crustaceans out of the shrimp cocktail and dip them in the hooch. She thought you'd want to know. What had you imagined, buddy? You're powerless against our machinations. And, by the way, I AM a man: I rub my hands impatiently at the prospect of my demise. Here she is:

VICTOR? THERE'S SOMETHING YOU SHOULD

Veen again here. Now she's dipping her tears in the blubber. We're a bit tipsy. We're having sea devil later on, shall I order a muscadet, or something fruity? You should know. Here she comes again:

THERE'S SOMETHING YOU SHOULD KNOW, EVEN THOUGH YOU DON'T DESERVE TO HAVE ME TELL YOU. SO I'M ONLY GOING TO GIVE YOU A HINT. YOU'LL NEVER FORGIVE YOURSELF IF YOU DON'T CONTACT US. I'M ENCLOSING ANNA'S ADDRESS. CALL US, CALL THE DOCTOR IF NEED BE. THAT I HAVEN'T WRITTEN BACK TO YOU IS YOUR OWN STUPID FAULT.

L

What handwriting, where does she come up with it, and what exquisite language! Don't you agree? Yes indeed, I'm a real Writer now! And I truly am fascinated by those Bratpeckers, but only a Mokum Tabernacle Choirboy would run off after such folk. *This is not America.*

Victor, I beg of you (just once): come back! Opposition is needed. A stiff north-easter. I can't form a front on my own. It still isn't too late, but in six months' time that monkey-doodle-business down in Amsterdam will be forgotten and there will nothing left to bitch about, let alone piss on. And seeing's how you're too far away to smack me one: what this country needs is regional rioting! Don't contradict me. The western hemisphere has dumped its sprouts. I let them burn on, and you should be in this with me.

That's that. I'm going to have dinner with your weepy sister, then we're going to Town to buy a wah-wah pedal (*Cry baby,*) and then I'm putting her on the boat. She has nothing more to say to you. Be well.
Veen

*

Paris, March 1990
(Postcard of 'The Wasteful Maiden' by Felix Labisse. Illustration torn from a gallery memo-book and glued to cardboard.)

Anna, dearest,
Me sorry, ugh! What the hell is going on?
V

*

Amsterdam, March 1990

Dear Victor,

That's Lisa, by the way, the damsel in that picture. Oh sure, you're so sorry. Well that's your problem. I'm keeping my nose out of it, and there's no way I'm going to tell you. It's like the only way I can see my family these days is to go to the movies, and now that I've gotten used to that, I plan to keep it that way. Everything that has to do with you and her and Pa and Ma goes right by me. That's fine with me. I'm busy enough. Art history isn't as nice as I expected. Do you remember how I went to the academy for an admissions interview? And how a bunch of guys with face fungus and one of those henna bitches with Gums and Patchouli (in '88!) were sitting in front of a whole slew of paintings and asked me: 'Which ones do you like?'

And me: 'None of them.'

And they: 'Well then, what *do* you like? Impr. or Expr., I mean, where do your affinities lie?'

And me: 'Late Kandinsky, early Monet, that's about it.'

And they: 'This isn't the place for you.'

Well, ditto bullshit here. Wasn't it your Franny who sighed: 'I'm a freak . . . and those bastards are responsible'? Same here. Oh well. I miss you a lot. We never get to yak (okay, I won't say 'yak' anymore). I want to talk to you and go to the movies and go hear bands, like we used to. Shall I tell you what I look like? Okay. My hair loose, all the way down to my

ass. Black jeans with purple and peach-colored patches
(I know I'm behind the times). Sixties' T-shirts, lamé
blouses, shoes with big square heels. But the tits will
never amount to anything. Thanks to Sis, who took it
all for herself. Write to her. I know you can do it.
Don't be such a baby. I love you.
Anna

*

Paris, April 1990

Peatsby,
   Please send me a few kilos of inflammatory material.
I haven't received any mail from Lisa for the last six
months. In exchange for the favor, here's an anecdote:
At the Gare du Nord, where I change my bills for
francettes, these two girls are always hanging around,
about fifteen years old, typical Veenian beauties.
Methinks they're in it for the money, and they seem,
in view of their apple cheeks, free of bubonics. At this
station it is my wont to purchase the best there is to
offer in dirty books. Last week the girls followed me
to the 'wideopenbeaverrack' and continued to observe
me while I made my purchase. I was drunk, and therefore randy and bold. I beckoned to them, asked them
in English what they were doing, and they replied that
they were up to 'nuzzing', just hanging 'round. So
I asked them, man-to-man: 'What do you do for
money?' Amazingly enough, they were still able to
giggle: '*Rien de trop, rien de manque.*' I flipped through

my most recent acquisitions, found a picture illustrating one of my preoccupations and showed it to the toddlers. Still capable of giggling but not of being amazed, the girls went into conclave and announced: *à titre gracieux*. At first I didn't get it. For free! You hear that, Veen, for free! No wonder God lives down here. They took me to a vacant lot behind a deserted, dilapidated building, forced open a door, took me inside, bummed cigarettes, stood there smoking a bit, staring at me brashly (in that East Groningen county-fair fashion), pulled down their jeans and stepped out of them, panties too, then peed in perfect unison on the stone floor. For free! Since that happy afternoon I occasionally take them out to dinner, just to be seen at a table with two such creatures. We barely understand each other, and I'm still not completely convinced they do it for money. And you think I'm coming back? In exchange for this story, I want information. You know. Tell me all you can, this messing around makes me nervous. All this I report to you in deepest secrecy. V

*

Gomorrah, April 1990

Alter Knabe,

I envy your ability to shit through your teeth. If you want me to come, why not just ask? I'll hop in the car Friday morning. If you're not home when I get there, I'll wait until you show up. I'm bringing – the world is too good to you – a letter from Lisa. So you can jangle your nerves even harder until then. Besides inflammatory materials, is there anything else you require? Just call me, leave a list with the receptionist. Don't even think of calling my parents. Meanwhile, I'm still waiting in vain in the tunnel café (where is she, goddammit? Has she forgotten everything about the way we do things?). I have to get out of here for a while, in any case.

Veen

*

Ameland, April 1990

Asshole,

Hille tells me he's going to visit you, and he wants me to come along, but I wouldn't dream of it. Anna at least got a card from you. Nothing for me. You're a coward! Traditionally speaking: I hate you. I'm writing to you so you'll be obliged to write back. Then we can talk further. By the way, what have you been writing to Hille to make him keep collapsing in laughter? Nothing about me, I trust? Remember this, dirty pig, he's more my friend than he is yours! So you'll be getting this letter from him, and I recommend that you do your best to pull yourself together, because now I'll get to hear what you look like and how you're doing. Write me *gefälligst, Dreckskerl! Vous nous manquez.*

Elisabeth van Ameland

*

Gomorrah, April 1990

Dear Abby,

I just got back and here follows my immediate report on the vicissitudes of his condition. (Go out and buy a phone!) Don't worry. About Victor. He really does live with a bunch of intellectuals. Pretty girls with no conception of hygiene (Of course, I'm a fan of young girls with tufts, but what the Parisian ladies allow themselves by way of wild hairs is too much, even for me.), two boys who purportedly read books but look like they model clothes for fashion brochures: five o'clock shadows (cultivatedly unconscionable) and dressed to a tee. The girls treat him like a trick poodle. He's writing a book about Kerouac; I was allowed to peruse it, it's giddy enough to give you the whirlies. He's looking good. (I am too, by the way.) So I kept my mouth shut about the situation in Oude Huizen, not because you suddenly changed your mind about the whole thing, but because I refuse to do your dirty work. For the rest, I have no idea what he's up to. He didn't ask about you. Not once. He took me out on the town, we went to the Louvre. In front of the portrait of John the Baptist he baptized me with a drop of Seine water he'd smuggled in. Such airs! We were both rather touched. We relived old times, as they say. (Although it's impossible to score dope in that town.) I nagged the hell out of him to come back with me, at least to attend my gig next week and then leave right away if need be, but with no success. Send me a tape, said the asshole. What else can I say? To recapitulate:

I don't understand at all. He lured me down there with depraved stories and dirty promises, thereby taking advantage of my sick bent to gossip, and once I was there he didn't want to know a thing. You get him, let me know. He said he'd write to you, but do we believe a fucking word he says? You'll find out, I guess. I'll pick you up from the boat on Thursday, the one that comes in at six. I've booked a room for you, so you can stay with me in Town after the show (yes, Lisa, separate rooms). Hang in there, little biddy.
Hille

*

Paris-on-the-Seine, Liberation Day 1990

All right then,
   You look like hell! What is this? Anoreksia Karenina? Do something about your weight, goddammit! Stop playing Brontë Schwestern, there on the wuthering heights of Ameland. Okay, okay, take it easy. I stood watching you across the room like a shy schoolboy. Incognito in Groningen; good name for a bad story (as Veen would say). Hey, old Veen up there on that stage. It wasn't bad. I came in (I'd let my beard grow and was wearing my powdered wig, oyez), sidled up to the rail (the girls behind the bar don't know me anymore) and peered around: you were standing up front and I just couldn't. What kind of commotion would we have encountered if I had?

Answer please! What will happen when you see me? Will you, traditionally and freely adapted from Veen's girl, start kicking me? Throw your arms around my neck in slow motion? (The assembled peoples part like the Red Sea, you come running down the path they've cleared, I let my glass fall to the floor with a crash? The crowd applauds and spontaneously gives birth to manifestos?) After about an hour I left and drove back in the DS I'd borrowed. So now tell me what's up.

Ludwig

*

Ameland, May 1990

Feigling, ewiges Schwein!

If it was possible to stamp your feet on paper, this would be it. It's only because I know you ('oyez' to you too), otherwise I wouldn't have believed it. An answer? Okay then: first I'd throw my arms around your neck, then start kicking. Satisfied? Do you mind my asking what brand of crowbar you used to get away? Do you mind my asking where you got the filthy gall to ogle me and then leave? Traditionally, then: is that so much easier for you? What's become of your sense of drama, your penchant for display? What's become of your predilection for filmic scenes? Don't give me that! In your eyes, this was the perfect display. Tell me about it, sweetheart! There are plenty of things I'll never forgive you for, but this takes the

cake! Here's what's up: The Boss is dying. If you want to see him, you'll have to hurry. I don't know what else to say to you. Drop dead!
Lisa

*

Paris, May 1990

Brat Packsby,

Nice show. I peeked around the corner. Postmodern, or Revival? From Floyd to Genesis to Young to Wim Sonneveld? Woe betide us: too young for the first Summer of Love, too old for the second: the eternal return. When it happens this fast, though, reality becomes a spinning top. You really did dedicate a song to me. I thank you for that display of affection. I thank you anyway. And now I want to ask a favour. Before long (as soon as possible), I have to go to Oude Huizen, that's right, now I know why. May I presume you'll drive me there? I wouldn't survive the bus ride. You can be Neal and jerk on the wheel, I'll be Jack the Rabid. I'll call your hotel with a date and time. Stay away from that girl! Knock it off. Burn that book!
V

*

Paris, May 1990

Dearest,

I'm going to East Groningen by way of Amsterdam. Do you still wish to receive me? If you have to study, or whatever, I'll just head straight on through. Let me know. We could go to the movies, and we could even yak a little. If it suits you, I'll be there on Saturday.

V

*

Amsterdam, May 1990
[Telegram]

Come here! A.

*

Paris, Printemps 1990

Beloved Empress,

Here's how it is: my sense of drama is safe in a locker at the Centraal Station in Amsterdam, my penchant for display is running thin. After I took Paris, I wrote you. You swore back at me. You let the doctor sell the house. You left for parts unknown. All this at the drop of a hat. This is what they call covering one's tracks. For years, you raised your finger at me and pointed out my status: homeless & injured ('I had a wonderful

diehood thanks to my fa– fa– family', remember?),
then, as soon as I looked the other way, you burned
my bridges behind me.

Have you ever wondered whether I'd Come Back
(capitals mandatory, according to Veen)? Obviously
not. As many thoughts as have pounced on us in unison and strangled us from behind, so this thought, too,
has given us hell: *es gibt keine Rückkehr*. And that
while everything in your world, *verzeihe mir*, your
universe, comes back eternally. *Mutti Mutti, er ist
wieder da!* So you're the one, Granny, who, excluding
the eventuality of repentance and reform on my part,
has made it impossible for me to come home. Could
it be you're having second thoughts? So what are you
cackling about, little witch?! Even in books, brother
and sister are unable to remain at Ardis and fade into
the woodwork.

Going away, the village manhood told me on
occasions too numerous to think about, is an art. And
a necessary evil. Don't ask them why. Ask me. All
the hero's handiwork is hoary. Are you listening? No
spectators on the sidelines shouting: ooooh, how
original!

The brother had a sacred failing/he went out a' holy
grailing/ I hope, he said, my compass ain't ailing./His
sis stayed behind and started railing:/ 'I want to be
part of this junk mailing.'/She kicked up a fuss with
much gnashing and wailing/ then asked herself: could
it be I'm derailing?/ Let's, said the witch, stick with
toothing and nailing/ I'll show him that my ass ain't
trailing!

And then, dearest, would you be so kind as to look up the possible declensions of the verb 'to kvetch'?

Enough chortling? Then on to the heart of the matter: what's to become of an old satyr with venal plans regarding a girl who is not only his sister but also his virile Waterloo? Please reply!

V

*

Amsterdam, May 1990

Sis,

V. was here. For two days. And he's just left for Oude Huizen. This is the last chance I'm giving you, and him too. I mean, this is the last time I'm going to get involved in that game you two play. I've got better things to do. Granny on the Warpath will be arriving soon. So that'll keep me congested for a while. What am I, an intersection? If you're able to bring yourself to go home and see him, then you don't have to be secretive. He knows I'm writing this to you. What am I saying? He knows better than anyone that I'm writing this to you. Once the two of you have blown off, I'll take Mama up to see the old man. I'll keep her here until I'm sure you two have fucked off. And this is the last gesture I'm going to make!

Anna

*

Ameland, May 1990
[Postcard: GREETINGS FROM NES]

Dear Anna,

I can't bring myself to do it. It's okay, leave us be. In another lifetime, when all of us are tossed together again to pick through the wreckage, we'll offer our apologies to you three times a day, after every meal. Kisses, Lisa

*

Rotterdam, May 1990

Dear Victor,

They tell me you've been back twice without coming by or letting us know. It's really hard for me to say all the things I need to say to you like this, but if you insist on playing hide-and-seek, there's no other way. I want you to understand why I couldn't stay with your father, just like I want you to understand (even though I *am* your mother!) why you couldn't stay with Lisa either. It's because the two of you drink. Do you understand what I'm saying? You two drink! Your father and you. I want to emphasize this. Whatever else may have gone wrong, all right, it takes two to make a quarrel. But if you can't talk about it, you're lost. There's no talking to people who drink. I know women who stay with their husbands out of fear. I'm not afraid. I wasn't then, and I'm not now. I resigned myself to my fate. Which also means that, when it was enough, it was enough. I love your father, but he's not the person I love, if you understand what I'm saying. Somewhere inside him is his former self. If you become like him, no-one will ever be able to stay with you. I promise you that. That boozing, son, is a way of putting on airs. I hate airs, and I've tried to raise all of you in the wisdom that they only cloud things. You have an eye for people who put on airs, but you, now don't get angry when I say this, are an enormous poseur yourself. I know this, I could always see it on your face, and I only have to think about you and I know it again for sure. Sober Groningers. It's the biggest misconception ever. But that's how it often goes. People who come to rely on a character trait, one they've been talked into, have to live with it. Do you understand what I'm saying? Nowhere is there so much drinking and grousing as among the men of East Groningen. Take it from your mother. You don't have to be like that. That you and Lisa, well, don't ask me. I know you care about her, and she cares about you, in a way that isn't healthy. But things like that, and I know what I'm talking about, things like that can't be changed in an instant. I think it's a really good idea that the two of you don't live together any more. But there's no reason why things have to go the way they're going now. The two of you are grown-ups. You both, because that's how life works, okay, laugh about it, you both have to find your place in life. That's all there is. It all gets a lot more complicated once you have children of your own. I know you've both suffered from the way things were at home. God! Everyone

suffers from whatever it was like at home. When your
father and I got married, we had children and that was
that (well, okay, it didn't go quite like that, but you
understand what I'm trying to say). Ever since, I've been
trying to figure out what's wrong with your father. I
never have understood. And now I don't have to understand anymore. He wouldn't want it any other way.
And I don't need it anymore. Take a good look at what
you're doing, boy. If you give in to your weakness
now, you'll never be able to be strong. That's what I
wanted to say to you. Anna tells me you're looking
good. I only hope so. I'm not going to beg you to call
me sometime. You have to figure that out for yourself.
But you're my son, and I think about you every day.
Love, your mother

*

Paris, June 1990
[Telegram]

Ma, I have no grievances, regrets, etc.
V

*

Paris, June 1990
[Telegram]

Lisa. What now?

*

Oude Huizen, July 1990

Victor,

What now? Have you lost your *vade-mecum*? I came here after you left, and then Anna and Mama came too. The doctor is drinking himself into the grave, slowly but with verve. Three weepy women at the kitchen table. Where were you with your smirk? Maybe I'm exaggerating.

Now I'm here alone with him, and we're waiting for The Boss to die. He has a housekeeper to take care of him too. The man is dying in silence.

For the first time in her life, by the way, our mother tried to comfort me. I've run up the flag; half-mast. One mustn't – that's her credo – exaggerate.

With regard to the question at the end of your letter, I have no answer. And I don't even want to think about coming up with one. That making love is so important to you, I'm prepared to believe that, but methinks there are adjacent fields in greater need of fertilization. Don't look so shocked!

Sorry.

That it didn't become important to me, that's what finally bothers you, isn't it? You're incapable of being ambivalent, and I'm not talking now about being half-and-half, let alone hermaphroditic (or what seems to horrify you most: being androgynous). When Victor partakes of unlawful communion, then it has to be the product of passion and lust, and not, for example, of passion and consideration. When Victor disappears, then it has to be the product of going away and abandoning all, and not of going away and reflecting, or of distance and a deep breath. When Victor dabbles at art, then it has to be the product of *Weltschmerz* and manifest destiny, not of preference and conviction. Don't try to deny it, you conceited ass! When Victor drinks, it has to be the product of background and protest, not of trying and failing, or of courage and fear. Victor wishes to lead his life irrevocably. Victor looks like a goddamn symbol, a little boy with no foot-hold, only a penchant for display. (Put that in your pipe and smoke it!) Victor clings to old rites, and when a new and original bond arises, he has no idea how to deal with it, because there's no book to show him how to quantify that bond, how to color it in and trump it up. Victor, in other words, is scared shitless of what comes down the pike. (And life, jerkwater, is what comes down the pike.) Even your mother – are you listening? – even your mother could resign herself to it. To what? To ineradicable ties. To – hold onto your hat – symbolic love and tenderness. We can forget about that symbolic bit as far as I'm concerned, as far as you're concerned too, I take it. I've got plenty of time to think, to remember, to make decisions. But what am I supposed to think about? The way I see you right now: standing at your pulpit in Paris, in the finest tradition of smirking Dutch writers allergic to their own culture, bellowing with a pained expression about everything you left behind. It's precisely the ones who leave who never seem able to shut up about what's happening back home. Pitiful, pathetic, tough titties! Now that I'm off and rolling, I may as well sideswipe you hard. There's one good thing about a united Europe: before long, all those peeved sourpusses will have to go all the way to Africa to establish their distance. That'll be a laugh, Grandpa. And I'd like to deepen the cut a bit: you, with all your pretensions, have responsibilities. You always tried to tell me that denying one's culture was a sign of indolence. But that's exactly what you're doing. You always tried to tell me – the ancient rite – that denying one's origins was a sign of cowardice. You dragged me by the hair through proud books. You tried to tell me that one should hate one's nest and love it: the only chance of development, of purification, of evolution. Yeah, sure, it looks fine on paper. Great. Just imagine. We were going to cultivate hope, we were going somewhere. To find redemption. Hoopla. Redemption, buddy, is getting up in the morning and taking a nice shit. Never thought you'd hear me say that, did you? For the umpteenth time: redemption, as described in your books, is a fairy tale. This life moves one step at a time. If you take my hand, I'll take yours (I know, it sounds like a song); if we don't do that, we just wobble a little more. No-one will lose any sleep over that, except for you and me. I know you lose sleep over it. I know that for sure. When I look at the doctor and his granny on the warpath, then I see how that wobbling goes, I mean, I can see where that wobbling takes you. People wobble in circles, until they get used to being alone. And where does that get you? Do you end up 'doing the things you always wanted to do'? Fat chance. People develop pride because they're not lonely. Aren't people lonely? Not as long as they don't want to be, that's the feat behind it. But loneliness is unimportant. Love is what's important. (It stopped being hip to sneer at that a long time ago, buddy!) Love, do you hear me? I'm tossing that word in your face, and at the same time I'm stating that I know you well enough to know you think you're capable of loving only once. (We're not talking about anyone else here, not now and not ever.) And who is it you've loved? It's already been me. So what are you going to do without me? Please reply.

And now, what am I going to do without you? I have my options (she said, examining her nails). You're aware of those options. One should suppose. But. I'm ambivalent. I want to have you. In songwriter's language: I want you near me when I call. I wonder whether anyone else in this century has ever actually been jealous of the Old Whazoo. But then, you're not really jealous. *Du bist verdattert.* And you'll be befuddled when they lay you in your grave. That's why I love you. And don't even think about imputing this to my fledglings-fallen-from-the-nest syndrome!

We, brother o' mine, have always used elaborate dialogue when talking about our love. That's conceivable, but unforgivable. Now all we have left is naked language. *Spielerei ist nicht verboten,* but may serve from now on only as ornamentation, not as peace offering. Here I'm presenting you with an accomplished fact.

Well, sir. This is all you've got. I'm writing this in my room. The windows are open. It's drizzling outside.

The garden doesn't smell like it used to. My old under-shirt is moth-eaten and my tits are starting to sag. That we all lived here together once is almost too much for me to believe. So you see: you're not the only desperate one.

Ugh! Blood brother,

Lisa

Oh, yeah: write to Mama. Do it!

Oh, yeah 2: write to Hille, he's in deep shit.

*

Paris, July 1990

Mother,

At thy bidding, and Lisa's insistence. You say you hate it when people put on airs. But who, goddammit all to hell, do you suppose I get these airs from? Precisely the fact that one sees someone else constantly beheading their own true nature makes one determined not to behave that way oneself. Do you understand what I'm saying? You say you're not afraid. It's essential – and I know this better than anyone – not to confuse running away with an act of courage. The fact that you don't want to stay with the old man is understandable, but don't expect a twenty-one-gun salute. Understand what I'm saying? If this was all a fairy tale, you would have seen through him and taken away his thirst. If it was all a fairy tale, you and I would be traditional, true-blue Groningers: sober and scornful, never even having heard of the phenomenon of 'posing', let alone chronically falling prey to it. Do you understand what I'm saying? When you say that all one can hope for is a 'place in life', you're probably quite right, but that's coming from a person who's getting on in years. I'll turn thirty this year, and who says I even know whether I want a place or not? I'm at the age to ponder the question endlessly (people in this century grow up later all the time), and a youngster has to do what he has to do. Don't even think of calling this an identity crisis. An identity crisis overcomes you at four or five, when you're sitting in the sandbox and wondering where this echo is coming from in your stomach, in the boundless hollow inside. In the sandbox. Understand what I'm saying? Well, all right, so I'm a poseur. I drink too much. And I can also state that, in accordance with the finest tradition of the coquette, I fuss over death. Why am I saying this? Because it makes finding a 'place in life' that much less important, and it ridicules the urgency of the search. A lifetime spent mucking about is no sorry achievement. Just look at your husband. He consumes tankfuls of high-test and gets one to the gallon while vegetating. You (and Lisa too) accuse me of fatalism. It's all just a bitter case of the giggles. And what's more: do you know what I've been doing since I transferred my abode to this town? Hold onto your hat. I've been missing the house I grew up in, my home, my native country, my family. This was all foretold me by the village bigwigs. One day everything will come thwacking down into place, and then you'll really get pissed off. Do you understand what I'm saying?

Love, your son

*

Paris, July 1990

Dear Beam MeBacksby,

Are you still in that pleasure garden? I never hear from you anymore. What's going on? And don't try to tell me I should be worried. *I hate to be the one who has to say I told you so.* If you don't respond quickly, I'll come and get you.

V

*

Paris, July 1990

'My sister, do you still recall
our only youth, we had a ball'

Sissi,

I bow my head. I'm sitting in my beloved Bois de Boulogne and don't know what to say. The tone you adopt makes me itch in places I can't get to. (And I've never been able to put my finger on this feeling!) Too bad about your undershirt, pity about the titties. So how's your ass? Ahem. The fact of the matter is that everything anyone could accuse me of I have long lumped together. And that lump is malignant. Bring on the metastases. Your question. I've been living without you for almost a year, and behold the healthy flush on my cheeks, see the spring in my step, listen to the smooth growl of my talent!

You raise questions, but provide no answers.

Why did you give up the house in Town? Why did you leave Town? Why did you let me go without kicking up a fuss? What are you trying to say in your songwriter's language? Do you have regrets? Did you seduce me? Do you regret the fact that you ever seduced me?

You toss the word 'love' in my face. Granted, that smarts. I'll try to adopt a tone that is foreign to me. I have to tell you a grisly secret. A major feeling of security has come my way; an ineradicable domesticity has grown within me. And this hearth of domesticity, which I hope to drag around behind me from now on, is need. Pure, pathetic need. There will never be a place on earth where I can't give in to, where I can't warm myself at, my need. Do you understand what I'm saying? You suffer from hope and confidence, you wander over fields of mud and through the dunes, and suddenly you miss me and home and back then. You want to warm yourself at me for a moment, because I'm the last little bit of back then, and I grow along with your life, so what's to stop you? Once you're warm, you can move on. I have nothing but my need. I see – it's a hackneyed form of suffering – nothing in this life. All right then: given, the drinking is a game of fear and courage. In a delirium you can see what dying is, or can be. And dying is a form of violence that combines joy and horror in the most hysterical form imaginable. I have no fear of death. I do entertain a bitter mistrust with regard to the hereafter! If beauty has to be wrested around the bend as well, I'll rise up from purgatory with my banner reading: Over My Dead Body! In my eyes, dearest, faith is fear. Dearest. Fear. And fear breeds intuition. We are not beasts (although life is beastly). We don't share in any progressive instinct, although you think differently: you've never, even though I am your blood and you are mine, been able to transfer to me even a grain of that instinct you call intuition. Only your existence makes me believe at times in a beauty that isn't slapped together. But supposing you're mistaken, that you're basing your life on a misunderstanding, a stray splash of light shot from its orbit and not intended for humans at all? Then we're pretty much 'up a creek'. Don't try to convince me of your brand of truth, then I'll never ask you that again.

I know what I have to do. I'll issue you with a full report. And I'd like to see you again too. But then I want to Go Away again. I'm going to fulfil my childhood dreams (or wade through my nightmares), my knapsack on my back, and in it my longing for you, and yours.

Ich liebe dich,
Ludwig

*

Gomorrah, July 1990

Fellah,

Just what I always wanted: to grant notoriety, by broadsheet and grapevine, to an imminent performance in Gomorrah by a band led by a former inhabitant of this dump. The name 'Veen' has been whispered. The girl in question reads or hears this. The big day arrives. Veen stands on stage, as Gonzo the lead-guitar player, and strikes the lyre till the stars fall from the sky. Everyone gets to make a wish, in other words. The rest is television.

Governing your own fate turns out to be quite a chore. The performance is scheduled for August and will take place in the open air, at the edge of my colonies, in the park where we, etc. I've become my own Carraway, though I did meet my old comrade and companion-at-arms Cobus in the tunnel café. He attempted, as of old, to shoo me away to more fertile ground; he refuses to intervene in the state of affairs.

If I look down from the stage and see she hasn't turned up, I'll toss my book into the crowd.

Pray for me.

Veen

*

Paris, July 1990
[Telegram]

Collapsby. No! I'm coming to get you.
V

*

Ameland, July 1990

'And who will render in our tongue
The tender things he loved and sung?'

My sweet,
    Come! Come a' kvetching! I'll go to pieces, but I won't sob. I swear I'll let you go. I left Town back then to leave it to you. It's your Town. Have you never realized that? I can't believe it. Yes, I seduced you, and I'll seduce you again. That, too, I promise. (I'm still on the pill. And you? Are you still clean? Will you have your blood tested? I remain a practical kind of girl.) God, what am I supposed to say? My ass is no slouch. Y'know. What am I supposed to say? If you think this is all there is – each of us with a life of our own – then all I can do is rest in it. Roil in it. Stomp in it. (Even though you, of course, are so horribly right.) But you said it. For the first time in that life of yours, you said you love me and I've got it in black and white! And I'll promise you something else. I'll always be here.
    When your ship touches shore in our country, I'll

be there. (Songs!) The old witch of Ameland, in her cottage on the heath. And don't even try to say I'm too young to decide that! Papa has agreed to give us the rest of our grandparents' capital. Something about taxes. We get it in cash and can't put it in the bank, I think, and before long The Boss won't be here to help us either. Before long, our only grandfather will be dead. I'm getting weepy, but you can't see me anyway. Promise me you'll come! In two weeks I'm going to Hille, he's giving a concert in his lost paradise. I beg you. Come afterwards to my island.

Elisabeth of Ameland

*

Gomorrah, July 1990

Old Fart,

Stay away, fat motherfucker!

Don't even think about rooting in my demise! See to your own extended emptiness. 'When the going gets tough, the tough get going.' Instead of coming to my aid, you act like you know better. What do you know about Going Back? What do you know about Finishing Things? In your pitiful little career you've written half a book about an old beatnik. What's that amount to? Life is either a piece of art or a piece of junk. Mine will be a drama with a curtain line. I take pride in that. And that's the whole trick, foul *Versager*: having something to be proud of! Dreaming is suspect, if I've read the addenda correctly; nightmaring isn't. And dreams (nightmares), old boy, *are affected by the experiences and impressions of the present as well as by memories of childhood,* and besides, *the most typical trait of practically all dreams … should be understood as a dismal weakening of the intellectual faculties of the dreamer, who is not really shocked to run into a long-dead* Love Affair. *At his best the dreamer wears semi-opaque blinkers; at his worst he's an imbecile.* An East Groningen dreamer-in-the-rough is as thick as a rotten plank, and written on it in flaky letters we read: 'Private: Keep Out (Art. 1, Veen's Code)', and: 'If you're reading this, you're retarded'. If I ever do awaken, it will be dead, floating in a pond with a bullet in my noggin. Admit it, you're jealous! If my life was entered in The Big Book right now, there would be a lot more story to it than yours. In your eye, buddy-guy.

I have, by the way, arranged the matter in Town for you. Contract enclosed.

I'm hiding out in my hotel room until the day of judgement. Every once in a while, Cobus comes by to work me over. You have the kind of tough-ass who, despite all faded glory, feels no homesickness for the playgrounds of our murdered school. Not that it impresses me, not that; it makes me sad. You have no eye for the romantics of schoolyards (however disgusting the school to which those yards belong), and that's why, for that reason alone, you don't understand a thing. So fuck you! Try talking about how things are between you and your sweetheart. I hardly hear from her anymore. That's how it's always been:

she's only had time for me when she didn't want to have time for you. I know something's going on. That's fine. Soon, old boy, you'll have to take over from me around here. Whether you like it or not. Nobility obligates.

See you in hell,
Veen

*

Paris, August 1990

Sis,

I'm leaving this burg. Cowboy Veen has rented me a house beside the tracks.

Yes, I'm still clean. I am not only chaste, but since I left I've also been celibate. Even the plague compels us to true love.

You won't go to pieces at all. You're unsinkable, that's the annoying thing, at times. And don't mourn The Boss. The man is ripe for death. Veen drove me to Oude Huizen that time. He went over to Stik's, and I went into the Bank. That harpy of a housekeeper asked who I was. I'm his heir apparent, I said, his brainchild. The old bitch was ready to call the police. Like in a bad movie, I walked right past her, down the hall, into the room and locked the door behind me. Death belittles: everything enormous about the man had disappeared, he was small and brittle, and that, little witch, is what I consider a mockery. Big men should grow on their deathbeds. Fairy tales. I sat on his bed and held his hand. The man wept. Was it from sorrow, rage, or exhaustion? He wasn't in pain, there was no-one he was leaving behind. Was he weeping with joy? I didn't dare to ask him. We let half an hour go by in silence. When I stood up, I didn't dare to ask him if there was anything I could do, should do. The distance between an old man and a little boy, when they're pissing on the potatoes together, is too small for words. The distance between an old man and a young man, in a room where death is being waited for, is too great for words. I hate life. He loved it. I would have liked to ask him why, but I already knew and I always have known. He cherished it and scoffed at it, the same way he scoffingly cherished his wife's quirks. Grim cherishing, tender scoffing. That is, if you'll excuse my saying so, a manly attitude. The manly attitude. The look he gave me when I went away was, how can I say this, pressing. Not clamoring, not oppressive, not pleading, especially not pleading. Pressing. I thought I read in it (but where can I look this up?): care for them, or care for *it*. It. Care for. I don't know. Care. In my eternal matinée, he was the Godfather, I the lost son. And I promised him in soundless words that I would Care. Everyone needs a reason, or a little shove. There's only one person I've always loved in all simplicity, and that's him. I could say it was because he took me seriously and more of that nonsense, but that wasn't it. The man took 'it' seriously with me around, even when I was just a little sprout crawling around the Bank. He sighed deeply when I was around and wasn't bothered by knowing that I could read those sighs. He knew his sighs were as easy for me to read as his words, maybe more so. Do you understand what I'm saying? He showed me the life of a man on earth. Naked, without costumes, without casting, without seeing me as an audience. There's an unspeakable simplicity in that. You can't have that within a family. We didn't have a bond. We had a pact. We're men. And that kind of thing doesn't create a bond, but an obligation; I can't put it any better than that. Around him, I've always been a man. Do you know what I'm saying? He didn't ask me to stand on my feet. I stood, and he nodded: ah, right, that's how it goes. I can't explain it. I won't miss him. I'll remember him in my steps. Everyone looks for a teacher. Mine always lived next door. I didn't go looking for him, and he didn't choose me. We shared the shadow of the same row of chestnuts. Me in the afternoon, he in the evening. And around six that shadow fell behind us, and we peed on the potato patch. There's nothing more I can say about it. Only coincidence brings us riches. And coincidence is a form of fate. You can curse fate. You only have to thank fate once in order to go on. A little shove and then on with fashioning life. I got my shove at his deathbed. I'm going to fashion my life, even though I hate it and view what I'll create only with fear. The only real form of protest, of blasphemy, as I see it now, is simply to be a man. Being a man is an art. Only talent brings responsibilities; that's a certainty. And certainties shouldn't be glossed over, because that amounts to calling off the hunt. And the hunt must go on. Hunting is the revenge, or the goal, of the hopeless: it binds them to the earth. Never again will I offer apologies for my pathos. My spirit I cover in war-paint.

You're my only love, and I'll see you again. Some day, somewhere, in some song or other.

Ludwig of Groningen

PART FOUR

Stürmisch bewegt

. . . An' there, where I was, it's summertime an' the sun's shining, but I'm not feelin' the heat, an' the land is there ahind the houses, from here you can see the marsh 'n' the mud, an' the gulls screechin' from the steeple. Gulls can't stay still, but today . . . it was a long trail've folk, I 'member now, an' the church bells ringin' hard enough to shudder all the walls of Oude Huizen. Real pretty, that long trail steppin' through the village, an' when they crossed the Hoofdweg old Bu joined 'em, with people mumblin' it was a scandal, the old Nazi – it was wartime when I said to him: 'None of my concern, Bu, but don't you reckon you got it all wrong, with them Germans? I mean, can't you see, no matter how long it takes, folks like that'll take a dive, any fool can see that,' but he was a policeman by then an' that was after his fashion, an' he turned a blind eye by occasion, but discussin' matters wasn't his way, still he never left, an' now he was bringin' up the rear, that's beautiful, but kind've sad too. I've never been inside a church, but that pealin' o' the bells I think's real pretty. That's for me. An' standin' round my grave are the sisters Prins, bawlin' to beat the band, aren't they pretty gals, just like their ma, dang, what a pretty thing she was, an' as I recall it: there weren't any children, no children at all, an' if Prins had up 'n' left we'd've never had any children in Oude Huizen, but he came back an' bought that place on the corner an' I was pleased, 'cause he was a real fine fellah, didn't know a hoe from a hatchet though, so I gave him some taters an' things, an' that gal, his wife, daughter've old Zonnebloem, 'n' farmer I had to call 'sir' at first, 'cause he was a man o' mark, that gal came back here from Amsterdam in the family way, an' all the rest had up an' left, but not him, an' that's how children come to Oude Huizen, an' there was no schoolhouse here since sixty, so it was like the whole village was havin' a baby. Victor had twenty grandpas 'n' grandmas after that week – Prins went somber on us right away, right after Victor came. Victor was made in the turlet've the train. Where *is* Victor? We had us a party, an' Prins was sittin' at Stik's knockin' 'em back, an' I says to him: 'What's eatin' ya, fella, that little one's yours, in't he?' An' he nodded, yeah, yeah. So I went: 'Well then! The days of putterin' around with that motoscooter o' yourn is ahind ya, fella, time to put your shoulder to the wheel!' But he was a medical man, an' his pa died, his ma did too, he got all that money an' I said: 'Or weren't ya plannin' to get hitched?' An' he went: 'I were.' So I said: 'Well then!' An' he – he's tied one on again. Drunk as us'al. Damn, it's like I'm hangin' in the tree. They're playin' music now. Yeah, that's how they do things. When Anthia died, Victor picked out some music too, real sad 'n slow. An' I figured to myself, bye now, 'cause she was doin' real poorly, an' when the life's finished then it's finished, that's the best 'n' worst on't. No more'n that. An' Victor, he said: 'Now she's gone home.' An' I said: 'Wha'?!' 'Now she's gone home,' he says. I went: 'What're you jawin' about?' I said: 'She's dead, boy,' an' he went all red an' says: 'Oh yeah, right.' Ah! They're throwin' sand on the box now an' I don't feel a thing. Prins 'n' his little sunflower's up in front, 'cause they became our children, really, Zonnebloem an' his missus died early too. She was all broken up, that pretty, pretty gal was all broken up back then, 'n' good time after the war, Prins an' his little sunflower they were maybe fifteen, sixteen, doin' the do out in that field an' we went: 'Those two're gettin' hitched.' Plain's the nose on your face, with some folks you can see it. So pretty, that, so pretty. There were lots more children back then. An' durin' the village fair, all pennants 'n' flags, an' she was the princess on the prettiest float, all cover'd in flowers, him walkin' along ahind her, an' each year the pennants looked less like pennants an' more like little scraps've paper, an', oh, the land . . .

. . . ho, wait a minute. They're goin' away, but what about me, where'm I goin'? I don't wanta go, I don't wanta go, I don't wanta go. Land. The churchyard's abuttin' on the marsh an' it's all black there, an' comes time it'll all be black 'n' mud, but now there's still land 'n' green 'n' the ditches 'n' the – there was al'ays that land far's you could see, when the boys were makin' hay. I wasn't any farmer, when Pa died I stayed alone with Ma, I had to tend the hogs 'n' the kitchen patch, an' I went to work at the office, up to Woudbloem, but summertime always choked me up. God, fellah, I'm hangin' in a tree!

. . . on my lonesome now, an' the churchyard's restful an' this here's my land, an' I got myself a village too, my own village, Oude Huizen; they never built up around it like everwhere else, where everthing's ruined in villages where I'd go, 'cause I went out to 'em, to 'praise a cow for collateral 'n' so, an' I always called 'em 'sir'. But when things changed 'n' all the farmers went poor, they came to me with hat in hand an' I never, no never, smirked at 'em, 'cause Anthia said: 'That's no way to do. That's jest no way to do.' Everthing 'round these parts is goin' to the dogs. Well, anyhow, everthin's goin' worse. An' I don't wanta leave. God, fellah, I'm like a whipped pup. Hangin' in a tree . . . an' the gravediggers standin' there lookin' at my box 'n' smokin', an' there, look there, here he comes, pokin' along, Victor boy, I was startin' to wonder, an' he looks up at the gulls on the steeple, yeah fella, they're sittin' still, an' he looks at my grave 'n' makes this gesture, like this, cockin' a finger from the hip: be seein' ya. I thought as much. I told ya – Didn't I tell ya? – I told ya: 'Take over quick, your pa's ailin', he doesn't have long to live.' An' God, boy, what's that in your head? He's all restless, he didn't want to stand there with his sisters, with all that bawlin', an' he turns around 'n' strolls off, an' inside that head've his is all this commotion, it's quiet an' empty on the Hoofdweg an' inside his head it sounds like: and I wondered how the same moon outside, over this Chinatown fair, could look down on Illinois, and find you there . . . what you goin' on about, fellah, China?

. . . they're sittin' at the kitchen table an' I'm stuck to the ceilin'. An' Liesje, what a pretty gal . . . so pretty, like a child come walkin' in from a world that isn't discovered yet, like the first in a whole slew that'd be comin' along . . . you expect 'em any minute now, an' I was out with the boys on the land an' there she came, old shirt, worn-out knees, not brown but white, 'n' still black on the shoulders, 'n' a shiner, an' I said: 'Been in a tussle?' She goes: 'Nope.' An' she looks me right in the eye, an' I hand out smokes 'n' say, jest for fun: 'Want one?' An' she nods. Big fat cigarette in her mouth, sure as sin, six years old an' just watchin' the boys. For hours. I say: 'Nice here, ain't it?' Don't know why I did. An' she goes: 'Yeaah.' I say: 'What's so nice about it then?' An' her, six years old, she says: 'It ain't for livin' on, it's for walkin' on.' Six years old! I said: 'Figger you're right 'bout that.' An' she climbs up on the combine an' looks at the boys, with that cigarette in her mouth, like an old coot, with her elbows on her knees. An' now she's sittin' at the kitchcn table an' the dog barks 'n' jumps an' she sees Victor standin' at the door, she's fixin' to get up but stays put, an' the whole family's lookin' at him so's he doesn't dare to come inside, an' then Prins says: 'Well, well.' An' Liesje wants to get up but can't. They al'ays were funny children. So alone. If you can see that, like a color, that lonesomeness, then it gets you. It used to get me when they were over at my place. Little Fikkie, kneelin' on the floor've the office, hours at a time, never sayin' a word. Eyes in his head like saucers. I'd say: 'Tell me what ya see, little fellah.' He said: ''Tamps.' I says: ''Tamps?' Him noddin'. I empty out an old postal service bag on the floor, an' the little gal's laughin', but that fellah was busy for hours with all those stamps on all those old letters. I said: 'Whatcha seein' now, little fellah?' He climbs up on the window an' points outside an' says: 'What's that out there?' I say: 'Summer.' He nods, just like 'n old coot too. He says: 'An' what's back behind there?' I say: 'Fall, but he's got a ways to go yet.' An' he says: 'When's he comin' then?' I tell him: 'Ten weeks' time.' An' he goes: 'That's dumb!' I say: 'Oughtn't he to come then?' He shakes his head no, not never. An' lookin' cross, just like his daddy, give 'em 'n gun an' you won't even know what happened. An' there's strange words soundin' in Victor's head, still about China. An' Lisa runs off upstairs, with him right ahind, an' Anna starts in cryin' again, an' I lie on the floor in Liesje's room when she hits him upside o' the head. What's this? That color lonesomeness makes the room all misty. I have to gulp. 'What took you so long?' Liesje says, 'where've you been, dirty rotten bastard?!' An' he says, no thinks: right close by. An' says: 'One more time,' an' she hits him ag'in, oh oh, she can cry somethin' fierce. Somethin' fierce. She's like her mother: al'ays real far away. The little sun-flower used to be real far away, in thought then. I'd come to her daddy's an' there that sixteen-year-old thing'd be with her head way up in the clouds. It gave you the chills. Liesje don't give you the chills, but she makes you sad. An' now she's howlin' 'n' yelpin' an' Victor's standin' there all white as a ghost, noise in his head, then he hugs her, an' she him, an' they kiss. An' then they let loose an' he's runnin' his fingers through his hair an' she looks at him like she's goin' to hit him ag'in, till she laughs real sad through the tears an' I think: that's pretty to see. That's how she is. An' then she hisses at him: 'Coward!' He nods his head, an' downstairs at the kitchen table Prins 'n' his little sunflower 'n' Anna are cranin' their necks, listenin' to what's goin' on up there. Then Victor takes Lisa's hand 'n' says: 'Come on.' They head back down, an' I flop through the ceiling. I don't wanta go. I'm stayin' here. There's plenty of room in this house. Prins, who crashes down into himself soon's he sees Liesje, says: 'Liesje, honey, do the honors, would ya'?' An' his little sunflower holds his hand tight an' that was a long time ago, 'cause it makes him bashful, he's almost dead already, that Prins fella, buddy, what're you doin' to yourself? I know. If that's how you're put together, like: this isn't what I want. Don't want what? I don't want a child. I know. I didn't want it either. A long time after the war we thought another war was comin'. Not from the krauts, but the Reds, those crazy Reds, not a war right here but one everbody could see, with flyin' bombs, like Hitler's Vs, I said to Anthia durin' the war: 'We'll jest wait,' an' after the war I said it again: 'We'll wait.' I was al'ays doin' that. Waitin'. It brought her a lot of pain. Until Fikkie came along. Then it was over, but by then it was goin' on '61 . . .

. . . 'He's back living in Town,' Liesje says to her folks, 'and you two knew it all along, didn't you?' But they didn't. An' they look at their son . . . he's a good boy, but things aren't right in his head, never were. It's enough to give you the chills. It's like it's fixin' to explode. In his head: like the tub's runnin' over an' the water's drippin' down the walls. It gushes 'n' gushes. Prins says: 'Well, cap'n, what's the word?' Victor says: 'Now, uh, I'm planning a trip, I'm going to, uh, to the Front.' They look at him, an' Liesje 'n' Anna are cryin' again, an' Victor smiles, thinks: war, war, war. But I see he's thinkin' that if he ever did find the front lines – is there a war on? – he'd shoot himself through the head. From courage. Now I feel like shakin' my head. 'Just shittin',' Victor says. 'How'd things go with Veen?' Nobody says a word. They drink, an' the little sunflower holds onto Prins's hand. I'm not lettin' my land go. No, he wouldn't, not shoot himself through the head. Why would he do that? He thinks: sweetest, my sweetest, an' he gets warm, strokes Liesje's hair, an' nobody says a thing. What's this? A color from

him 'n' Liesje. Like mornin' mist on the land, after a cold
night in a hot summer . . .

. . . 'You think he's gone to heaven?' Anna asks Liesje,
an' she says, real calm all of a sudden: 'Sure, what do you
expect, dumbo?' Heaven? I been tryin' to die for days now,
but it won't take. They drink. They're sad about me. They're
real fine children, all five of 'em. Al'ays were. And so pretty,
ya got pretty 'n' pretty. Liesje's way off, she's comin' from
somewhere. Like she was strollin' in after wanderin' 'round
for years, in that old undershirt o' hers, and with a shiner.
Victor runs his hand over his hair. Gets a smack from Liesje.
They smile and turn warm, and real happy. Their color's
fadin'. They drink. Liesje says, after one last sob: 'So,
Granny, how're you getting your kicks these days?' The
little sunflower blushes. 'Hey,' Prins says, all shy-like, 'try
'n' behave, would ya?' If Prins'd been my son, what could
I've done? I hear the mire in his head. I hear it like a boot
in wet mud. It's pure 'n' simple: there's those that wanta
live, they get gobbled up by the future, and there's those
that try to get out've the thing's maw. That feel it chompin'.
This is real serious. Victor feels it chompin', doesn't wanta
escape, doesn't wanta get gobbled up either, just wants to
keep feelin' that chompin', pissin' his britches to be gettin'
swallered, pissin' his britches to be gettin' spat out. What
now, boy? Prins's *been* spat out.

. . . Prins and his little sunflower go sit in the yard. Liesje's
on the phone. Anna and Victor head upstairs. I let go've the
ceilin' an' trickle up the stairs ahind 'em, up in the attic
all've a sudden, jest hangin' there in mid-air. They're sittin'
at a bar. 'So how are you holding up?' Victor asks. 'Man,
don't fuck around,' Anna says. Hard kid to figger. Al'ays

was. Victor's got himself a bottle. He drinks like his daddy, but in his head it's diff'rent; he's laughin' now inside his head. Anna's cryin' ag'in, real quiet. 'Can I come and stay with you?' she asks. Victor gets up, picks her up off'n the stool, she puts her legs 'round his waist, head on his sho'lder, an' lets him rock her. She was never like that before. So little. 'Sweetheart, don't feel bad about The Boss.' 'I don't,' Anna says, 'it's not just that. You're all here, and if I don't watch out you'll be gone again, like that, and I always thought I didn't give a shit, and now here we go again.' Victor puts her back on the stool, tosses that drink down his craw – I could stand a brace myself; that gin burnin' in your gullet – and says: 'We grow old and sentimental, but never mind, tomorrow you'll be fed up with it again.' 'You think so?' Anna says with a sob that sounds like it's comin' from her gut. 'I hope so, for your sake,' Victor says, and shrugs his sho'lders, and it's not his own voice that's shoutin' in his head: shore leave, shooore leave! And that's what's in his head: noise you can't figger out, with words poppin' up you can't figger out either. 'Are you really going away again?' Anna asks. Victor nods, runs his hand over his hair 'n' lights a cigarette; I try to snuff up the smoke, but I can't. 'Where to?' 'The Weimar.' 'Wha'?' 'Berlin.' 'Oh.' The commotion in Victor's head starts buildin' up again. It's runnin' over and drippin' down the walls. The Weimar? Lisa sticks her head up through the floor, I curl 'round a beam. What a rumpus! I think I'll be stayin' here. I don't dare go into the house. What's goin' on in *my* house? 'I guess I'll just get lost, huh?' Anna says with a sob comin' up from her gut. 'Yeah, do that,' Lisa says. That's Liesje for you: like a knife through a hog's bleeder. We smuggled the pig from up to Slochteren down to Oude Huizen, at dusk, on the back of the bike, Old Zonnebloem was laughin' so hard he fell in the ditch, swine 'n all; we slaughtered it in the bill'ards room, on old newspapers; everybody got some, nobody ever went without in Oude Huizen, we used to make fake coupons in the office. No nerves, just blocks've ice for a head. Krauts were the stupidest people we ever saw, dirty, mean, smelly and dumb. That Hitler, that's what we thought, must be a right pecul'ar fellah. The little Jewish gal went away after the war. Anthia cried for a whole year. I said: 'We'll jest wait, we'll wait a tad.' 'So, mister,' Liesje says, warm, real warm, 'and now out with it.' Anna's gone. 'Childhood dreams,' Liesje says. 'Yeaah . . .' Victor says. They're real shy. What's goin' on? They're sittin' at that little bar and lookin' at each other like, like . . . like they just came out of the field where they were doin' the do! I see it on their faces; they're in love! God, fellah, I see it on the color that's changin'. That lonesomeness is jest blowin' away. They're smilin'. Hold me tight, that's what I read in those heads've theirs. But they're stayin' put, and I lay me down on the floor in a corner. I always thought love was a likely thing to look at. It's so . . . uh, so like . . . the world's packed with it, 'specially on television. It'd been a warm wind blowin' everywhere, and no barkin'll keep it from the door. Where I am now is warm and blustery, but I'm still alone. It's real cozy here, that passin' away isn't all bad. Just takes so long. Dyin's somethin' else again: that's like . . . well, it's like gettin' sucked down into warm mud. But then, real strange, you hear this suckin' sound and you plop up out've the mud, and that's even stranger, your life's lyin' atop your life and you see all kinds of things stickin' out, sort of like, uh . . .

this 'n' that could've been otherwise. What I saw was that we could've, or should've, had children, I don't know, and that those children, two I think, that there'd be a son livin' at the bank and another one who'd be . . . I can't recall. An' I, no, we could've gone away, to some other village where they were buildin', but I saw that straight away, that wouldn'a been right, this is my village, my village an' my land, and I don't wanta go, summer's still on, and hayin' – and Liesje says: 'So?' And Victor empties his glass 'n' says: 'I live in a house by the side of the tracks.' 'Sure, asshole,' Liesje says, 'chicken-shit, and what are you gonna do about it, huh?' Victor shrugs and runs his hand over his hair. 'Knock that off,' Liesje says, but quiet, and the tears are flowin' from her eyes and she's not even cryin'. 'Don't,' Victor says. It makes me gulp. Just like on television. 'So say something,' Liesje says. 'How are your tits?' Victor asks. Land's sake. They laugh an' hug an' kiss, and it's pecul'ar, but awful pretty. 'Now stop that blubbering,' Victor says, and lays his hands on Liesje's sho'lders and pushes her down onto the stool. Liesje doesn't say a thing, just lets the tears go, and the noise in Victor's head is differ'nt, quieter, and all've a sudden I know: it's music. Champion of the noise-box. It's music that keeps tryin' to get out've that head. Liesje's drinkin' now too. Out've his glass. 'How did things go with Veen?' Victor asks. Lisa lifts her chin, real pretty, tosses her hairs and lights a cigarette. I don't smell nothin'. 'She showed up,' Liesje says, 'I saw her, she's twenty-five, pregnant, and looks like she's sixteen, absolutely unfair, Hille played well, but at 'Cortez the Killer' it all went wrong, voice gone, you know how it goes: there's this line in that one, I don't know, and man, I turned around and ran out of that park and caught the first bus that came along, I mean I can put up with a lot, but this was too sick for words, that poor guy, it was hor-ri-ble!' Victor nods. 'I tried calling the hotel, must of been a hundred times after that.' Liesje shrugs her sho'lders 'n' shakes her head. 'Should we go looking for him?' Victor asks. Lisa nods. 'Shall I call his parents?' Lisa nods again. 'So out with it,' she says then. Victor thinks: well, here we go. 'I'm going to Berlin.' 'When?' 'In a week or two.' 'Alone?' Victor nods. 'Can't I go with you?' Victor says nothin'. Liesje sighs, looks at him 'n' says: 'But what are you going to do there?' 'Find inspiration,' Victor says. 'What?' 'I'm going for the nightlife,' Victor says, 'there's cabaret there, real cabaret, all the musicians are going there.' Liesje lets the tears go. Lots've tears in this house, awful lot've tears. Before Prins bought it, no one lived here for a long time. 'Cause it's such a dark place, I figgered. And wetly. Before that, 'nother doctor lived here. Doctor Oudenaarde. Died back in '54. They're holdin' each other's hands now. Shy, no, restless. In his head: And I know she's living there and loves me till this day. He asks: 'When are you leaving?' 'Tomorrow,' Liesje says, 'I want to stay with Papa and Mama until tomorrow.' 'Ah,' Victor says, 'and, uh . . . what's the situation now?' 'What do you mean?' She sounds angry now. Her mouth's a long, thick line. Victor says nothin'. 'So ask!' Liesje says. Victor says nothin'. 'Ask if I'd like you to come and visit me!' Liesje says. 'Would you like me to come?' 'Sure I would, you lame wimp!' 'Excuse me?' 'Blowhard, fruitcake, retarded swine!' Land's sake. She's laughin' ag'in. He is too. 'Why didn't you come by, after that letter?' 'Things to arrange.' 'Sure, Grandpa, and now you're going to tell me God's dead, you know I looked for you in Town? Like that mad cowboy of ours, peering around on the market square and stuff?' 'Hmm.' 'Hmm, he says!' Victor gets up, walks through my danglin' jambs, puts on some music an' takes Liesje's hand. They dance. They laugh. They're gettin' hitched, that much's sure . . .

. . . an' I dribble out the skylight and hang over the yard and dandle in a birch and I can't feel the sun. There's an echo in my innards. The first nasty feelin'. Am I dyin'? I'm not lettin' go. Never not. My guts are cryin', no, they're yelpin' like a dog off yonder. I know that sound, but I can't recollect . . . Prins and his little sunflower 'n' Anna 'n' their mutt are down below me. The quiet here's good 'n' fitly, and the little sunflower is sittin' calm too, but in her head somethin's sayin', it's herself: I'm leaving, leaving, leaving. I have to leave. It's what she says. But why's she wanta leave? I lie down under a tree, and 'tween it all I hear the commotion in Victor's head, like it was pourin' through the house. I see him in the front room, right out the walls, he's put on that funeral music and he's pickin' up the phone. I look straight through the house and see Café Stik a' lurin' at me. 'Hello, this is Victor, is Hille there?' Voice in his head: 'Pardon me? Hille? No. He's not here. He's in Town, I guess.' 'Do you know where, exactly? I mean, where he's staying in Town?' 'Well, at the house on Ooststraat, in the Indische Buurt, he's been living there for years.' 'But didn't he do a concert, with his band, in the park?' 'Sure, but that was a couple of weeks ago. We haven't seen him since then.' 'So you don't have any idea where he is?' 'Well, no, but if I happen to see him, do you want me to give him a message?' 'Would you ask him to get in contact with me, with Ameland?' 'Ameland?' 'Um-hum.' 'Well, okay, Victor, wasn't that the name?' 'That's right.' Victor sits down in the front room an' I hear the music crashin' against the commotion in his head, like ice breakin' up down at the waterworks. The racket makes his pa get up an' go look where it's comin' from. Prins sticks his head 'round the corner of his own room. 'Everything okay, fella?' 'Fine.' Prins sits down too. An' in the yard Anna's sayin' to her ma: 'You going to stick around for a while?' An' the little sunflower sighs. An' Prins sighs. An' Victor sighs. 'Isn't it about time to crack the beer?' Victor asks. Prins nods. Victor fetches a brace o' tall boys from the kitchen. They drink. The music's crashin'. And Liesje's gone to lie on her bed, an' she's clenched her fists an' she's comin' real close. Like she's movin' up to me, peerin' 'round an' lookin' for me. 'So what was it like, there in Paris?' 'Great, uh, you could say: enlightening.' Prins nods. Victor sighs 'n' says: 'How did that go, that business with the house in Town?' 'Well, your sister came here and said: sell the bastard, and I says to her: why would ya' do that?' She says: 'Victor wants it that way, and so do I.' 'Aha.' 'So that wan't the case?' Victor shrugs his sho'lders. 'So tell me,' Prins says. 'Why don't you tell *me* something,' Victor says, 'I mean: what do you think of all this?' Victor's made've ice. His head's about ready to bust again. What is this? It looks like shame, but it's not. There's light spatterin' out've his head, an' Liesje's lurkin' 'round, no, she comes glidin' in. Prins says: 'To be perfectly frank, cap'n, it seems to me that it doesn't make a bit o' difference anymore who does what with whom, technically speakin' there's a kind of doom hangin' over any kind o' love, and then what the hell dif-fer'nce does it make what someone does with his immediate family?' 'Goodness, aren't we in touch with the times.' They

smile. 'Nature's degeneratin',' Prins says. 'Tell me about it.'
''Parently that improves the race, with time.' 'Is that so?'
'By rootin' 'round, maybe people build up resistance.' 'Meta-
phorically speaking?' They smile. 'I want,' Prins says, 'for
all of you not to be unhappy, and that's a heavy wish to
tote around.' *Ich weiß.* 'When you went away, I was –' 'I
know, don't tell me.' 'Figger we could use a shot along with
this?' 'Absolutely.' The bottle's on the table. 'So now what?'
Prins asks. 'I was hoping you could bankroll me.' 'Oh yeah?'
'I need about six grand.' 'Well well.' I see Liesje slidin' down
from the peak've the roof, her body's spinnin' an' she smiles
'n' she's six again, like an old coot. What's she up to, ferchris-
sake? I look in her body, but it's still lyin' on the bed. What
is this? Liesje sees me, I think. Her hand's tryin' to touch
me, but she's still aways away. Girlie, girlie now. I go 'n'
hang in the tree and touch her hand with my fingertips.
Hey, sweetheart, calm now. But she *is* calm, calmer'n I am.
That touch calms *me*! The yelpin' in my innards stops. She
tumbles away again. 'I need to buy something.' 'A car? But
what happened to that heap o' yours?' 'Sold it, needed the
money in Paris.' 'But I sent you money.' 'Do you really
want to know?' 'No, I spose not.' 'I took a crash course while
I was there.' 'In what?' Victor says nothin'. 'But what do
you need to buy?' Victor waves him off. I see Liesje come
glidin' into the house an' I follow her 'n' sit on her bed an'
put my hand on her forehead while she's slippin' into her
body. An' she opens her eyes with a smile 'n' looks at me.
Girlie, girlie now. But no, she doesn't see me. She hears
somethin' comin' from the front room, jumps up 'n' runs
down the stairs. Plops straight down in Prins's lap. All the
color goes out've his face. 'You talk to Hille?' 'His parents,

they don't have the slightest.' 'What's that?' Prins asks. 'A friend of ours, he's disappeared in his paradise lost and regained.' 'Aha. Well, doesn't get much better'n that, does it?' 'That's what we're wondering,' Liesje says.

I mosey through the house, leave it, go outside, look at my place, feel the calm in my guts, feel somethin' callin' me, hear someone tuggin' at me, but I look out across the fields an' the sun's shinin' an' I wish summer'd begun or that I could see the hayin' an' the boys out on the land. Used to be, back when the land was still good 'n the farmers were rich, it stretched out all the way to Town, to the Win- schoter Canal, out to Germany, an' Oude Huizen lay at the foot of all that land like it grew out've our yards: Schaaphok up north, waterways down below, and out east, all Europe, ahind us, in front of us. Front of us, Victor thinks. 'Hind us, I think. Victor's goin' away, goin' there, there where the krauts came from. The Weimar? Anna says: 'Mama, what are you gonna do now?' 'Honey, I'm leaving as soon as I can.' 'Why?' 'I can't stay here anymore.' 'But why not? Is it Papa?' 'No, that's not it, not anymore I guess, I don't know, sweetheart, I, uh, it's just so, uh, so dead here, you know what I mean?' Anna nods. 'And you? How's school?' 'Oh, okay, I don't understand what Victor has against Amsterdam, it's pretty fun, I have to admit.' 'Victor has a way of putting on airs.' 'I don't think that's it, Mama.' 'You don't? Well then don't ask me, you know, he wrote me a letter that made me really sad.' I can read bits've letter in the little sunflower's head. 'Why was that?' 'I think he's really angry with me.' 'He was born angry.' 'He puts on airs.' 'You can't dismiss whatever you don't understand as "airs".' 'Don't try to be smart all the time, okay? He blames me for all sorts of things.' 'Like what?' I read bits've letter in her head. 'Oh, that I, oh, I don't know exactly.' 'Stop talking shit, would you?' 'Well, that I went away, or no, that it didn't help anything.' 'Oh, and I suppose you thought otherwise?' Anna laughs, not angry, not sad. Strange child. 'I don't want to talk about it.' 'Oh, that's great. Very grown-up of you, an "A" for inappropriate response.' 'I mean, I have my own life now . . .' 'Sure, why not, to each his own.' 'Anna, don't act so callous.' I read bits've letter in little sunflower's head, but don't see a thing that looks bad. She's not so quick on the uptake anymore, she used to be, but after her first baby she pulled her head down out've the clouds and stopped thinkin'. She was tired. She is tired. 'If you ask me,' Anna says, 'you're one of those people who expects a standing ovation. The question is, from whom?' 'Anna.' 'Is it because you don't have any outraged old folks behind you, cheering because you finally left that lush in the lurch, is that why you keep bitching about doing the right thing? Is that it?' 'Anna, Christ, don't act so high and mighty.' 'And hoopla, as Sis would say, we're back to that again.' 'Try to keep a civil tongue, would you?' 'Blow it out your ear, Mommy dear, civility would clash with the curtains around this house.' They look at each other. Anna with her little dolly-face, the sunflower with her old lines. But in the little sunflower's head there are proud thoughts ringin', only she barely hears 'em herself. She says: 'You know what I find disgusting?' 'Do me a favor and introduce it to the group.' 'Blecch, I mean, you know what I really find disgusting? Parents who ask their children if they've done something wrong, with one of those guilty crucify-me looks, that's just the worst, you know?' 'Sure, I guess I'd call the paramedics if you said you thought that was normal.' 'And you know why?' Anna gives her a welcomin' smile. Strange, hard child. 'Because –' 'Because,' Anna says, 'somewhere along the line we all do something wrong, sure, okay, I'm glad Victor can't hear this, because you've left something out here, if I may prattle on buddy and sissy's behalf, and that is that if you make children, you'd better do your best BECAUSE OTHERWISE!' 'Oh, right, and I suppose I haven't.' 'What are you blabbering about, where's your can of worms, you're goddamn fishing around!' 'Anna!' Little sunflower's shakin' her head. Says quiet-like: 'What are you trying to say?' 'You figure it out.' 'Wha'?' 'Why don't you stay here?' Anna says. 'I don't want to –' 'Don't talk shit, you want to, you're just afraid you'll never leave, what you really want is for all of us to say we'll go skipping off, bright-eyed and bushy-tailed, so you can slink off to Rotten-darn alone and get on with your moping.' 'I'm not –' 'Mop-ing! You're down there moping!' 'I'm not moping.' 'Listen up, Granny, all four of you are moping, all four of you, and if you ask me that's just a little bit ridiculous, spreading your wings, okay, you have to do that, you're supposed to do that, with all due thanks to *Ladies' Home Journal*, but then to hang around and mope, what's the point? God, I think I could use a drink myself.' 'Don't go doing that.' 'No, you're right, what I need is to bang like a shithouse door in the wind.' 'Anna!' 'What about you?' 'Wha'?' 'A drink, hey, take it easy.' 'Okay, a little one then.'

. . . 'How 'bout 'n' little walk?' Prins asks. And Liesje hops up off've his lap an' says: 'Just a minute.' And she comes out into the yard an' grabs hold've Anna by the back o' the neck, an' Anna says: 'Your little displays of affection,

if you'll excuse my saying so, old batsy, are pretty lame.'
'Is we tipsy?' Liesje says. 'Mama, Papa wants to take a little
walk, why don't you go with him, then Victor and I can
make dinner.' Anna busts out laughin': 'This is really pitiful,
am I the only one around here who reads books or what?'
'Don't listen to her, listen to me,' Liesje says, 'do the doctor
a favor, would you, let him out for a stroll.' Little sunflower
thinks: my vagabond jacket. Then she gets up. Anna's
creased up laughin'. Liesje gives her a soft smack up against
the head. Little sunflower's shy. Liesje shouts: 'Pappaaa!' So
loud everyone in the village hears. The dog sits up 'n' looks
at little sunflower, head to one side.

... they've forgot all about me. It's like I'm bein' called.
But the sun swings 'round and the shadow falls from the
chestnuts, and I don't wanta look at my yard. And Victor
comes walkin' out've the house 'n' thinks about me ag'in,
'n' walks along the hedge 'n' across the gravel to my place
'n' my yard, and I'm not lookin', but then I look anyway
'n' see him pissin' on my 'taters, even though it's too early,
an' I left him the house – he's rich now if he sells it, but I
know he never will, 'cause he's thinkin about houses all over
the world an' now he's got one that's his alone, big enough
for him 'n' a wife 'n' children, 'cause he's the one who has
to put down children in Oude Huizen 'n' keep the place
from dyin' out. And in his head I see children in my yard
an' in the 'tater patch, and I hear the tearin' inside him and
he says to the land: 'Not just to see if from the rotten seed
a healthy root can grow.' And he looks at the horizon with
my place, his place, ahind him, an' he cries without a sound
'n' no tears. Then he lights himself a cigarette 'n' says:
'Inbreeding for the advancement of the race, yet another

road closed to us.' And he's peerin' 'n' peerin' out across the land, like we al'ays did, and he says: 'Of course, adoption is an option, eh, what's black and hangs around the farm? A free-range Negro.' He giggles. And I shout: go out 'n' get hitched, but that can't be, I realize that now, 'cause she's his sister. His kin. And I look the other way.

His kin. Then. But from where I am it's diff'rent, and when I see them the way they were dancin', then it's diff'rent too, then it's not his sister but his – like Prins and his little sunflower, so you think: they're gettin' hitched, and that's lovely. An' his life lyin' atop his life I see that everthing stickin' out leads back to her, all dead ends; turn back's what he's gotta do, time after time. Jest look, boy. But when I was alive I didn't see it either. That's the cruelty of it. That blindness. I want to shout to him, but I don't know what to say. And Victor looks at his hands spread out, wiggles his fingers and hums. And what's comin' up in his head is runnin' out over my field.

. . . I think I need to get away from here. I feel homesick, but I don't know what for. Wish I could talk to Anthia. I go rollin' through the air and don't know where I have to go. In the kitchen I see Liesje, she's wearin' her old under-shirt. Anna's got her head down on the kitchen table, she's asleep. She's dreamin' about a boy, and she . . . land's sake. I'm not goin' to watch that. Liesje's washing lettuce and cutting tomatoes. Love apples, she thinks. I sit down on the kitchen table. Once we shot a freak billy down at the swamp and Lisa never forgave us, and whenever I ran down a pheas-ant and Anthia fixed it, and then Liesje heard about it from the little sunflower, who never could keep her trap shut, she wouldn't talk to me for a week. Running down a pheasant's a real trick. You sort of have to hit it at the head, so it scrambles into the field while it's out cold and falls right there. If you drive over the thing whole, then the gut's open and you got a mess you can't do much with. A hare's even more of a trick. Hare basted in butter. Nothing's better than that. I'm not hungry. I'm homesick. I see Victor going into Stik. Anna wakes up all of a sudden, slides back and forth in her chair, looks at Liesje and says: 'Mmm, think I'll catch a shower.' 'Go get Victor.' 'First a shower, I'm sopping right out of my pants.' 'Anna, Christ!' Anna gets up and goes upstairs. Liesje walks into the yard, looks at my place, thinks: uh oh, he's flown the coop. But I shout from the kitchen: Stik! And Liesje thinks: oh, I bet he's at Stik's. And she looks at me. But she doesn't see me. Then she shakes her head and walks down the garden path. I go off after her, cross the Hoofdweg, and we go into Stik's and I start yelpin' like a puppy when I see the propeller on the ceilin', and I don't smell a thing, that's the worst of it. Victor's at the bar, and Stik's boy's behind it, and they're talkin' about me and old Stik, and how I used to pull the drunk ones out've the bar and bring 'em home, because the women in the village always called me: 'Boss, if the hubby's 'round, 'n' if't he'd be at Stik, send 'm home, wouldya?' So I dragged 'em out of the bar and drove 'em home in the Cortina. Liesje's standing in the doorway, looking at Victor, in her old undershirt, and Victor sees her, no, smells her, and looks up and laughs, happier than I ever saw him before. '*Déjà vu*,' he says. And her: 'What, man?' And she walks over to sit next to him and he says to young Stik: 'Give the lady 'n' popsicle, raspberry-flavor.' And young Stik says: 'Don't make 'em anymore.' And Liesje says: 'What're you blathering about?' And Victor's happier than ever before and thinks: similitudes. Music's running out've his head and rushing over the bar and across the floor. Liesje gets a half of Oranjeboom. And I mosey through the bar and tumble through space and don't even feel the warm air off the propeller anymore. This is all taking an awful long time, I'm getting awful tired, I thought dead was dead. 'So,' Young Stik says, 'what are you two plannin' to do, stay at the folks' place here in Oude Huizen?' Liesje and Victor look at each other. 'First, two drops o' the pink,' Victor says, and he and Stik say cheers and drink up, and I'm feeling left out. I want to go back. 'He's taking a trip,' says Liesje, her mouth like a line. 'Oh, like that, huh,' Stik says, 'and where to?' Victor mumbles and looks at Liesje. 'They're not sagging,' he says. 'Wha'?' Liesje blushes. 'Jackass!' 'How's that?' Stik says, and then: 'How's the guitar comin'?' 'Gave it up,' Victor says. 'Pity,' Liesje says, 'a real pity.' And Victor grins and says: 'No more noise-box.' 'But,' Stik says, 'Liesje-girl, what are you gonna do, you goin' back to your island?' Liesje nods. Looks at Victor. 'I bet you've got yourself a lover-boy there,' Stik says with a grin, 'yeah, those islanders, they're pigs for that.' Liesje smiles and looks at Victor. 'Is that right?' he asks Liesje, 'have you got one lined up? As once before?' 'Don't be precious,' she says. And Victor looks at her and holds back words. Then he says: 'Two drops o' the pink.' I'm goin' away.

. . . and Prins and the little sunflower are standing by a ditch and it's like I'm flying over, being pulled along by something, but I latch hold've 'em . . . and the little sunflower says: 'What if I stayed, just for a week?' 'Hmm,' Prins says. They're tired. And she says: 'So what's Victor supposed to do with that big old house?' 'Let's tell him about it first, he has to figure it out for himself.' 'But the children already have so much money, it's not good for them.' 'Don't start naggin',' Prins says, 'mind your own business. Besides, what's money anyway?' 'It's my business too,' the little sunflower says quietly. 'Whatever you want,' Prins says, 'is that what you want?' Little sunflower blushes. Prins looks at her, with love and aversion. 'I want . . . I mean,' he says, not angry but tired, 'I druther you just beat it.' 'I know that,' she says softly, 'that's just it.' 'Wha'?' 'What are you planning?' 'Plannin'? I'm not plannin' anything, never have either.' 'You swear?' 'What is this? What's got into you now?' Little sunflower sobs. She points: 'Remember when we . . . ?' Prins turns around and walks away. She tags along behind him. Something's pulling on me, but I want to see this, I want, I want to shout but I don't know what I'd say. If he was my son, I'd punch him for a loop. You don't do that, like he's doing, you just don't do that. She's trying to point and he's walking away. Anthia would say: 'That's no way to do.' She grabs him by the sleeve, sticks her hand in with his in the pocket of his coat and they walk on. The dog bobs up out of a dry ditch. I see their hands clenched in that coat pocket. I have to latch onto them, otherwise I'll be blowing away. She says: 'What're you going to do?' He stops, pulls the hands out of his coat, looks at her, runs his hand finally, finally, over her hairs and says, surprised: 'Nothin', what's got into you?' She sobs. They look at Old Zonnebloem's farm. Empty, in ruins. 'Well,' Prins says, 'come on, this isn't good for a body.' He takes her hand. They walk on and she sobs. 'Come on then,' Prins says, 'out with your remember-whens.' She laughs through her tears.

'There,' she says, pointing to the top of the canal running to the fen, 'that's where we made Anna.' Prins nods. 'We really thought we were something, back then, didn't we?' Prins nods again. 'Still doing it in the grass.' She laughs again through her tears. 'There was nothin' better'n in the grass,' he says. She nods. They look at each other and smile and walk on. 'Oh, and remember when, sorry about this, remember when your father caught us and acted like he didn't see, and your mother walked around for a week with a face like a tomato and kept getting the giggles at the table?' Prins nods and sees his father giving him a swift kick in the pants, pushing him into the shed and saying: 'Ye'd be leavin' afore the gospel, I takes it?' And him: 'Aw.' And the old Prins: 'Man, man, what'd you be comin' to . . .' And he shrugs, and his pa says to him: ''Ye was shruggin' them sho'lders atides yer still in yer ma's belly, so's she could hardly walk from the bumpin', that won't get ye much'n anywhere, fellah, shruggin' like that.' They stand at the foot of the canal and the little sunflower looks at Prins, and the dog lies at their feet, and everything's empty and the land stretching all the way to the horizon. She pulls him onto the ground. She pulls him down hard onto the ground and he falls on his ass and laughs, for the first time in years. And she sobs and pulls off her old jacket and hugs him, and he struggles but lets it happen, and half undressed they do the do in the grass at the edge of the canal, and the dog lies next to them and looks the other way, and she's sobbing and sobbing and they do it real slow, and then he rolls off of her and she says: 'I'm leaving tomorrow.' And he nods. And I want to yell something but I don't know what . . .

. . . and Victor and my house suddenly come to mind, and

I shoot off again from where I was and sit down on the kitchen table again and see Liesje and Victor crossing the Hoofdweg. When they come into the kitchen, Victor says: 'What are we going to do about Veen?' 'I've been thinking about it, and we should just leave it be, he'll hate us if we find him and, to tell the truth, I bet he's found a room somewhere in Gomorrah; it's his juice, let him stew in it.' Victor nods, holds back words, rubs his hands together, says: 'What are we going to cook – you think the old man still had half a steer in his freezer?' 'Pa keeps whole sides of beef these days.' 'Is that so?' Victor opens the freezer and fishes out a roast and tosses the frozen lump on the counter. 'Here's to late-but-excellent dining.' 'Fikkie?' 'Hmmm?' 'Be sure to make yourself right at home.' It bursts down the walls inside his head, waves of commotion, it flows into a puddle and sounds pretty and Liesje hugs him and he sticks his hand up beneath her undershirt and lays a hand on one of her breasts and says: 'My Waterloo.' 'Don't say that,' Liesje says, holding him tight, 'I am still able to receive you.' Victor bursts out laughing, gets loose and sits down next to me at the kitchen table. 'So tell us about Ameland.' Liesje starts cutting tomatoes again, gulps the gladache out of her throat and says: 'When Pa sold the house, he had to invest the money again and I was, well, I was pretty upset, so he says: take a vacation, like that yellow belly . . . that was you, God knows he was *angry* at you, the sweetheart . . .' Victor shakes his head, thinks: Don't tell me. '. . . and I wanted to go to Ameland, well, because I had nice memories of it, you, uh, you remember that . . .' 'Tell me a –' 'Okay, all right already, and I was staying in an apartment and there were these little houses for sale, so I called Pa and said: if you don't know what to do with your money anyway, why not buy one of those, not such a bad investment, and no sooner said than done, so I went and stayed there for a while, and one day he came to visit and saw me there in that dollhouse and he said: honey, are you sure you really want to teach? So I say: I don't know, and we talk, we talked about us, we really did, and he says: if you want that windbag back, then just stay here, he says: I don't know whether providence smiles on it, but you've got my blessing, he says: the further you are from home, the more homesick he'll get. That's what he said.' 'He said that, did he?' Liesje turns around, looks at us and grins. 'God, buddy, he loves us, you wouldn't believe it.' 'Oh yes I would.' 'Oh yeah? Well, anyway, that's how it went.' 'And you're going back tomorrow?' 'Yep.' Victor's holding back words, but they slip out anyway: 'Is it okay, uh, if I go with you?' Liesje throws a tomato at us, it splatters on the table. Then she comes over to us and sits on Victor's lap. She lays her head on his shoulder and their hair mingles. 'What's going to happen now?' she asks. And now Victor wants to say words, but something's keeping them in; he's pressing down. The little sunflower and Prins are standing in the doorway. They look and smile and blush. Liesje jumps up, blushes too. And Victor blushes too. And Prins gestures, like he's saying: well there you have it. And I'm tired, and it's like I hear my friend Zonnebloem saying: 'Drawp o' the pink, Boss?' I want to go home . . .

. . . I must've dozed off, and the dusk, the August dusk, soft and fragrant and warm – I catch a whiff of something, finally I can smell the land, the fragrance is hanging in the kitchen, I can smell the evening – dusky August evenings when the ditches smell different, when the sun starts smelling of water, when the smoke from burning weeds makes the evening smell of distance, of land going on forever, when the tang of conifers drops over the village, when the cats of Oude Huizen start mewling in the yard, when the farm dogs howl because evening's come, when the boys on their motorscooters come by, from other villages, on their way to other villages, when you know you'll have to wait a whole other year for summer, when you know the land will turn to mud, black, wet, chilly and old, when the gulls come back from the shallows and attack the garbage dumps, the whole country around here is being built up on garbage, someday that'll start stinking for good, but now you can still smell the evening, evening in August . . . and I want to go home, and they're sitting at the table and eating and drinking wine and they're quiet and thinking about me and I love them, I look at the children, the family I never did have, and they're all unhappy too often, except for Anna with her dolly-face, but now they're peaceful and not too awful sad, and they're thinking about me with a love that makes me warm and makes me gulp, and I hear Zonnebloem saying: 'Come awn, Boss, come awn o'er here,' and I see how Liesje squeezes Victor's hand under the table just for a moment, so that Anna says: 'We all saw that.' And they smile shyly, except for Anna, and Prins says: 'Victor, boy, you've got a house o' your own.' And the children look at him, and Victor says: 'God help me.' And Liesje says: 'Well, only if you insist.' And the music flows out of Victor across the kitchen table and he looks through the walls at the bank and thinks: I'm too vain for words, because I knew this all along. And Prins says: 'So what are we going to do with it?' 'Leave it,' Victor says, 'don't do a thing with it, just leave it.' And I always knew that, because it's for his wife and children, and for Oude Huizen. Or for him, and her, and children. Later. Liesje. 'And then,' Prins says, 'this gentleman has the gall to try and borrow six grand from his old man.' Everyone looks at Victor. Victor says: 'For a piano.' They all look at him. 'I'm, uh, going to compose.' He blushes. 'I wrote this thing in Paris, in *Klavarskribo*, in uh, braille, as it were.' Everyone looks at him. '"Ugly Notes": that's what it's called.' It sounds in his head, like a whole crowd all shouting at once. His commotion. 'Aha,' Anna says. 'Is that so?' Liesje asks. Victor looks at her. His head and the back of his neck deep red. 'Pathos,' he says, 'completely acceptable in music.' They all look at him. 'That's all.' It sounds in his head and it's shrill and ugly, like a fight. But then suddenly quiet for a bit, and like a funeral. And then shrill again and ugly. My song, he thinks, *und ich bin der Welt nicht abhanden gekommen* . . . And Liesje says again: 'Is that so?' And he nods and Prins lifts his glass and says: 'To airs.' And they drink a toast. And the little sunflower looks at Victor and he looks at her and they smile shyly. And I hear her father talking to me: 'Boss, fellah, come awn now.' And I'm tired and feel the wind plucking at me. I just wish I could go home. 'Well that's good news,' the little sunflower says, 'but Victor, so much money?' 'Mama!' Anna says, 'for once in your life, try *not* to bellyache!' And Liesje says: 'Will you be staying here for a while?' And the little sunflower shakes her head no. And Prins says: 'One mustn't exaggerate.' And the children say in unison: 'Oh, is that so?' And the five of them laugh, awkward and shy. And Liesje says: 'Victor and I are going to Ameland tomorrow.' All it takes is some getting used to, she thinks then. 'Oh,' the little sunflower says, 'well, huh, that's good to hear.' And the children say in unison again: 'Oh is that so?' And the little sunflower chokes on her wine and Prins pounds her on the back, grinning, and thinks: praise the Lord, or whoever, tomorrow I'm on my own again, and he thinks about a bottle, and the bar up in the attic, and the view out of the skylight. And I'm hanging in front of the skylight and see the evening over the fields and the sun going down where the land ends, and something warm runs through what's left of me; dying's one thing I guess I won't get around to, and as I'm flowing out the skylight and smelling the evenings for once and for all, in my head I see my old friend Zonnebloem: he nabs me by the elbow and says: 'Hey, ol' fellah, ye 'members whan . . .'

AFTERWORD

A joke in Book Two was lifted from an episode of *Fry & Laurie*. A joke in Book Four is one I wangled from an old friend, who unfortunately could not remember whether he'd made it up himself.

All similarities between passages and perplexities in this novel and those in other works of art, living or dead, are purely coincidental, except in those cases where the writer intends an allusion.

NANNE TEPPER, Groningen